Praise
American 1

"*American History* is a thrilling epic tale of two families—crossing an ocean, a continent and spanning a century. An ambitious undertaking skillfully executed by a writer deserving wide recognition."

—Steve Hamilton, Edgar Award-winning
author of *Dead Man Running*

"*American History* is a beautifully written, ambitious crime epic. Abramo delivers an immersive, emotional and suspenseful gem that reminds us of who we are. A page-turning pleasure."

—Michael Koryta, *New York Times* bestselling
author of *How It Happened*

Praise for the Novels of
J. L. Abramo

"*Coney Island Avenue* is not just a thriller—and a good one at that—but is also a look into the lives of the policemen and women. Abramo does a masterful job of integrating the personal lives of his characters into the story without slowing the pace of the thriller."

—Sandra Dallas, *The Denver Post*

"If grit, hard guys, and the rhythm of the mean streets is your thing, *Brooklyn Justice* has got them in spades and J. L. Abramo is your man."

—Reed Farrel Coleman, *New York Times* bestselling
author of *Where It Hurts*

AMERICAN HISTORY

J. L. ABRAMO

AMERICAN HISTORY

Down and Out Books
3959 Van Dyke Rd, Ste. 265
Lutz, FL 33558
www.DownAndOutBooks.com

Cover concept by J. L Abramo
Cover design by Lance Wright

ISBN: 1-946502-70-7
ISBN-13: 978-1-946502-70-4

for

Ferdinand Charles Cataneo

one of the good guys

AUTHOR'S NOTE

The family name Agnello is also the Italian word for lamb. It is pronounced an-yello—the agn spoken as in lasagna.

The family name Leone is also the Italian word for lion. It is pronounced ley-ō-nē—the o and final e spoken as long vowels.

AGNELLO/LEONE FAMILY TREE

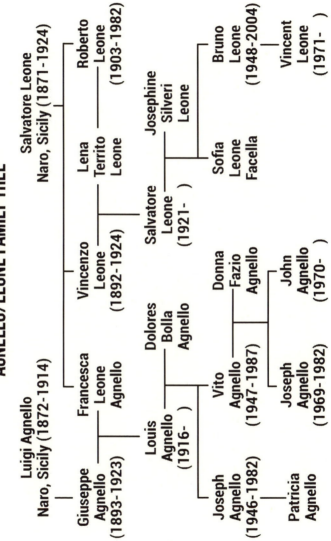

OTHERS

ALFREDO CATALANO
A New York lawyer, adoptive father of Louis Agnello

SERGIO AND SOPHIA BOLLA
Friends and neighbors to Giuseppe Agnello
DOLORES BOLLA AGNELLO
Their daughter, Louis Agnello's wife

FRANK BONNER
A prison inmate in Colorado
LINCOLN BONNER
His son, a Denver police detective

ROSA LEONE SILVERI
MARIA LEONE
Daughters of Vincenzo and Lena, sisters of Salvatore

HANK SIMS
A friend to Vito Agnello
KATY SIMS
His wife
AMY SIMS
Their daughter

THEODORE HARDING
A friend and business manager to Vincenzo Leone
RICHARD HARDING
Theodore's son, a San Francisco prosecutor
JACK HARDING
Richard's son, a San Francisco police detective
MARTINA HARDING
Jack's daughter

BENITO LUCCHESE
Business associate of Roberto Leone

SAMMY ORSO
Long-time security for the Leone family

*If we could read the secret
history of our enemies,
we should find in each man's life
sorrow and suffering enough
to disarm all hostility.*

—Henry Wadsworth Longfellow

Genealogy

Sicily. Late Nineteenth Century.

They were born less than one year apart, in a poor village full of boys so like one another they could all have been brothers.

It was the 1890s. The Gay Nineties for much of the Western World and, in the New World across the Atlantic, a time for casting off the restraints of the Victorian Age.

In the rocky hills surrounding Naro, on the ancient island of Sicily, time seemed to stand still. For Vincenzo Leone and Giuseppe Agnello, the approach of the twentieth century had little consequence—and offered less promise.

In another time and place, these two boys could have been friends.

Amici. Compagni. Fratelli.

The two young boys often crossed paths, and there was a mutual attraction—although part of their curiosity to know one another was likely encouraged by the taboo. Both had been educated from birth to mistrust and forswear the other and as they grew to adolescence they succumbed to the prejudices of their fathers—blindly accepting the ageless dissension between the two families if not totally adopting the fierce hatred.

Vincenzo Leone and Giuseppe Agnello might have spent their lives in the hills of Agrigento, working the miserly earth and perpetuating the blood feud that had existed for so long no one could remember when it began.

Or why.

And, as both approached adulthood, this looked to be their fate.

But each young man, independently from one another, had a common dream.

To escape.

To escape the barren land.

To escape the senseless and violent antagonism.

To escape the archaic island prison.

All that was needed was a catalyst, an inspiration, a reason to break away from family and home, a motivation too strong to resist.

And the incentive came for each of them in the form it had taken for all ages—for as long as restless sons struggled to gain a foothold on manhood.

Romance.

PART ONE

SELF DEFENSE

*Yet I, this little while ere I go hence,
long very little now, in self-defense.*

—Adela Florence Cory Nicolson

ONE

John Agnello. Colorado. 2005. Thursday.

The heavy gate closed loudly behind me.

I was on the *outside* this time.

It's not easy doing the same thing for five years.

More difficult when you are someone who has rarely done anything for that long a time.

Someone who couldn't complete high school, who never held a job for five years, who never kept a lover for five years.

Or a friend for that matter.

Particularly when the same thing you have been doing is jail time.

Of course, there were the years I spent living with my parents and then only my father—before I left school and home and city and began running.

I would not have had to leave school and take to the road if I hadn't killed a man.

But I did.

It was self-defense.

I was just not confident that a court of law was going to see it that way.

Years later, when I had to kill another man, it was also self-defense and a court of law *nearly* saw it that way.

And I earned a five-year prison sentence.

Now that I'm out, I know it won't be long before self-defense rears its ugly head again.

I suppose I can avoid it for a while, but I'd rather get it over and done. I just need to stop the right man this time, before he kills me or has me killed—so I can stop defending myself, stop running and hiding, and avenge my father whose death perpetuated this historic killing spree. Then, maybe I could hold onto something for longer than a few months at a time. And if I can get through it without returning to prison, it would be a terrific bonus.

But first things first.

He knows I'm getting out. The wheels are in motion.

I have to dodge the bullet long enough to develop a plan. I'm going to have to move quickly. And often.

And reach out for help.

I'm hoping help is still available.

It's been a long time since I reached out, and a long time since I was any help to someone else.

It's about time for a little give and take.

They say *time waits for no one.*

I'm gambling they are wrong.

I'm wondering as I walk out through the prison gate in a freshly pressed suit with two hundred dollars in the lapel pocket, holding my breath and trying to suppress an urge to hit the dirt, how far I will make it away from this spot to begin with. I walk across to the shuttle that will take me downtown and climb aboard. I have no choice.

I make it off the shuttle intact and move into the Greyhound terminal.

The worst is over for now. I'm out of the open. If anyone was tailing me they missed their shot because I'm in control now.

I have developed a rearview mirror.

I know how to disappear now.

And I do.

If he wants me, he will have some searching to do. I've bought some time. I'll need a safe place to rest, safe for a time.

I'll need cash, and I'll need information. I can keep moving. I've got that down.

I have a chance, maybe even a good chance, of getting to him before he gets to me.

There's always the possibility he hasn't sent anyone out at all. Instead, he's just going to sit back and wait for me to come to him. So be it. I never imagined either of us was likely to benefit much from the element of surprise.

This is one of those things that are inevitable.

Him or me.

Or him and me.

I pulled what cash I had out of my jacket pocket and headed straight for the ticket window. I bought a one-way bus ticket to Phoenix and I crossed the terminal toward the men's room, loosening my tie as I walked.

Lincoln Bonner. Colorado.

Imagine taking a large slab of concrete and dropping it onto a beautiful natural setting.

Why imagine it? You have seen it before.

This particular eyesore was surrounded on three sides by rolling green meadow generously spotted with white and yellow daisies north and south as far as the eye could see and west to the foothills and the Front Range beyond.

The huge sign across the entrance to the parking area read *Arapahoe County State Correctional Facility.* The lot was large and not full—but there were enough vehicles, likely belonging to staff and visiting attorneys by the look of the makes and models, to enable me to park among them inconspicuously. A two-lane blacktop designated as State Route number something or other ran north and south, and the prison sat in all its cement and barbed wire deformity on its eastern side.

I was early, so I curled up with a Camel straight and the *Denver Post* and waited.

Watching the prison gate.

Finally, I saw them leading him out. He looked as if he was trying hard not to look worried. I think if I threw a bottle cap his way he might have hit the ground.

Two guards escorted him to the entrance—the exit in this case.

Without ceremony, he left the confines and the heavy door closed loudly behind him.

He crossed the road, where a twenty-passenger shuttle van was parked with only a driver aboard. The vehicle was idling and set to give him his free seventeen-mile, twenty-five-minute ride to downtown Denver.

With any luck, a one-way trip.

I waited a few minutes and pulled out slowly. A sign read *Thank You for Visiting.*

You're welcome.

I knew exactly where the van was heading. I took some time overtaking it and, after passing, sped up to arrive at the destination first. Twenty minutes later, I was parked behind the Greyhound terminal among the buses and taxis with a borrowed RTD parking permit displayed on my windshield. I entered the terminal from the boarding area, sat down with a cup of coffee from a vending machine, and opened the *Post* to the sports section.

Ten minutes later he came in, pulled some money from the lapel pocket of his freshly pressed suit, and walked straight to the ticket window. After the transaction, he surveyed the area and headed for the men's room.

It was time for my move.

When he walked out the back doors to the boarding area a few minutes later, he had lost the jacket and tie. I sat in the truck with the engine running and watched him walk toward me.

The handgun sat on the seat beside me.

He came to the passenger side, opened the door, and slid in. I pulled out of the parking area, turned onto Blake Street, then onto Speer Boulevard toward the interstate.

"Thanks for the ride," he said.

"No problem."

"Did it look like anyone followed you?"

"No, didn't look like it. Where to?"

"Cheyenne."

"Cheyenne it is," I said. "Why did you ditch the jacket?"

"Never liked the fit."

"There's a denim jacket behind the seat that may fit better."

"Thanks, but what I could really use is a decent cup of coffee."

"Got you covered."

"And a Camel, if you don't mind."

"How's my father?" I asked, as I held out the package of cigarettes.

John Agnello answered me with something like reverence in his voice and we headed north on I-25 toward Wyoming.

John.

As with many life experiences, you could have little idea of what being locked up in prison is like unless you have been there.

I'm not being arrogant. I say this because I know this.

Before I was awarded room and board at the Arapahoe County State Correctional Facility, I thought I knew what to expect. I had read the books and seen the scenes, from Dostoyevsky to *Cool Hand Luke*.

Nothing prepared me.

And it was not the horrors that surprised me, though I witnessed many. What I wasn't prepared for was the sense of being totally alone. Even someone like me, who had spent ten years basically unattached and overly cautious of intimate human contact, felt the unique solitude from the moment the prison gate closed behind me.

When you are born you come into the world completely dependent on those who came before, and a newborn left on its own will perish.

In many ways, prison is very similar. You are dependent on those who came there before you, dependent on those on the inside, because no one outside the walls of this new ward can reach in to help you. And if no one on the inside steps forward soon to claim responsibility for your survival, you will perish like the abandoned newborn.

I came very close to that fate when Frank Bonner took me under his wing.

Franklin Bonner was in the fourteenth year of a life sentence, no chance of parole. Murder one. I will not go into the details of his crime, except to say I would have done the same in his place. Of course, I might not be the best judge of appropriate behavior. Nonetheless, to me the man was a saint and a savior. For five years Frank Bonner nurtured me like a mother, protected me like a strong father, and kept me safe and sane.

Why Frank adopted me I really can't say. I certainly couldn't do a thing for him.

In the great scheme of things, I was just a temporary visitor and he was there for the duration.

Nothing I could do or say would change the fact he was never getting out, so what *could* I do for him?

I could respect Frank and ultimately love him, and I guess it meant something to him to have been able to earn that respect and that love.

But it wasn't about what Frank Bonner could do for me, which turned out to be a lot. It was about what he *would* do for me whenever he could and about what I *would* do for him *if* I could.

I would have gladly let Bonner walk out in my place five years after we met. And Frank knew it.

So, when the day finally approached for me to leave him behind, I asked if there was anything I could do for him on the outside. Frank said no, and he thanked me for asking.

And when he asked if there was anything he could do for me, I told him there was.

Because even when you feel you've been taking and taking, when you need help who can you trust but someone who has been giving and giving?

I told him what I needed and he told me he would see to it.

And when I walked out of the prison gate and crossed to the shuttle that would take me to downtown Denver, I had no doubt I was covered.

And, less than an hour later, I was in a pickup truck sitting beside a total stranger named Lincoln Bonner who held out a pack of cigarettes and asked me how his father was.

And I simply said, "Frank is doing well."

It seemed enough for Lincoln to hear.

He appeared to understand it.

"There's a truck stop up ahead, do you want that cup of coffee?"

"Sure," I said, "I'd love that cup of coffee."

I lit the cigarette and stared out at the highway.

The Rocky Mountains to my left, the Great Plains to my right, five more years of my life behind me—and the prospect of resolution or extinction ahead of me.

Lincoln.

John Agnello and I had a great deal in common. Then again, we could hardly have been more different.

John grew up in the most populated city in the country. I was raised in a small rural town on the eastern plains of Colorado.

John tried to save his father's life but could not. He's been running since. My father tried to save my life, and he did. He's been locked in a prison cell ever since.

John and I are nearly the same age and the years have often been unkind to us both. I would have to say, though, I'd rather be in *my* boots at this point in time.

Since John Agnello was seventeen years old he has been looking over his shoulder, anticipating yet another test of his ability and desire to survive. And, after a five-year hiatus, he is about to test those skills again.

Since I was twenty-one, I have been working at taking advantage of the life my father allowed me to continue, while dealing with the knowledge of the extreme price he paid to do so. When I got past my guilt, I realized my responsibility. I've devoted myself to making certain Frank Bonner's sacrifice for his son was not in vain.

There is nothing I wouldn't do for my father. I would not want to have to break the law—but he would never ask that of me.

I broke the law when I was a younger man, and he rescued me.

Since then, I've pledged to uphold the law—as a police detective in Denver, it's what I do every day.

My father doesn't ask much of me.

He always insists I not blame myself for his situation. He asks me to bring books for him to read, he prefers history. When he asked me if I could help a friend who was getting out of prison, I did not hesitate to say I would.

The last time I visited my father, he pointed Agnello out to me.

John and I glanced at each other just long enough to guarantee future recognition. John sat with my uncle, across the visitor's hall. My father had arranged the visit.

It was the only way he could get John into the room while I was there, because John never had visitors of his own.

So, my father asked Uncle Jimmy to get onto Agnello's visitor list and to come out to see John that day. So, I could do for my father what he *would not* ask Uncle Jimmy to do— pick John up when he got out and take him wherever he needed to go.

"And that's all I'm asking you to do for me, son," my father said. "If there is anything more you can do for John after that, it's completely up to you."

I know my father well, I knew he meant exactly what he said—so all I expected to do was to get John Agnello to his chosen destination. Cheyenne.

Over coffee at a café off the highway, John had trouble getting past talk about the weather. Eventually, he warmed up and began to tell me about how much my father had done to help him survive the past five years.

"I don't think I'm exaggerating," Agnello said, "when I say Frank saved my life."

And *that* was another thing we had in common.

Whenever he spoke of my father it wasn't a matter of telling a son what he wanted to hear about the virtues of his old man, it was a matter of someone needing to express his feelings about a man who had been much like a father to him.

Maybe it was the talk of family that eventually got him talking about himself.

I had the waitress fill my thermos with coffee for the road and we walked back to my truck. As we merged into the highway traffic, John began to tell me a fable.

The story of how he had come to this point in his life.

And the hundred or so years it had taken his family to get him here.

TWO

Sicily. New York. Philadelphia. 1915-1919.

In 1915, while the First World War raged throughout Europe, Giuseppe Agnello and Francesca Leone left Sicily for America.

To be more precise, they escaped—marrying against the wishes of their respective families.

The Agnellos and Leones had been bitter rivals for generations, and their feud had been bloody at times.

The young lovers had no use for this particular war and made their own sacred truce.

They left by ship from Palermo, headed for England and passage to New York.

Purchasing steerage space with money Giuseppe Agnello had saved and borrowed, the newlyweds departed Liverpool in April.

Three years earlier, the White Star's *Titanic* had begun a similar voyage to New York—but never arrived.

The ship they boarded in Liverpool was the Cunard Line's *Lusitania.*

They landed in New York City through Ellis Island, and joined a group of Italian immigrants already settled in lower Manhattan and willing to help them get started in their new lives.

Soon, Giuseppe was working on the docks at Chelsea Piers, the Agnellos rented their own small flat, and Francesca was carrying their first child.

The Lusitania did not fare so well.

On its return trip in May, it was fired upon and sunk by a German U-boat off the Irish coast. Of the nearly twelve hundred passengers, fewer than eight hundred were saved.

Among the dead were one hundred twenty-eight citizens of the United States, beginning an outrage in the country which escalated feverishly throughout the next twenty-three months. On April 6, 1917, the United States entered the war against Germany and its allies.

When Giuseppe Agnello left Italy in March of 1915, he barely escaped being drafted into the Italian Army.

Only months later, Italy entered the arena, declaring war on its longtime enemy, Austria.

In 1917, as a newly established citizen of the United States, Agnello could no longer avoid the world conflict. Giuseppe was enlisted in the United States Army and was shipped back to Europe to fight in France on the Western Front.

Francesca soon found it too difficult to remain alone in New York with her small child. She chose what she felt was her only option, though she knew it would greatly trouble her husband.

Francesca took their son and traveled to live with her brother Vincenzo and his family in Philadelphia.

Vincenzo Leone had immigrated to that city in 1913. Although Vincenzo had tried to locate his younger sister in America for nearly two years, he had been unsuccessful.

Francesca, on the other hand, knew how to find her brother and arrived on his doorstep with her son, Louis, in July of 1917.

Vincenzo Leone ran a small importing business that was suffering from wartime trade difficulties, but he had done well enough to build a fine home for his wife and two daughters with ample space for his sister and her son. Though he first kept distant from the boy who carried the name of his family's perennial enemy, he began to warm up to the child in time. As much as Leone loved his two girls, he still waited for his wife to give him a son.

In November 1918, the Germans signed an armistice—ending the war.

Private Giuseppe Agnello would soon be returning home to his family.

At the same time, another war was being fought on the home front. The Spanish Flu plagued the world and was ravaging the city of Brotherly Love. In October alone, nearly thirteen thousand Philadelphians died from the pandemic.

Vincenzo's wife, Carmella, succumbed to the virus in her seventh month of pregnancy. Every effort to save her failed. Francesca, who vigilantly tended to her brother's wife through her battle to survive, contracted the disease herself. On November 11, Armistice Day, Francesca Agnello lost *her* struggle for life.

Francesca left behind her widowed brother, Vincenzo, his two young daughters, and *her* two-year-old son.

Vincenzo Leone soon sold his home, gathered the three children, and relocated his business to the booming wharf of San Francisco.

When Giuseppe Agnello returned to New York City in January 1919, he found his wife and son gone.

Agnello stood in the hall outside the tenement apartment where he had left them. The stranger who opened the door moments before had no idea of the whereabouts of his family and quickly retreated inside. Giuseppe clutched a small canvas bag containing all he had managed to return from the Front.

Giuseppe was wearing his only outer clothing, an Army uniform beneath a long wool coat and a cloth cap. He had fifty dollars to his name and he stood for nearly ten minutes in the dimly lit hall, staring blankly at the closed door, before he gained enough of his wits to seek out his former neighbor in the flat on the floor above.

Sergio Bolla welcomed his old friend warmly with an embrace at his door and ushered Giuseppe into the rooms. He took the small bag from Giuseppe's hand and placed it gently at the foot of the door side table, then he guided the stunned soldier to a seat at the kitchen table and poured two glasses of wine.

The two men had worked side by side at the Chelsea docks up until the time of Giuseppe's induction into the Armed Forces. Sergio had a slight limp, due to a childhood accident, which did not disable him at the job on the docks but did excuse him from military service.

Bolla called to his wife, who had been occupied putting their children to bed for the night, and asked that she please prepare a meal to sustain their guest.

Sophia Bolla began to reheat the evening's supper and she put together a fresh green salad.

Giuseppe took a few sips of the homemade wine, and tried to calm himself enough to question his host.

"Thank you for your generosity, my friend," Agnello said, holding out the wine glass in a gesture of respect to Sergio. "I pray you can comfort me further with news of where I may find my wife and son."

"I fear I can be of very little help, *mio amico*. Francesca left for the city of Philadelphia, several hours south of here, just more than a year ago. She did not say which family she was joining. She had a difficult time here alone with the child and told us there was a place of refuge for them in that city. We have not heard from her since. She did leave a communication for you which I have kept safe, and also left some of your clothing which I agreed to store here in anticipation of your return."

As Bolla solemnly spoke, he retrieved a folded piece of paper from a small ceramic bowl in the kitchen cupboard and handed it to Giuseppe.

Giuseppe unfolded the message and read it. It was a short

letter, testifying his wife's love for him. Although it did not name the family she had gone to live with, it did hold a street name and house number in Philadelphia where she and their son could be found.

Agnello bolted to his feet as if ready to cover the ninety miles at a gallop, beginning immediately. Bolla reached out and placed his hand firmly onto Giuseppe's shoulder to keep him from running out the door.

"My dear friend," he said, "it is late. You look very tired and you must be famished. Please allow us the privilege of feeding you, and providing a sleeping place. You need your strength. In the morning, we will be able to think more clearly, help you gather your belongings, and plan for your travel arrangements. Drink some wine, it will relax you. Do not worry, you can be on your way early tomorrow in a much better condition. We have money if you need some help in that regard. You can repay us at a later time."

Agnello sat down again and looked deeply into Bolla's eyes.

"I do not know the words to thank you."

"You can thank me by eating heartily," replied Sergio. "Sophia, please bring the salad and I will serve the pasta, it should be warm enough."

Giuseppe took a deep breath to control the urge to cry over his fate.

He did not wish to embarrass his benefactors after their abundant kindness.

The following morning, Giuseppe woke up much calmer and with great resolve. He devoured the large breakfast set out by his friends, and the great activity of the three Bolla children in the small apartment was stimulating. He longed to see his wife and the son he hardly knew—his boy who surely would not remember him. Agnello fought to suppress any thoughts that were less than optimistic. Sergio told him he could be on a train to Philadelphia within an hour. Giuseppe quickly gathered some of his belongings, aided by a small satchel the Bollas had kindly loaned to him, and he accepted Sergio's offer to accompany him to the train station.

Arriving at Philadelphia's Broad Street Station less than four hours later, Giuseppe asked directions to the address Francesca had identified. He was told it was a long walk, but nevertheless within walking distance. As anxious as he was to see his family, he decided to conserve his money by going on foot. Giuseppe had accepted the loan of twenty dollars that Sergio insisted he take. Agnello's intention was simply to collect Francesca and the boy and return to New York, where his former job would be waiting for him and where an apartment would not be difficult to find. He moved briskly through the city streets toward his destination, closing his coat tightly against the chilling January wind.

As Giuseppe approached the house, his anxiety suddenly grew. This was a strange place, and he had no idea what he would find here. He did not know who his wife had turned to for help in his absence. He used the knocker on the door to announce his presence.

The man who opened the door had dark skin, and his clothing and parts of his face and hands were covered with white paint. Giuseppe discovered that the man was painting the house for the real estate broker who was handling its sale. The painter had no knowledge as to the whereabouts of the former inhabitants, but did give Giuseppe directions to the office of the broker. Agnello stared at the new address in his hand, and the confidence and courage he had gained from the Bollas dissolved into uncertainty and fear.

The broker's name was Johnson, and he greeted Giuseppe guardedly. He could offer Agnello no help. He had purchased the house from its former owner and was preparing it for sale at a profit. His dealings with the seller were therefore complete, and he had no knowledge of the seller's present location. He was not in a position to supply a name since he considered that information to be confidential.

Giuseppe pleaded with Johnson, explaining to him the disappearance of his wife and young child and his need to find them. Johnson was a cynical man, had seen and heard too many stories of wives going off from their husbands and the trouble it could cause between men, especially these hotheaded immigrants. He decided he could not give Agnello any name, it was in fact illegal for him to do so, and only a court order could budge him from his resolve. Johnson recommended Giuseppe go to the legal authorities to begin such a process.

Johnson expressed his regrets and asked to be excused to attend to pressing business.

Agnello left the small office and started aimlessly down the busy street.

Giuseppe eventually came out of his haze and called his friend Bolla from a public telephone. Sergio tried to calm Giuseppe and demanded Agnello not remain in the strange city alone, but return to them on the next train. Bolla assured him that he could help, but only if Giuseppe proceeded through legal channels from Manhattan with the help of a lawyer from the old country who Sergio was confident they could rely on. Giuseppe entrusted his fate into his good neighbor's hands, promised he would return to New York City, and solemnly made his way to the train depot.

It took nearly a year for Giuseppe to learn that Johnson had purchased the house from Vincenzo Leone. During the period of waiting, Agnello worked incessantly. His single mindedness was an attempt to distract himself from his torment. His goal was to earn and save enough money to be able to offer a comfortable life to his beloved wife and son when at last they were reunited. Giuseppe's optimism was fueled entirely by willpower, aided by the support and encouragement of his good friend Bolla, the lawyer Catalano, and the close-knit Italian community.

Giuseppe now understood why Francesca had left with their son—he could appreciate the solace she could hope to find with her brother. But why had Francesca not tried to contact him in all this time? She could surely have hoped to reach him through Sergio and Sophia Bolla.

With no idea about how or where to begin, Giuseppe enslaved himself to an all-consuming mission.

To find Vincenzo Leone, and with him, he prayed, his precious family.

THREE

Colorado. Thursday.

Lincoln Bonner glanced at the rearview mirror in his truck and realized his initial assessment may have been incorrect. He was fairly certain the large black sedan following a hundred yards behind was the same vehicle he had seen when he and John Agnello had stopped for coffee earlier. They had just passed the exit for Fort Collins, thirty miles from the Wyoming border. If they were being tailed, he wanted to know before they reached Cheyenne.

Lincoln touched John's knee, interrupting the recounting of Giuseppe Agnello's history.

"I think we have company," he said.

"What should we do?"

"We should make sure."

Lincoln took the next exit off the highway and he drove west toward the small town of Wellington, Colorado, making note of a wooded area he had noticed as they drove over a small bridge crossing Boxelder Creek.

There was one picnic table at the edge of the woods, and it was deserted.

Lincoln drove down the main street of Wellington and stopped in front of a grocery and sandwich shop.

The black Cadillac passed them and turned left at the next intersection.

"Let's get lunch," Bonner said.

John climbed out and walked into the grocery. Lincoln kept an eye out for their tail. A few minutes later, John returned with sandwiches and cold drinks. Lincoln pulled away and turned left where the black sedan had turned. They spotted two men in the Cadillac, parked at the curb with the engine running, and Bonner continued around in a circle and headed back toward the creek.

"Think they'll make a move?" asked Agnello.

"You'd know better than me. I suppose it depends on whether they're more interested in finding out where you're headed or in keeping you from getting there."

"This might be a good time for you to bail out."

"I promised my father I would get you where you needed to go. You said Wyoming, so you're stuck with me until then. Besides, what would you defend yourself with, a sandwich?"

"Why don't we just drive through and I can take my chances in Cheyenne?"

"I would rather not be responsible for leading them to your door. These guys had to be following me since we left the bus station, if not before. In any case, by now whoever sent them knows I'm on your side. I'd rather deal with it here in Colorado, where I'm still an officer of the law."

"So?"

"So, we sit at that picnic table," Lincoln said as he pulled up to the creekside parking area, "dig into our lunch bag, and see what develops."

Lincoln stopped the truck and killed the engine. He took the grocery bag from the seat between them and dumped it into John's lap. He picked up the weapon that had been lying beside him and replaced it in his shoulder holster. They left the truck and walked a few hundred feet to the table at the edge of the trees.

"I sure hope I don't have to kill anyone," said Lincoln.

"Sometimes it's unavoidable."

"So I've heard."

"You want the roast beef or the tuna salad?" John asked, as they settled on the benches opposite each other at the weather-beaten pine table.

Lincoln watched the road and the small bridge across the creek for any sign of the black Cadillac sedan. Then, he turned his attention to the wooded area behind them.

Lincoln could see another road on the far side of the trees.

"My guess is it will come from back there," said Lincoln, nodding toward the woods, "and that one of them will stay with the car in case we make a run for it. Either we sit here and wait, or I take a stroll in and check it out."

"How about we sit for a while?"

"Okay, I'll have the tuna," Lincoln said, placing his firearm on the bench with one hand as he reached for the sandwich with his other.

John was about to pop open a can of root beer when they heard the sound from the near tree line to their left.

Bonner grabbed his gun, jumped to his feet, and moved to the other side of the table.

The two men threw the table over on its side and ducked behind just as a shot rang out.

Then two more shots in rapid succession.

The first bullet missed high, the second splintered the top of the bench, and the third crashed through the table between the two men.

"Well, the bait worked just fine," said John. "What's the plan?"

Lincoln caught sight of a movement in the trees and fired four shots in that direction.

The sound of a body falling heavily to the ground was unmistakable.

The gunfire ended.

"Think you got him?" asked John.

"We'll soon find out."

Lincoln headed into the trees, Agnello at his heels. They

came upon the body almost immediately, and John quickly determined the man was dead.

"Nice shooting."

"I missed three times."

"The one in the head did the trick."

"Recognize him?" asked Lincoln.

"I know the type."

"Follow me."

John followed as Lincoln moved through the trees toward the back road.

In a few moments, they spotted the black sedan.

The man in the car seemed to have no intention of getting out. He sat behind the wheel ready to speed away as soon as his partner returned, or to hightail it alone if things didn't work out as planned.

Lincoln told John what they needed to do.

A few minutes later, Agnello was walking down the road toward the black sedan from the front—waving his arms madly in the air. John had the driver's undivided attention when Lincoln appeared at the car window and pressed his pistol against the man's temple.

"Put your hands behind your neck, slowly. I'm going to open the car door and you are going to step out, slowly. Clear?"

The man nodded as he raised his hands. John came up to the vehicle as Lincoln opened the door and the man got out.

"*Come stai?*" said John, looking into the man's eyes.

Before the man could answer a blow to his head brought him to the pavement.

"Ouch," said John.

"Take the car and beat it out of here. I'm going to have to stay and do some explaining. Sorry I couldn't get you all the way to Cheyenne, Dad won't like this."

"You did more than enough, tell Frank I said so."

Lincoln took a card out of his wallet and handed it to John.

"Call me if you need me," he said.

"I'd rather keep you out of it from here on."

"I'm already in it and, from what I understand, you don't have a wealth of help out here. And you never finished the story of the Agnellos and the Leones. I hate to be left hanging."

They heard the wail of sirens, responding to the gunfire.

"Go," Lincoln said.

"Thanks."

Agnello climbed into the Cadillac and threw it into gear.

"Ditch the wheels as soon as you can."

The black sedan drove away and Lincoln headed back through the trees to the overturned picnic table, leaving the driver of the Cadillac unconscious on the road. He cleared one of the sandwiches and one of the drinks to the nearby trashcan and waited for the police to arrive.

Two Town of Wellington cruisers pulled into the parking area. Bonner stood with his hands over his head, holding up his detective shield.

FOUR

Lincoln Bonner. Colorado.

The dead body in the trees belonged to Paul Sacco of Oakland, California, or at least that was what his driver's license suggested.

The gray-haired gentleman sitting across the interview table was Sheriff Melville of Wellington, Colorado.

"You're a little far from home, Detective Bonner," he said.

"I've been further."

"And you say you didn't know Mr. Sacco."

"He never gave me the opportunity."

"So, you stopped to enjoy your lunch and you were alone."

"Yes, as I said earlier, I was alone."

"Detective Bonner, please understand we don't get much of this kind of thing around here. I just want to be clear about the facts. By the way, what brings you to these parts?"

"You mean so far from home?"

I wasn't trying to be a wise guy. I wasn't playing the hotshot big city detective to the local yokel. It was simply not relevant and I really wanted to get on my way. To his credit, Melville gave me the benefit of the doubt.

The driver of the Cadillac, who I'd knocked out cold on the road, never surfaced. I had nothing I cared to say about him, and I was sure the feeling was mutual. I certainly didn't envy him.

Maybe I *was* being a bit of a wise guy, but to borrow a

27

psychological term it was a defense mechanism.

I had just killed a man and that is never a thing to inspire humility.

"I apologize, Sheriff. I'm still a little shook up. I really didn't expect a shooting match today. I took the drive up here to get away from this kind of thing, as you call it. I well understand you have a job to do and I'm trying my best to help."

If I couldn't be truthful, I could at least be civil.

Twenty minutes later I was in my truck headed back down to Denver.

I wondered how it was going for John Agnello—he would be in Cheyenne by now.

For a moment, I felt fortunate not to be in his shoes, always wondering what was around the next corner, always wondering when the confrontation would come.

Then I realized I had likely put myself in the same boat.

I also knew I would have to give my father bad news.

John Agnello. Wyoming.

Thirty-five minutes after leaving Lincoln Bonner, I was crossing the state border into Wyoming. I had a couple of hours before my meeting at the state capitol. I took the Lincoln Way exit off the interstate and followed Route 30 into the city. At Fifteenth Street and House Avenue, I parked the sedan among the cars scattered just north of the railroad yards. I walked one block east to Evans Avenue, then up to Seventeenth Street.

I walked into Antonio's Ristorante Italiano shortly after three in the afternoon.

The restaurant emptied as the last luncheon guests walked out past me. The staff was busy setting up for the next shift. A handsome man of around sixty greeted me graciously. He said they would not be serving dinner for another two hours. I spoke with him in Italian, explaining I had traveled far to get there and it had been a long time since I had enjoyed a homemade *pasto Italiano*. The man looked into my eyes.

"*Vieni con me*," he said, and led me to a table in back.

A teenager, who appeared to be a busboy and possibly the grandson of my host, collected the dishes from his own lunch and disappeared into the adjacent kitchen.

I sat at the table alone as the old gentleman, who had introduced himself as Antonio Caravella, followed the boy.

A few minutes later, Antonio returned with a basket of hot crusty bread, pats of butter, and a small lettuce and tomato salad covered in vinegar and olive oil. He handed me a white cook's jacket and returned to the kitchen.

I had spent much of my pre-adolescence in my Uncle Joe's restaurant in Brooklyn and I understood that the jacket was intended to discourage others from doing what I had done—wandering in and interrupting preparation for the dinner patrons.

I put the jacket on over my shirt, and I gratefully dug into the salad and bread.

Soon Caravella returned with a large plate of ziti Sicilian, pasta tossed with sautéed eggplant topped with marinara sauce and mozzarella, and a side dish of meatballs.

"*Mille grazie*," I said.

"*Prego. Come ti chiami?*"

"Agnello. Giovanni Agnello."

"*Bene. Mi scusi*," he said, indicating he needed to return to his work, "*mangia, per favore.*"

He left me to attack the food. It *had* been a very long time.

After refusing an offer of seconds, I paid my bill and thanked Antonio again for his warm hospitality.

"Agnello is the lamb," he said as he escorted me to the door.

"*Sì.*"

"*Attenti il leone*," he said. "*Buona fortuna*, Agnello."

I could use some good luck, I thought, as I walked out of Antonio's and up Evans Avenue toward Twenty-Fourth Street.

I could see the dome of the state capitol building when I reached Twenty-Third Street.

When I turned left at the next corner, it was straight ahead.

I had known Hank Sims most of my life. Hank and my father had done a tour of duty together in Vietnam during 1966 and 1967. They were both just beyond adolescence at the time, and from very different worlds—until they were thrown together into the same nightmarish one. Hank and Vito remained good friends for more than twenty years, up until my father's death in 1987.

It was to Hank's ranch I ran when I left New York after Dad was killed, and he welcomed me like a son of his own to a spot where I would never be found. I often wonder why I didn't simply remain there—at the same time knowing, only too well, I wouldn't rest there for long this time either.

I came to the front of the capitol building ten minutes before our scheduled rendezvous. Hank pulled up in a 1953 Chevy truck at exactly five, rolled to a stop, and pushed open the passenger door.

He was a genuine cowboy, and I will never forget the first time I laid eyes on him. I was not more than seven years old, and Hank sat atop a huge black stallion, looking to me to be closer to the sky than to the ground.

I thought he was a god.

Lincoln Bonner would have enjoyed meeting Hank—they had a lot more in common than I had with either of them, at least from a cultural standpoint. Each had a tough but quiet Western strength that was not at all like my hot-blooded New York City variety.

"You look good, kid," Hank said. "How do you feel?"

"I feel safer," I said, settling into the seat beside him.

He put the truck into gear, and we started toward Iron Mountain.

FIVE

San Francisco. Russian Hill. 1921.

Seven-year-old Rosa Leone sat on the front porch of the large Victorian minding her six-year-old sister Maria and brother Louis. It was late May.

"Louis," she called, "stay away from the road."

"You're not the boss," he called back.

Vincenzo Leone walked out of the front door and placed his hand gently on Rosa's head.

"Louis, you listen to your sister. *Vieni qui,* I have good news."

Since coming to San Francisco, a little more than two years earlier, Vincenzo had prospered. His small business grew after the end of the war. There was less competition here than there had been in Philadelphia for the products he imported to the United States through his contacts in Sicily.

Vincenzo had subsequently opened a family restaurant, Naro, and that business was also doing very well.

A year earlier, a beautiful dark-eyed Italian girl came to work at the restaurant.

Lena Territo lived with her parents in the North Beach neighborhood, her father was a successful tailor.

Vincenzo and Lena began courting and soon they were married. Vincenzo was grateful he had been so fortunate in finding a loving young woman to help raise his children.

"Come, Louis," he called again, "*pronto!*"

Louis, who had turned five two weeks earlier, joined his father and the girls on the steps of the house.

"You have all been blessed with a baby brother," Vincenzo told the three children.

An automobile drove past the house, throwing up dust as it rolled by. It was becoming a more common occurrence and soon Vincenzo would be unable to allow the children to remain in front of the house unattended. The back of the house was protected however, and offered a magnificent view of Alcatraz Island, the Bay, and the Pacific Ocean from its perch atop Russian Hill.

"What is the baby's name, Poppa?" asked Maria.

The girls could not remember their mother very well, but they had fallen in love with Lena as deeply as their father had. And they could not remember when Louis was not their brother. Louis had no idea he was an Agnello, not a Leone, by birth.

"His name is Salvatore," said Vincenzo, "named after your grandfather in the old country."

Louis also bore his grandfather's name, inherited from Luigi Agnello who was killed in Sicily by his mortal enemy, Vincenzo's father. Now the young son of Giuseppe Agnello was known to himself and all others as Louis Leone, with no knowledge that across the continent his true father had been desperately trying to locate him for two long years.

"Can we see baby Salvatore, Poppa?" asked Rosa.

"Soon," said her father. "Now come inside and have your dinner."

The children followed Vincenzo into the house. As the girls ran to the kitchen, Vincenzo stopped the young boy with a firm hand on the shoulder, and Louis looked up into the man's piercing eyes.

"You now have a brother and must promise to always protect him."

"I promise, Poppa," said Louis, and he ran to catch up with his sisters.

New York City. 1923.

Nearly two years later, Giuseppe Agnello sat alone in his two-room residence as he usually did each evening after a modest dinner. He seldom had guests and almost never left the rooms after returning from his work on the docks. Aside from Sergio Bolla, who lived on the floor above, he had developed no close friendships. Giuseppe's days were spent in hard labor, often including weekends when he was offered the opportunity to earn extra wages. Giuseppe continued to live frugally, saving his earnings for the time when his wife and child would rejoin him. He recalled that his son would be seven years old in a few days. As he sat in the dark room, Giuseppe thought of little else. Agnello clung to hope, but years of futile searching were loosening his grip.

A knocking at Giuseppe's door aroused him from his indolence. He rose to answer the call.

Agnello opened the door to find Sergio Bolla and the lawyer Catalano.

"*Buonasera*, Giuseppe," said Sergio. "Please excuse this imposition."

"You are always welcome my friends. Please come in."

"I am afraid I cannot, *mio amico*, it is time to put our children to bed," Bolla said. "However, Alfredo has need to speak with you."

"Of course, please enter, Signor Catalano."

Bolla excused himself once again and Catalano followed Giuseppe into the small apartment and to the kitchen table.

"Please sit, Signor. May I offer you espresso?"

"That would be good," said the lawyer, "*e per favore, mi chiamo Alfredo.*"

"*Bene*, Alfredo. *Prego, si accomodi. Mi scusi, un momento.*"

Catalano sat as Agnello moved to fetch the coffee.

Minutes later, the two men sat across from each other at the small table.

"Giuseppe," the lawyer began with little ceremony, "I need to hear from you about your father."

"With all respect, Alfredo," Agnello said, surprised by the request, "I prefer not to talk of these things."

"I fear I must insist. I have some news, but I must know your mind before I can talk with you of my knowledge. Please trust me."

It was all Giuseppe had to hear.

"What would you like to know?"

"I need to hear about your father's death."

Catalano silently listened to Agnello's narrative.

In the rocky hills of Agrigento in Sicily, near the small village of Naro, the Agnello and Leone families had feuded for years over questions of power and land. Power so local and land so desolate that few people from outside their world would appreciate the concern. But to these Sicilians, a respected name and large estate were everything, were all a man could claim and proudly pass on to his children.

A small piece of ground lay at the border of the lands controlled by the two clans, and the dispute over these few rocky, infertile acres was as gravely important to the two families as was the dispute between Germany and France over the Alsace-Lorraine.

In their blind stubbornness, both padrones, Salvatore Leone and Luigi Agnello, had selected this particular plot for their eldest sons, Vincenzo and Giuseppe. It was no matter that the two sons had different feelings as to the worth of the inheritance—the fathers battled fiercely for their birthright.

When Vincenzo Leone left Naro for America in 1913, his father blamed Agnello.

As strongly as Vincenzo insisted his decision had nothing to do with the land dispute, Salvatore refused to accept it. He obstinately believed that had the question of ownership been settled in his favor, his son would have happily remained in the bosom of his ancestors. Vincenzo's motives were far more practical and much less complex. Vincenzo wished a better life for his wife and his infant daughter than he could ever hope for in Sicily, and an escape from the relentless vendettas.

Salvatore Leone's hatred of the Agnello's, and his delusion that a resolution of the property question would bring his son Vincenzo home, eventually turned to violence.

Less than a year after Vincenzo's departure, Salvatore lay in ambush on the dirt road outside of Naro and assassinated Luigi Agnello as he passed in his horse cart toward his home.

The cry for vengeance rang through Agrigento, from all quarters of the Agnello lineage. And the responsibility for retribution lay on the shoulders of Agnello's son, Giuseppe. It was an ancient and solemn duty—the eldest must avenge his father's murder. But Giuseppe had more significant and personal concerns. He was in love with Francesca Leone. And as much as Giuseppe understood the requirements of his tradition, he could not consider taking the life of Francesca's father.

As Giuseppe spoke in public of his patient plans for reprisal, he spoke in whispers to Francesca during the moments they could covertly meet—planning their elopement.

Giuseppe and Francesca were secretly married by a sympathetic priest and left Naro late the same evening, filled with love and hope for a peaceful new beginning in America.

The lawyer Catalano understood that hate, like love, had the power to span oceans.

He needed to know Giuseppe Agnello's mind.

"Do you regret your failure to retaliate against your father's murderer?" the lawyer asked, hoping not to offend.

"Never. I hold no love for Salvatore Leone, and for his actions he will one day have to answer. But not to me. He remains the grandfather of my beloved Louis, and I have decided long ago to leave retribution to the hands of God."

"And your feelings about his son, Vincenzo?"

"I always believed that in other circumstances he and I might have been *a compagno*. I am certain he was a great comfort to my dear wife in her time of need."

"And if you found that in some way Vincenzo Leone was responsible for keeping you apart from your son?"

"*Non capisco.* I don't understand."

"Listen to me carefully, my dear friend," said Alfredo. "I have learned from the Immigration Service that Roberto Leone has recently arrived in New York."

"The younger brother of my wife?"

"*Si*, and he has requested permission to travel to San Francisco in California to join his brother."

"*Grazie a Dio!*"

"Giuseppe, *attenzione*," Catalano continued. "When asked if he had other family beside Vincenzo here in America, Roberto claimed to have none."

"But, *sua sorella*, his sister, *Ma Francesca?*"

"The denial worries me," said the lawyer sadly.

Giuseppe buried his face in his hands, trying to maintain his dignity.

"However, I still remain hopeful we will find your wife and son."

After a short silence, Agnello dropped his hands into his lap and looked steadily into the lawyer's eyes.

"It is all I live for," he said.

Catalano looked at Giuseppe, then gazed around the room. The unkempt appearance of the surroundings and of the man validated Agnello's somber avowal.

"Then you must remain strong and persevere. Have patience for a short while longer. We will wait to see where Roberto Leone leads us."

San Francisco. 1923.

Vincenzo Leone observed the two boys from the window in his study.

Salvatore waded in a small pool, barely three-square feet, which Vincenzo had fashioned from wide planks of wood and thick rubber of the kind used to make automobile tires. As Salvatore sat and splashed in the twelve inches of water, Louis stood just outside the box and watched the younger child like a lion guarding his cub. Vincenzo looked on with pride. He had come to deeply love his sister's boy, and he rejoiced in the addition of a true son of his own. The two male children were devoted to each other. Louis, guiding and protecting. Salvatore, constantly at his brother's heels, like *uno cucciolo*—an adoring puppy. Confident that the boys were safe, Vincenzo sat down at his desk.

Vincenzo removed the letters Francesca had asked him to post to her husband during the weeks before she died.

He had never mailed them.

These letters, written in his sister's hand, along with her son Louis, and a photograph of Francesca taken in Philadelphia, were all Vincenzo had left to remember his precious *sorella*.

Vincenzo held the letters tenderly for a brief moment, returned them to their hiding place at the bottom of the desk drawer, and went outside to join his sons.

SIX

Roberto Leone. New York City. 1923.

Roberto Leone sat on the cot in the small room at Ellis Island, a room much like a prison cell. He was being held for a two-week period of quarantine, to determine the condition of his health before he would be allowed to enter the country and continue on to join his older brother in California. He was both impatient and nervous—Roberto had not seen Vincenzo for nearly ten years.

Roberto was the youngest of Salvatore Leone's three children, only ten years old when Vincenzo left Naro for America. When his sister Francesca ran off with Giuseppe Agnello two years later, Roberto became Salvatore's only remaining child. As such he was terribly spoiled by his father, and thoroughly indoctrinated in the traditional and often archaic Sicilian ways. In particular, Roberto was constantly reminded of the importance of family honor and hatred for *la famiglia* Agnello. Through all those years, Salvatore Leone had continued to blame the Agnellos for the departure of his eldest children and he instilled in young Roberto all of his bitterness and animosity.

At nineteen years old, Roberto had internalized all of his father's rage.

And he took the mission to America on behalf of his father very seriously.

Roberto lay down on the hard cot and silently prayed he would be able to carry out his father's wishes. Salvatore was very ill, and he desired above all to see his oldest son again before he died.

Roberto vowed to do all in his power to compel Vincenzo to make the voyage back to Sicily before it was too late.

On top of that, there was the matter of Giuseppe Agnello—the man Salvatore Leone had raised his youngest son to believe was responsible for the death of Roberto's beloved sister, Francesca.

Giuseppe Agnello. New York City. 1923.

Alfredo Catalano sat across the table from Giuseppe Agnello in the small coffee shop, thankful he had convinced his client to meet him here and so avoid having to return to Agnello's oppressive rooms.

"How are you, my friend?" asked the lawyer, after ordering a demitasse of espresso.

"Struggling to remain hopeful, and anxious for news," said Giuseppe, cutting through the formalities.

"*Capisco benissimo.* Roberto Leone will be released in seven or eight days. Leone has, as is required, given the address of his destination to the immigration authorities. I have learned the location of Vincenzo Leone and with that, I pray, the whereabouts of your wife and son."

Although Catalano had long feared Francesca Agnello had not survived, he could not bring himself to dash Giuseppe's hopes in any way.

"What can we do now?" asked Agnello.

"I will arrange for confirmation that your family is residing with Vincenzo Leone in San Francisco. Meanwhile, Giuseppe, you must collect all documentation of fact identifying Francesca Leone as your legal spouse—and Louis as your true son."

"I possess no such papers. There was no written document of our marriage, and the certificate of my son's birth is in the possession of my wife."

The lawyer sighed deeply.

It was no longer possible to avoid considering the worst case, and he could find no way of introducing it diplomatically.

"If, God forbid, Signora Agnello is unable for any reason to testify to these facts, you will need other verification. Your good friend Bolla and his wife are willing to state their knowledge in writing, and with your permission I will ask them to do so."

Giuseppe simply nodded and tried to express his gratitude.

"I fear my fortitude is wearing thin," Agnello admitted. "I have trusted my fate and the fate of my loved ones into your hands and I do appreciate, beyond words, all of your help and guidance. As hard as I try being patient, I am more and more of late urged to take control *di mio destino.*"

"I understand. Please allow me a little more time," Catalano pleaded. "*Poco tempo, per favore.*"

"*Va bene,*" said Giuseppe.

Agnello would wait only a short while longer.

San Francisco. 1923.

The family gathered around the large dining table in celebration of Louis' seventh birthday. Vincenzo Leone was disappointed that the delay at Ellis Island had prevented Roberto from being present for the occasion. Hopefully, his brother would arrive in time for Salvatore's second birthday—two weeks away.

Vincenzo Leone was by all accounts a successful and well-respected man. His business ventures continued to prosper and he had been unusually well received in the predominantly Anglo-Saxon community. He had grown to love his sister's child without reserve. His adopted son Louis would be heir to Leone's hard-earned prestige and fortune.

Lena held Salvatore on her lap and watched how her husband fussed over and pampered the older boy. She understood Vincenzo's devotion to his eldest male child, and she loved his three children dearly, but she also understood that her own son Salvatore would always be second. She had found a husband who was both a fine man and a good provider, and for that she was grateful. But she could not, as hard as she tried, dismiss the nagging feeling that she and Salvatore would never hold as strong a place in Vincenzo's heart and heritage as did his first wife and his first son.

Soon a stranger would be coming in to their home, another connection to Vincenzo's life before she became part of it, and Lena feared Roberto Leone's arrival might demand more of her husband's attention and devotion at the expense of herself and her child. Her husband, seeming to read her thoughts, gave Lena a reassuring smile from across the table, then came over to her and took Salvatore lovingly into his arms.

"*Mio figlio adorato*," he said loudly, much for his wife's benefit, "soon we will celebrate *your* miraculous birth."

Lena's heart lightened at the sight of the child wrapping his arms around his father's neck in a tender embrace.

"*Poppa, vieni qui*," called Louis gleefully from across the room, "hurry, come to see what Rosa has given to me for my birthday."

Vincenzo returned the child to his wife's lap and rushed back to the older boy's side.

New York.

Roberto Leone boarded the train for the trip across the country and the reunion with the older brother he barely remembered. Having spent his entire life in a small village on a fairly isolated island he would be overwhelmed by the vastness of this land, and could only vaguely imagine the opportunities it presented.

Roberto had been well versed by his father in the importance of power, and the young man saw before him a landscape where such power could have real meaning.

The lawyer Catalano's cousin, who had recently settled in San Francisco, would be waiting at the end of Roberto's momentous journey.

San Francisco.

On the morning of Salvatore Leone's second birthday, Lena Leone had taken all four children with her to do the shopping for the celebration. At her last stop, to pick up the specially prepared cake, a woman not much older than Lena entered the bakery just behind her and the children. The other woman was carrying a small child of her own. Lena had not noticed the same woman had been outside the grocery store and the meat market as well.

Lena left Rosa to mind Maria, Louis, and the basket of groceries, and moved to the counter holding Salvatore in her arms. As the baker Sabatino went to the back to retrieve what he promised would be *una torta magnifica*, the woman who had been following Lena came up to stand beside her at the display case.

"*Buongiorno. Uno figlio bello,*" she said.

Lena was initially startled and suspicious at being approached and greeted by a stranger.

When Lena turned to look at the other young woman, who spoke Italian and also held a young child, her misgivings faded.

"*Grazie.*"

"How old is he?"

"Two years today."

"Bravo. My Mario will be two years old in July. *Come ti chiami, per favore?*"

"Lena Leone."

"*Mi chiami* Rosalie Catalano."

"*Bene.* The oldest girl is Rosa, and her sister is called Maria, so much like your son's name," said Lena, indicating the three other children waiting impatiently near the bakery door. "The older boy is Louis."

The two toddlers had by now become very interested in each other.

"You are so young to have such a large family," said Rosalie. "*Congratulazioni!*"

Lena surprised herself by being so forthcoming as to explain that the three older children were not hers by birth but by marriage, her husband having lost his first wife to influenza some years ago.

"They are fortunate to have such a beautiful and loving new mother," said Rosalie with a kind smile.

"*Grazie, molto grazie.*"

Signor Sabatino returned with the cake and both women expressed their delight in his artistry.

"It was good to meet you," said Rosalie, "*buon compleanno!* Salvatore."

"*Arrivederci,*" said Lena.

"*Buona fortuna,*" said Rosalie.

Lena put Salvatore into Rosa's care, placed the cake into the basket, and started out of the bakery—the four children following.

"*Pronto,* Luigi," Lena called to the seven-year-old, who was lagging behind.

Rosalie and the baker watched them leave the shop.

"*Si, Signora?*" Sabatino asked Rosalie when they had gone.

"*Biscotti, mezza libbra per favore.*"

When Michael Catalano returned home from work that evening, he was greeted by the wonderful aromas from the kitchen, a warm embrace from his wife, and a tug on the leg from his son, Mario.

Michael picked the boy up into his arms and followed his wife as she hurried back to her cooking.

"Tell me what you have learned," he said, sitting at the kitchen table and placing Mario on his lap.

Rosalie dropped the pasta into the boiling water and turned from the stove.

"It is true, there is a boy in the Leone family who appears to be near seven years old and is called Louis," said Rosalie Catalano. "Signora Leone admitted that the older children were not her own, but were those of Leone's first wife who died of the influenza. However, she did not say the boy, Louis, was the son of her husband's sister."

"Perhaps she is unaware the boy is in truth Leone's nephew."

"Surely Leone would tell his new wife," said Rosalie, turning back to attend to the pasta and the sauce simmering beside it.

"Not if he hoped to maintain the boy's position in the Leone house. To others of the family the boy would always be an Agnello, regardless of who his mother was. And to his new wife, if it were known, Louis would be a threat to her own child's rightful place as eldest son and heir. Leone has tried to do something honorable, for the love and memory of his sister, which I'm afraid could ultimately be dangerous to Louis."

"You seem certain the boy's mother is deceased."

"I'm afraid there is no other explanation for what we have witnessed. I would guess she was also a victim of the deadly flu."

"If Leone truly loved his departed sister, he would have reunited Louis with his actual father, as I am sure his sister would have wished."

"Leone's wife died without leaving him a son, possibly he feared he would never have one and believed it was fate that his sister left a male child into his care."

"Call it what you will, fate or honor, but I only see more tragedy ahead."

"I must wire my cousin Alfredo in New York," Michael said. "*Rapidamente.*"

San Francisco.

Vincenzo Leone sat at the head of the grand table in his palazzo on the hill, having every reason to feel abundantly fortunate. His businesses were thriving and he planned the opening of a large salumeria, a grocery for retailing the delicacies his company imported from the old country for the growing Italian-American population of San Francisco. He had a beautiful wife and four fine children, all in good health. And two days earlier, his younger brother Roberto had joined the household, in time for tonight's celebration of Salvatore's second birthday.

Yet, with all of these blessings, Vincenzo sat feeling anxious and distressed.

The brothers had been at odds almost immediately upon Roberto's arrival.

The news of his father's poor health deeply concerned Vincenzo, but a trip to Sicily to visit his parents was out of the question.

The importing company, supervision of the restaurant, and the preparations for the new delicatessen demanded most of his waking hours.

To travel now would be impossible.

Leone tried patiently to explain to his brother the importance of these endeavors to the entire family, including Roberto himself—who Vincenzo had planned to name proprietor of the salumeria. When the younger man could not or would not understand it had caused the brothers to lose their tempers and raise their voices, frightening Lena and the children.

To compound the antagonism, Roberto Leone began to ask many questions concerning Giuseppe Agnello and their sister Francesca.

"Had Agnello not taken Francesca from our midst, she would still be alive in Naro—in the bosom of our dear, brokenhearted mamma," insisted Roberto.

"That is our father talking," Vincenzo Leone answered angrily. "You are young, *non capisci*. Giuseppe Agnello and Francesca loved each other deeply and always treated one another with great respect."

"Then why did Agnello abandon our sister? Go off and leave her to die?"

"Agnello was called to serve his newly adopted country and answered the call nobly. Our sister died tending to my wife, Carmella, all the while keeping the young children and myself safe from the illness. Agnello cannot be blamed for Francesca's unselfish care."

"Why do you defend the enemy *di nostra famiglia*?" said Roberto.

"Roberto, *arresto!* You are in my house now, I am your older brother and you will submit to my wishes. Forget about Agnello, consider him *a morto*, he is no longer a concern to anyone in this family. I will hear no more of this hateful talk in our home."

At that, Roberto left the room and had not spoken of these things again, had not said much at all, keeping within himself his continued desire to satisfy the will of his father.

Roberto's silence grieved Vincenzo, and the subject of Giuseppe Agnello had brought back to mind a fear he had somehow managed to ignore for a long time.

Now, two days after the terrible dispute with Roberto, Leone sat during the birthday festivities and contemplated in solitude a probability he could no longer deny—that Giuseppe Agnello was still very much alive, and was without doubt desperately in search of his wife and child.

"*Mio marito*," said Lena, lightly touching Vincenzo's arm from her seat beside him, "*che cosa*? You are so quiet and solemn on this happy day."

"*Scusa, mi amore*," Vincenzo said, adjusting his demeanor to relieve his wife's concern, "I was thinking of business matters when I should only be thinking of our joy and good fortune. Now, where is Signor Sabatino's *torta gloriosa*!"

At the other end of the table, Roberto Leone was lost in his own thoughts.

The discord between the brothers had left Roberto feeling less welcome in Vincenzo's home than anticipated, and the prospect of having traveled so far to end up nothing more than a grocer did not inspire him.

What did excite Roberto, rather, were the stimulating conversations he had shared with Benito Lucchese during the journey west. Benny Lucchese, who had boarded in Illinois, had approached Roberto soon after spotting him. Lucchese was attracted by something he saw in the young man's eyes— by the way Roberto ravenously took in the vast countryside racing past the windows of the train. Lucchese saw in the newly arrived immigrant something he was always on the lookout for, a young man with raw ambition. With the help of his associations with powerful men in Chicago, including Alfonse Capone and Frank Nitti, Lucchese was in the process of setting up the largest illegal liquor operation on the West Coast, controlled from San Francisco.

And Benny Lucchese needed good help.

Foregoing many of the details of the job description, Lucchese invited Roberto to look him up if he found himself in need of lucrative employment.

Thanking Benny for the generous offer, Roberto Leone wished his new acquaintance good fortune as they amiably parted at the train station.

Lena returned carrying the marvelous cake, with its two lit candles, and placed it on the table in front of the wide-eyed children.

Roberto Leone watched his brother from across the room—

Vincenzo so absorbed in the excitement of the occasion.

Roberto decided that on the following morning he would pay a visit to Benny Lucchese.

SEVEN

New York City. 1923.

Alfredo Catalano received the news from his cousin in San Francisco with great sadness and dread. Michael and Rosalie had learned what the lawyer had long suspected, that Francesca Agnello was no longer among the Leones. Catalano had since confirmed, through laborious scrutiny of thousands of death records, that both the wife and sister of Vincenzo Leone were among the many fatal victims of the Spanish Flu when the epidemic ravaged Philadelphia in late 1917. The lawyer discovered that Giuseppe Agnello's wife had not been listed under the name of her husband, but was identified instead as Francesca Leone. Nearly two weeks after hearing from his cousins, Alfredo knew he could no longer delay relating the news to Giuseppe.

Catalano did not look forward to fulfilling this duty.

Under different circumstances, the news that Louis was alive and well might have helped to ease the grief Catalano was now forced to inflict upon his client and friend. The reality of the situation, however, was far more complex and distressing. Catalano had retrieved a copy of Louis Agnello's birth certificate from the New York City archives and also had in his hands signed affidavits from Sergio and Sophia Bolla attesting to their knowledge of Giuseppe's paternity. It was now clear Vincenzo Leone had claimed his sister's child as his own and would not give the boy up easily. The lawyer was building a legal case for the return of the boy to his true father, but these things took time. The American judicial system was intricate and slow moving, all the more so when two different states were involved.

All the more so when the parties involved were foreigners.

Giuseppe Agnello came from a culture where disputes were decided among the families involved and not by courts of law. When he heard of his wife's death, his total focus would be directed toward a reunion with his son.

Would Giuseppe be willing to wait longer, after more than four torturous years of searching, to finally see his son again?

Would Giuseppe stand idle while strangers, with little invested in the outcome, argued over the future of his legacy?

Could Catalano somehow convince Agnello it was in his best interest, and in the best interest of the child, to allow the legal process to run its course and not try to take matters into his own hands?

The lawyer was not confident that Giuseppe could be deterred and, moreover, Alfredo could not say with certainty how he would respond if it were his own child in question.

It was with this trepidation that Catalano approached the door to Giuseppe's apartment on a Saturday morning in early June.

Giuseppe took the news of his wife's death with great dignity. Although he was silent for some time, he sat calmly and nobly while Catalano explained the situation in regard to the child.

When Giuseppe finally spoke, the lawyer saw even more clearly the weakness of his argument.

"What you are saying is if we begin this legal action there is no way to know how long it will take to be judged or even know if it will be resolved in our favor."

"*Si, esattamente.*"

Catalano could think of nothing else to say in response to the sadly accurate assessment.

"I cannot wait."

"Giuseppe, *per favore*," said the lawyer, "allow me at least a short time to explore the chances of our success through the courts before you do something you may regret."

"How long?"

"Only a few weeks. I will devote all of my time and energy."

"I will wait only until the end of this month, and meanwhile I will make arrangements for my travel to San Francisco. I have great respect for you, Signor Catalano, and I will always be indebted to you for your generosity and your vigilance on my behalf. I beg of you, with no offense intended, do not offer false hope."

"I have always been honest with you and will remain so," said the lawyer, not at all offended but extremely moved.

"*Grazie.* I will wait for your word. You must now excuse me for I need privacy, *pregare Dio* for the soul of my dear departed wife and the fate of my son."

With a nod of farewell, the lawyer left Giuseppe to his solitary prayers.

As the last days of June 1923 approached, Alfredo Catalano was weary and discouraged. With the assistance of a fellow lawyer in San Francisco, through daily telegraph wires, he had learned that Giuseppe Agnello's chances of a speedy, legally dictated reunion with his son Louis were slight at best. Catalano could promise only many months of litigation with dubious success. The jurisdictional barriers, the formative years the boy had spent among the Leones, and the quality of life offered to the child in a prosperous home with a maternal presence and other young children, could easily outweigh biological considerations.

Possession, even in the case of an innocent child, looked to be nine-tenths of the law.

Alfredo had come to the conclusion that perhaps Giuseppe's

only hope of regaining custody of his son was to somehow whisk Louis away. And as difficult as it was for Catalano to make such an admission, being a man with great respect and faith in the law, he had come to the point when he felt he could no longer withhold the unhappy truth.

Alfredo asked Sergio Bolla to accompany him for moral support. Together they would visit Agnello.

Catalano decided he would do all he could to assist Giuseppe in whatever he chose to do.

Alfredo had been assured by his cousin Michael in San Francisco that Agnello would be welcome to stay at their home if he made the journey.

The lawyer wished he could do more.

On Saturday morning, the last day of June, Sergio greeted Catalano at the Bolla home with visible concern.

The previous day, Giuseppe had left work before noon, complaining he felt ill.

That evening after supper, Bolla had rapped lightly at Agnello's door to see how his neighbor was feeling and had received no response.

Guessing his friend had gone to bed early, Bolla did not persist.

Before the lawyer had arrived, Bolla had attempted to rouse Agnello once again, to no avail. Sergio was worried Giuseppe was more ill than he had appeared, and expressed his anxiety to Catalano.

Alfredo asked Sergio to join him in another attempt, and the men hurried to Giuseppe's door. After minutes of persistent, disregarded knocking, Sergio ran back to fetch the spare key to Agnello's apartment, which Giuseppe had left in Bolla's safekeeping.

Upon entering the rooms, Sergio and Alfredo knew immediately that Giuseppe Agnello had gone to fetch his son.

San Francisco. 1923.

Roberto Leone had spent less and less time at the house of his brother over the past several weeks, and had been little involved in the plans for the imminent opening of the new family business.

Vincenzo was distressed and angered by Roberto's behavior, demanding to know where his brother had been spending all his time and insisting Roberto prepare to take more responsibility for the operation of the salumeria. As his younger brother became more distant and uncommunicative, Vincenzo became more infuriated.

"I fear my brother will soon exile me from his home."

"*Non preoccuparsi*, do not worry, before long you will be able to afford a fine home of your own," Benny Lucchese assured Roberto, "but first, you must make peace with Vincenzo."

Suddenly, Roberto was not only willing but appeared enthusiastic about joining in Vincenzo's business enterprises.

After an enlightening diplomacy lesson from Benny Lucchese, Roberto had taken his older brother aside and apologized for his childlike behavior.

"I have been ungrateful, *fratello*, and what is worse, disrespectful. I humbly ask your pardon. I have been troubled over the health of our dear father and I have neglected the reasons he wished me to journey here. Above all, our father desires I provide help and comfort to you and will also learn from you and be guided by your strength and industry. He has placed me into your trusted hands, and I want only to make you and our father proud. Please forgive me, brother, and allow me that opportunity."

"*Si! Certo!*" said Vincenzo, embracing Roberto. "Together we shall make the name of Leone one to be respected for generations."

"*Mille grazie, fratello.*"

"We will begin immediately. Let us go to see the progress of the salumeria, and you must assist me in choosing the inventory. The construction is nearly complete, and we need to order our merchandise without delay."

"I wish also to learn all about the governance and receiving of cargo shipments, so as to be of the greatest assistance," said Roberto.

"Brother, I will teach you everything you will need to know to operate *l'impresa familiare* and together, in years to come, we will teach our children. And if you are a rapid learner, perhaps I will feel free to visit our father before too long with the confidence you will be prepared to oversee in my absence."

"You will be able to depend on me," said Roberto, "*Io promessa.*"

Two weeks after the reconciliation with his brother, Roberto Leone gave Benny's plan a trial run. Along with a large shipment of goods for the soon to open grocery and delicatessen came two wooden crates labeled as imported balsamic vinegar.

They passed through customs without suspicion, the officials being familiar and trusting of the Leones and their businesses.

On the evening of the delivery, Roberto worked alone stocking the shelves of the new salumeria while Vincenzo was busy at the family restaurant.

Benny appeared soon after dark.

"Did it go well?" asked Benny, as Roberto let him into the storage area at the back of the shop.

"With no difficulty," said Roberto, pointing to the two crates near the door.

Benny went to his knees, pried open the lid of one of the crates, and laughed heartily after removing the cover and revealing its contents.

"The finest whiskey from Ireland and Scotland. *Fantastico!* We must celebrate with a drink."

"Of course," said Roberto.

"*Compagno*," said Benny Lucchese, passing a bottle, "this is only the beginning. We are going to be very rich and powerful men. *Salute!*"

EIGHT

San Francisco. 1923.

Roberto watched his brother from the kitchen window. Vincenzo was in the backyard constructing a cedar chair, using lumber left over from the building of bulk food bins for the delicatessen scheduled to open its doors in two days.

The two brothers had visited the store the previous evening. Vincenzo was extremely pleased with the work Roberto had done in setting up the inventory and told his younger brother so.

The shelves were neatly stocked with imported goods including olive oils, jars of marinated vegetables and stuffed peppers, tins of sardines and anchovies, canned tomatoes, caponata, dried fruits, and bread sticks.

The cedar bins were filled high with dry foods in bulk including lentils, garbanzo beans, dried pastas, short and long grained rice, semolina flour, and roasted coffee beans. Large glass jars on shelves behind the long counter held dried herbs—oregano, basil, parsley, and rosemary—alongside jars of sundried tomatoes and capers.

Large salamis and provolone cheeses hung in the front window.

In the refrigerated display case were wheels of Romano and Parmesan, prosciutto, ham, and other slicing meats and cheeses.

Every morning there would be deliveries of fresh produce including tomatoes, garlic, peppers, artichoke, broccoli rabe, and escarole—along with milk and cream from the dairy, and breads and rolls from Signor Sabatino's bakery.

"*Stupendo!*" said Vincenzo, wrapping his arm around Roberto's shoulder.

The two men stood briefly out front, Vincenzo looking proudly at the large sign above the entrance. *Salumeria Leone*— painted in the colors of their homeland, red and green against a background of white.

Also, prominently displayed, was an American flag, as were many other flags like it up and down Columbus Avenue on the eve of the day of American independence.

Early the next morning, Lena took the two girls and Salvatore to the home of her parents, where she and her mother would prepare the foods for the delicatessen case the following day. Marinated olives, fried eggplant, sausage and peppers and onions, stuffed artichoke, fresh tomato and cucumber salad in virgin olive oil and balsamic vinegar, and other traditional dishes.

Louis had remained home and watched with fascination as Vincenzo assembled the chair, and Roberto observed both father and son from the window. Soon Roberto lost interest and turned away, his mind afire with thoughts having little to do with the shop opening.

Since the successful smuggling of two cases of whiskey a few weeks earlier, Roberto Leone and Benito Lucchese began making very big plans. The ships carrying food orders from Italy originated in Naples and then stopped at Liverpool in England to drop cargo and take on products from England, Ireland, and Scotland before continuing on to America. At Naples, falsely marked cases of fine wine would be set among the Leone shipment, and at Liverpool similarly disguised cases of Irish and Scotch whiskies, beers, and English gin would be added.

These very valuable imported alcoholic beverages would find their way into the most distinguished and respectable homes in San Francisco, and demand extremely high prices from the socialites who refused to humble themselves with rancid homemade wine, flat bitter beer, and bathtub gin.

On this morning, Roberto was about to meet Benny and see for the first time the warehouse Lucchese had leased to store their contraband. Roberto called to Vincenzo that he was leaving for a few hours, and young Louis ran back into the house to bid his Uncle Roberto goodbye.

Giuseppe Agnello had arrived in San Francisco on July third. As anxious as he was to see his son, he realized it was too late in the evening to visit the Leone home. He was directed by a railroad steward, a fellow countryman, to a transient hotel on Columbus Avenue in a neighborhood increasingly populated by Italian immigrants.

The location of the hotel would put Agnello closer to his destination, on Union Street directly down the hill from Vincenzo Leone's residence.

Giuseppe tossed restlessly until exhaustion finally overtook him and he fell into a deep sleep, waking much later than he had planned. Once again, he was compelled to delay his journey. He was well rested but famished. He walked from the hotel to a small diner, just next door, which the manager of the hotel had recommended.

Agnello gazed up at the American flag waving above the restaurant entranceway.

After a hearty meal of peppers, onions, and eggs with crusty bread and strong coffee, he returned to the street. It was then Giuseppe noticed what he had not seen the night before—the large sign above the doorway of a shop directly across from the hotel, Salumeria Leone.

Giuseppe crossed and he peered into the shop window, impressed by its wealth of goods. The salumeria was locked up and deserted. Agnello walked to the corner of Union Street and started up Russian Hill.

. . .

Louis begged his uncle to take him along. Roberto insisted he could not, and after playfully roughing the boy's hair he walked out onto Hyde Street.

Louis went to the window and saw Roberto hesitate for a moment on the front porch to take a deep breath of the brisk air before bounding down the steps to the sidewalk. Roberto was filled with excitement about seeing the warehouse and he stepped toward Union Street just as Giuseppe Agnello turned the corner and suddenly stood before him.

"*Buongiorno. Per favore*, I am looking for the home of Vincenzo Leone."

"May I ask who is calling?"

"Giuseppe Agnello."

Roberto was overwhelmed with emotion.

He was so visibly affected that even the boy at the window could not help but notice his reaction. A wild assortment of urges rushed through Roberto's mind and body, not the least of which was to strike the other man down where he stood.

Giuseppe actually took a few steps back away from the younger man, surprised and confused by the odd look in Roberto's dark eyes.

Then suddenly, Roberto Leone regained control, his demeanor changed and he forced himself to smile and speak.

"Please forgive me. I am Roberto Leone," he managed to say, "and you, I believe, are the husband of my dear sister."

Giuseppe wished to ask many questions. Was his wife alive, the news of her death somehow mistaken? Was his son perhaps in the very house they stood before? Why had the Leones cut Giuseppe off from his family?

Something about Roberto's initial reaction troubled him, so Agnello also controlled his emotions.

"Yes, I am Francesca's husband. I wish to speak with your brother."

"Vincenzo is not presently at home. I am on my way now to join him. I welcome you to accompany me."

"*Grazie*," said Giuseppe Agnello.

The boy, Louis, watched as the men moved away from the house. The two men walked silently, side by side. Roberto led Giuseppe back down Hyde Street toward the wharf where Benny Lucchese waited for him at the newly leased warehouse.

The Port of San Francisco and the majestic bay spread out before them as they reached Jefferson Street and turned east toward the Embarcadero.

Not a single word had been spoken between the two men, as both were lost in their own thoughts.

Giuseppe, hopeful and anxious about finding his family at last.

Roberto, concerned only with fulfilling the wishes of his father.

Giuseppe was momentarily startled when the reports of fireworks set off by holiday celebrants along Fisherman's Wharf disturbed the silence.

Roberto Leone had not flinched.

As they approached the warehouse, Roberto marveled at its location, a stone's throw from the shipping docks where cases of alcoholic beverages would be arriving regularly amid cargo consigned to Leone Importing.

Giuseppe followed as Roberto walked around to the far side of the large building, which faced the piers. Two wide load-in bay entrances flanked a large metal door that led to a good-sized room that would serve as an office, where Benny Lucchese had already set up a desk and a few armchairs.

Benny was seated at the desk when Roberto rapped lightly on the window.

Benny's pleasure at the arrival of his partner turned to surprise and dismay when he opened the door to discover Leone had come with another man.

"*Che cosa?*" Lucchese asked.

"This is Giuseppe Agnello, from my hometown of Naro. He is here to see my brother, Vincenzo."

Lucchese was confused, but decided to play along.

"*Buongiorno*, Signor Agnello. Please, sit. Signor Leone is occupied, but I am certain he will be pleased to see an old neighbor," said Lucchese. "Roberto, come with me, I will take you to fetch Vincenzo."

Giuseppe took a seat and the other two men moved from the office out into the open warehouse area.

"Fantastic," said Roberto, taking in the wide expanse of the open interior.

"What is this about, Roberto?" demanded Lucchese.

"Let me have your *pistola*," Roberto said calmly.

"What are you talking about? Who is this man?"

"He is the mortal enemy of my family. He is the man who took my sister from her heartbroken parents against their will and then left her alone to die. He is the man who I am sworn to my father to destroy."

Benny reached under his jacket, produced a large handgun, and passed it with care to Roberto.

"Do it out here," he said coldly. "I do not wish the office to be soiled."

Benny stationed Roberto against the wall beside the doorway and returned to the office.

"Signor Agnello," Benny said, "please come. Vincenzo will see you now."

Giuseppe rose and moved toward the door, stopping beside Lucchese before passing through.

"*Per favor,*" said Lucchese, "after you, Signor."

Giuseppe stepped through the doorway and looked out into the empty warehouse.

Roberto stepped behind Giuseppe and put a bullet into the back of Agnello's head.

"For Francesca, and *mi padre*," he cried, as Giuseppe fell

to the ground.

"*Rapidamente*, Roberto," said Benny Lucchese as he came up beside Leone, removed his jacket and began rolling up his shirtsleeves. "We must clean up this mess you have made."

NINE

New York City. 1923.

It had been many months and there was no word from Giuseppe Agnello and no clue as to his whereabouts.

Alfredo Catalano could only be certain the boy Louis was still residing at the Leone home—as was reported to him by his cousin Michael and Michael's wife, Rosalie, in San Francisco.

The police in that city had offered no assistance—refusing to question Vincenzo Leone about any knowledge he may have had regarding Giuseppe Agnello's disappearance.

Leone was a respected businessman and there was no local interest in troubling him over the fate of a New York longshoreman who had left home one day, like hundreds of others, and had never returned.

Alfredo Catalano could offer no proof to the San Francisco police that Giuseppe had ever actually reached the West Coast. The lawyer chose not to mention to the authorities the intent of Agnello's journey, having no desire to alert Vincenzo to the fact there were others who were aware of the true relationship between Leone and the boy, Louis.

The New York City police, among whom the lawyer had many friends, would have liked to help but had no authority.

All Catalano could think to do was to confront Leone himself, and he was reluctant.

Alfredo enlisted the aid of his cousin, as well as a fellow attorney in San Francisco, to keep an eye on the Leones—in the faint hope something might be revealed concerning Giuseppe Agnello's fate.

Now, after nearly half a year of unrewarded optimism, Alfredo resolved he would write a letter to Vincenzo Leone to ask directly if Giuseppe had ever arrived at Leone's door.

It was most likely Catalano would never receive a response, but Alfredo felt he had to do something.

San Francisco.

As the final days of 1923 approached, Vincenzo Leone had much to be thankful for.

The family importing business continued to grow very rapidly.

Sales had reached an all-time high and Leone had taken on a manager, Theodore Harding, who was both innovative and trustworthy. Thanks to Harding's invaluable insights, the company had grown far beyond its initial catalog of goods, which had originally included only foodstuffs.

Leone Importing was now importing and marketing products as diverse as books written in Italian, Spanish, and French, superbly crafted European cookware and coffee brewing systems, and fine decorative Italian ceramic tile and marble.

Ristorante Naro, named in honor of Vincenzo's birthplace, prospered as well. The restaurant was operated by Lena and her mother, and it demanded little of Vincenzo's attention.

In fact, the women often asked him kindly to stay out from under foot.

The children spent much of their time there. The girls helping in the kitchen and dining room, Louis tossing a rubber ball against the wall of the building, and Salvatore strapped into a high chair playing with his food.

Perhaps what most pleased Vincenzo, however, was how well Roberto was doing. The delicatessen was thriving, and its success could be credited entirely to Roberto's hard work. Roberto had also taken on the responsibility of cargo pickup and delivery for all three enterprises. Vincenzo was impressed with his brother, just twenty and already in possession of maturity and diligence well beyond his years.

The confidence Vincenzo had in the abilities of those around him, along with the approach of the far less active post-holiday season, had him considering what he would have thought impossible only six months earlier.

Leone decided that when the family came together for Christmas dinner he would make his intent known.

On Christmas eve, after a traditional seafood dinner that included steamed mussels, shrimp scampi, deep fried calamari, stuffed clams, cold octopus salad, and pasta with lobster sauce, Roberto asked to be excused to join a few of his young friends in celebration. Vincenzo was happy to see the young man making a life for himself in his new homeland and, though he refrained from saying as much, he looked forward to the day when Roberto would take a wife and start a family of his own. Vincenzo wished his brother a safe and enjoyable evening, then he joined Lena in attempting to coax the excited children to bed.

Roberto walked down Union Street to Powell and around to the rear of a building just off Columbus Avenue. He knocked three times at the door and a moment later Benny Lucchese ushered him in. He entered the large open room, teeming with people holding drinks sold at the long bar operated by Benny and Roberto. It was more active than usual due to the holiday, but was always busy and extremely profitable. On top of that, nearly all the libation purchased by San Francisco's affluent, in greater quantity lately as the city prepared to usher in the New Year, came from their warehouse. Roberto Leone had done everything possible, within the limits of Leone Importing Company's normal shipment volume, to smuggle in enough contraband liquor to meet the great demand.

The warehouse fronted as the headquarters of L&L Supplies, a purveyor of construction materials, which was a lucrative business in itself.

San Francisco was still in a steady process of rebuilding nearly two decades after the great earthquake leveled most of the city. Vincenzo did business with L&L—but he had no knowledge that the large initials painted above the warehouse doors represented the surnames of Lucchese and Leone's own brother.

And tucked behind rows of lumber and concrete, shelves of nails and hand tools, rolls of wallpaper, drums of paint, and pallets of Florentine hand-painted ceramic tile and fine Italian marble purchased from and delivered by Leone Importing, were cases of premium whiskies, wines, liquors, and beer from the British Isles, Western Europe, Mexico, and South America.

Benny Lucchese stepped behind the bar and poured two tall glasses of scotch, handed one to Roberto, and made a toast.

"*Salute. Buon Natale*," said Lucchese, "to a bountiful Christmas."

"And a wealthy New Year," said Roberto.

"I have something special for your brother," said Benny, reaching below the bar and placing a bottle of the finest imported Italian anisette in front of Roberto.

"Vincenzo will appreciate this considerably, but where will I say it came from?"

"A gift from a satisfied customer. I am confident he will accept without much protest."

"*Grazie.*"

"*Prego.* Now drink up so I may refill your glass. A pair of gorgeous ladies across the room are anxious for our company."

The two young women were lovely and eager to please their handsome and successful hosts. Benny was jubilant and charming, with no thought in his mind but to enjoy the moment.

Had Roberto been as clear minded as Benny, he would have marveled at his envious position—with a pocketful of cash and a pretty girl at his side. But Roberto was preoccupied with thoughts of another beautiful young woman who had captured his heart the instant he had first set eyes upon her nearly seven months earlier.

Roberto Leone had fallen hopelessly in love with the wife of his brother.

Vincenzo spent early Christmas morning with Lena and the children, opening gifts around the tall decorated tree in the Leone living room.

Roberto Leone slept late that morning, after a long night out.

Roberto had left presents under the tree for his brother, his sister-in-law, and his nieces and nephews. Vincenzo had to firmly insist, over the protests of the children, that those packages not be touched until their Uncle Roberto was among them.

The Leones had invited Theodore Harding and his wife, along with Lena's parents and sister, to join them for the late-afternoon holiday dinner. Lena's mother and sister arrived early to assist Lena in preparing the food and in arranging the large dining room table to accommodate the seven adults and five youngsters. Lena's sister Anna was ten years old, the same age as Rosa, and the two girls helped place china, silverware, and linens at each setting.

When Roberto finally emerged, there was a second round of gift giving to the delight of the children.

Roberto presented his older brother with two luxurious wool cardigan sweaters, hand-knit in Scotland, and the bottle of Italian anisette.

Vincenzo Leone was truly awed by the magnificence of the clothing, and appreciative of Roberto's generosity.

His reaction to the liqueur was another matter.

"Where did this come from?" he asked with great concern.

"An acquaintance of mine was able to acquire it for me, as a special favor."

"It is against the law, Roberto. Please do not take offense, but I cannot allow it in my home. It places us in peril, and it is extremely dangerous for you to associate with such an acquaintance. Please forgive me, but I must dispose of this immediately."

Roberto Leone stood in disbelief and humiliation as his brother emptied the bottle into the kitchen sink.

The women removed what remained of the feast after everyone had eaten far more than they could comfortably digest. The children had retreated to the living room to become acquainted with their bounty of holiday gifts.

Sally Harding placed bowls of fruits and nuts on the cleared dining table and then rejoined Lena and Lena's mother in the kitchen to help store leftovers and clean the supper dishes.

Vincenzo, his father-in-law, and Theodore Harding entrenched themselves in a lively three-handed Pinochle game. Roberto stood apart from the activity, and for the most part from the festivity. He had been silent at dinner and had eaten sparingly.

The incident with the anisette had dampened Roberto's mood, but it was Lena's radiance and her energy, as she gracefully entertained her guests, which disturbed him more.

He had so often caught himself staring at her that he could hardly wait for the meal to end so he could escape his self-consciousness.

Roberto now sat alone on the front porch of the house in a state of near turmoil.

After the food and dinnerware had been put away, the women returned with coffee and Italian pastries—cannoli, Baba ricotta, grain pie, cheesecake, and an assortment of biscotti.

Vincenzo called to his wife and asked her to fetch Roberto for dessert. Leone wished his brother to be present when he made his important announcement.

Lena removed her apron and straightened her dress. On her way through the foyer she stole a glance in the hall mirror. She arranged her hair and decided she looked fairly attractive considering all that it had taken to play hostess to the family and guests since early morning. Lena went out the front door, quietly moved behind Roberto where he sat on the porch, and placed a hand on his shoulder. He was startled by the physical contact and turned abruptly. Then, realizing who had touched him, his eyes met hers with an unguarded passion that both surprised and disturbed her.

"Roberto," she said, turning her eyes away, "Vincenzo wishes you to return and sit with us for coffee."

Roberto rose and she looked back to him. It seemed as if he were about to speak, but he stood silently and waited for her to lead.

Lena reentered the house and Roberto followed behind.

When everyone was seated at the table, passing around the platters of baked goods, Lena and her mother poured espresso.

Vincenzo finally spoke out.

"My family, my friends, I am blessed to have you all around me on this holy day. I wish to thank Theodore and Roberto for all of the help they have provided in building upon the prosperity of our enterprises. It is precisely my faith in the abilities of these loyal men that has allowed me to contemplate doing what I had thought impossible only a short time ago. I plan to travel to Sicily after the New Year, to visit my ailing father."

The declaration took all by surprise—and left Lena, Roberto, and Theodore with much to consider.

For Lena, it would be the first separation from her husband—it would leave her alone to see to the needs of the four children.

For Harding, it would be a grave responsibility, to solely protect the interests of Leone Importing during Vincenzo's absence.

For Roberto, it presented conflicting emotions.

However, he temporarily suppressed his disconcert and voiced his enthusiastic support.

"*Bravo, mio fratello*, this is wonderful news," said Roberto. "You will bring great happiness to our beloved parents."

Vincenzo looked to his wife, who had remained silent. She returned his smile, hiding her disappointment in not being told of his decision before he had made it public.

Once the excitement generated by the announcement subsided, all attention turned to the splendid pastries, strong black coffee, and small pockets of conversation. Lena's mother assured her daughter that she would always be nearby to assist with the children, and Sally Harding also offered her support. Lena's father informed Roberto that if help was needed in the salumeria, Lena's cousin Nino was available to provide assistance.

Vincenzo leaned over to Theodore Harding, asking for a short meeting in the study to discuss preparations for his departure.

After thirty minutes, during which time they thoroughly discussed the implications of Vincenzo's trip, he and Harding started back to the dining room.

"Vincenzo," said Theodore, stopping Leone in his tracks, "I had nearly forgotten. A letter was delivered to the office yesterday. I first thought it to be a business correspondence, and then I realized it was personally addressed to you."

Theodore reached into his jacket pocket and handed an envelope to Leone.

"It comes from an attorney in New York City," said Vincenzo. "What could this possibly be?"

"Why don't you take a moment to read the letter?" said Harding. "I will tell the others you will be joining us shortly."

Vincenzo handled the envelope as if feeling its weight and stepped back toward his desk.

"It is Christmas day and, whatever it is, it can wait until

tomorrow," said Vincenzo, placing the letter among the other papers covering the desk. "Come, my friend, let us attend to the happy celebration."

He draped his arm across Theodore's shoulder as they left the room.

On the final day of 1923, Roberto and Benny sat in the storage room of the delicatessen, arranging the procurement of an unusually large shipment of contraband alcohol to be included in the following scheduled Leone Importing delivery.

The stockpile of alcoholic beverages at the L&L warehouse had been drained by the brisk holiday sales, necessitating an extensive and speedy replenishing. With the imminent departure of Vincenzo to Italy, Benny and Roberto felt less inhibited about radically increasing the shipment. As they worked out the details, Lena's cousin minded the store out front. Roberto had hired Nino Territo just after Christmas, to allow himself the additional free time to attend to L&L business concerns.

That evening, Vincenzo Leone took time to catch up on paperwork before giving the evening over to celebrating the coming of the New Year. He had spent a good part of the past week putting all of his business affairs in good order to ensure that Lena, Roberto, and Harding could most effectively tend to their respective responsibilities in his absence.

As Vincenzo shuffled and organized papers on his desk, he came across the forgotten envelope from New York.

Leone's hands began to shake as he read the letter from Alfredo Catalano.

The discovery that Giuseppe Agnello had detected Louis' whereabouts deeply disturbed Vincenzo, even though Agnello had never arrived at the Leone home.

And the knowledge that this lawyer Catalano, and perhaps others, knew of the true relationship between Leone and the son of his sister was equally distressing.

Vincenzo came to a decision instantly, placed the letter into his pocket, and hurried to inform Lena.

Vincenzo found her in the kitchen trying to persuade Salvatore to eat his dinner.

"I have decided Louis will accompany me to Italy," Vincenzo Leone told his wife.

TEN

San Francisco. 1924.

Theodore Harding, wielding his brand new Graflex Century Graphic 23 camera, took a family portrait outside the Ristorante Naro.

Vincenzo Leone, standing proudly beside his wife Lena—who held their two-year-old son, Salvatore, in her arms.

In front of their father and Lena stood Rosa and Maria and, between the two girls, Louis.

Salvatore was staring with adoration at his older brother.

Rosa and Maria had begged to see their father and Louis off at the train station, but Vincenzo insisted the girls say their goodbyes at the restaurant and remain there with Lena's mother.

Later, Roberto, Lena, and young Salvatore stood with Vincenzo and Louis on the platform during the remaining minutes before departure.

Lena held tightly to Salvatore's hand, sensing the boy would fight to accompany his father and brother when Vincenzo and Louis boarded.

Vincenzo voiced his trust and appreciation to his younger brother, who would be taking care of the family and the family business in Vincenzo's absence.

It was mid-February, 1924, and Vincenzo had spent the past six weeks preparing his younger brother for the responsibilities at hand.

The letter from the lawyer in New York had disturbed Vincenzo deeply, and had puzzled him as well.

Vincenzo had considered asking Roberto if he had knowledge of a visit from Giuseppe Agnello—however, as close as he came to confronting Roberto on a number of occasions during the weeks since he had read the letter, he could never form the question.

Vincenzo could only agonize about how close Agnello had come to finding Louis, wonder why Giuseppe had failed to complete the pilgrimage, and act on the instinctual feeling that the boy was somehow in danger.

He knelt down to give young Salvatore a hug and a kiss and then rose to enfold Lena in his arms. Salvatore latched onto Vincenzo's leg and Lena had to pry them apart.

Roberto had looked away self-consciously while husband and wife embraced—and Louis stood by patiently.

After the five-day train trip across the continent, Vincenzo and Louis would be spending a week in New York City before the sea voyage to Italy.

Vincenzo would handle import business and wished to explore the city he had passed through only briefly before moving on to Philadelphia years ago. Particularly the large Italian-American neighborhoods along Tenth Avenue, near to the Chelsea docks, and Little Italy in lower Manhattan.

The uniformed station master called for final boarding. Vincenzo took Louis' hand as he moved toward the riding car. He had stepped up and lifted Louis onto the landing when he suddenly remembered the photograph.

Vincenzo turned to his wife.

"Lena," he cried, surprising her with his urgency, "there is a photograph of my sister, which I planned to carry to my mother in Sicily. Please send it to New York immediately, so it may reach me before we sail. You will find it in the lower right-hand drawer of my desk at home. Promise me you will not delay."

"I promise. I will post it today to your hotel."

"*Grazie. Arrivederci*," said Vincenzo, disappearing into the train car with Louis.

Moments later, the train began to move out of the station. Vincenzo and Louis stood together at an open window, waving.

On the platform, Lena flailed her arms about in farewell, Salvatore wailed inconsolably, and Roberto stole glances at his sister-in-law.

The train had finally pulled out of sight and Roberto had taken Salvatore up into his arms to console him.

The small boy worshiped his uncle, and was soon calm again.

"*Per favore*, Roberto," said Lena as they moved toward the station exit.

"Anything."

"Take Salvatore to my mother at the restaurant. I must return to the house to find your sister's photograph."

PART TWO

MYTHOLOGY

There is a weird power in a spoken word.
And a word travels far—very far—
deals destruction through time
as the bullets go flying through space.

—Joseph Conrad

ELEVEN

In the spring of 1939, Lena Leone called the family together to celebrate the eighteenth birthday of her son, Salvatore. Her mother arrived early, as usual, to help prepare the banquet. Her father had passed away two years earlier. Anna Territo, Lena's sister, attended with her fiancé, who she had met at the school where they both taught newly arrived immigrant children. Rosa was there with her husband and their two-year-old daughter. Rosa now helped to run the restaurant with Lena. Her husband, Thomas Silveri, operated a small shoe repair shop with his father. Maria Leone, now twenty-four, rode the bus up from Los Angeles where she worked as a dresser for a motion picture studio. Maria was close to completing her evening college studies in costume design.

Lena's two daughters, Antonia, twelve, and Roberta, ten, helped their mother and grandmother spread the icing on the large birthday cake.

After the feast, Lena's two young girls begged their father to take them down to Columbus Avenue for lemon ices. Lena reminded Roberto that he had promised the girls, and she ushered the three out the door with an admonition to not be too long.

"We will return shortly," Roberto said, "I need to have some words with Salvatore on this important day."

Salvatore, Thomas, and Anna's fiancé, Stephen, began a hand of *Briscola*—a card game imported from Italy—while the women prepared coffee and dessert.

Soon Roberto and the girls returned. From the kitchen,

Lena watched the two girls run into the house holding their prized cups of lemon ice, their father behind them. Roberto met Lena's eyes briefly, walked to the dining table, and poured a cup of espresso.

Roberto moved behind Salvatore and looked over the young man's shoulder as Salvatore played out a hand with Thomas and Stephen.

When the last trick was made, Roberto placed his fingers on Salvatore's arm, interrupting the card playing.

"*Scusi, Signori*," Roberto said to the two other men, "Salvatore, I wish to speak with you *personalmente*."

Salvatore rose from the table and followed Roberto to the study. Roberto had been a father to Salvatore since the boy was a toddler. It was now time to relate to the young man the fate of his birth father, Vincenzo Leone.

"What I say to you today I do not wish disclosed to your older sisters. It is only between us, the men of the family. Do you understand?"

Salvatore was not certain he did, but he nodded nonetheless.

Roberto then proceeded to tell the boy of Vincenzo's death—and of the violent conflict between the Leone and Agnello families which had begun years ago in the old country. Roberto told Salvatore of how Giuseppe Agnello had taken Francesca Leone from the bosom of her family and abandoned her and their child. How Vincenzo had taken his sister and nephew into his home and how, after Francesca's death, Vincenzo had raised the child Louis as his own. And finally, he told Salvatore of the terrible day in New York City when Giuseppe Agnello had murdered his father and tore Louis away from the only family he had ever truly known.

Salvatore listened silently—shocked, agitated, and angered by the ghastly revelations.

"Does my mother know of this?" the young man asked.

"Yes, Salvatore. However, you must not speak of it to her. She has not, even after all this time, overcome her horror. She need not be reminded."

"And what of this murderer, Giuseppe Agnello?"

"Agnello has been dealt with. It took many years to track him down, but at last I discovered his whereabouts. I realize this is horrible for you to learn, and that is why I have waited until your adulthood to reveal what you have a right to know. And I wanted also to assure you your father's death has been avenged, in the hope it is of some consolation."

"Agnello has been killed?"

"Yes, Salvatore. And please forgive me, but I insist on withholding the details."

"And Louis?"

"Out of respect for my dear sister, Louis has been spared. But I must warn you, Salvatore, and please take what I say to you now very seriously. Louis Agnello will always be your enemy. The hatred has been bred into him. Louis and his descendants will always be a threat to the Leone family. God willing, you will never be confronted with that danger. However, if it does threaten you, you must be prepared to handle it without the slightest hesitation. You must trust me in this, and swear on the soul of your dear father never to leave yourself or our family unguarded."

"I swear it," said Salvatore solemnly.

"*Bene.* Let us now return to the others. Your mother and the girls have created a marvelous torte. I have said what needed to be said. Now let us put it out of mind and enjoy the celebration."

Roberto rose to leave the study.

Salvatore followed, the young man trying his best to show appreciation for the great effort that had been expended in his honor.

As to putting what he had heard that afternoon out of his mind, even temporarily, Salvatore found it impossible.

It haunted him from that day forward.

Salvatore Leone never came to know the truth from the myth.

TWELVE

The truth was this.

Fifteen years earlier, 1924, after watching the train that would carry Vincenzo and Louis to New York leave from San Francisco, Lena and Roberto parted company outside of the train station. Lena returned home to search for the photograph her husband wished sent to him in New York.

Roberto carried Salvatore to the Ristorante Naro and placed the child safely with the boy's grandmother and his sisters. Roberto then walked from the restaurant to the salumeria. Roberto found the delicatessen bustling with activity, everything well in hand under the able management of Nino Territo and his two young sons. After a short time, Roberto became restless and decided to return to the house to look in on Lena.

Roberto found his sister-in-law sitting at the desk in Vincenzo's study.

Lena held what appeared to be handwritten pages in her lap, and was visibly upset.

Roberto moved quickly to her side with great concern.

"Lena, what is wrong? You look deeply troubled."

"My husband has deceived me," she said, her voice shaking.

"*Non capisco*," said Roberto.

Lena passed the letters with trembling hands.

Roberto recognized immediately that these were letters written by his sister, Francesca. He looked over to Lena and saw tears forming in her eyes. She looked away to hide her emotion. Roberto had a strong desire to embrace and console Lena, but feared such a gesture would only add to her discomfort.

Instead, Roberto sat in the chair across the desk and began to read.

Before long he understood the reason for the woman's suffering.

"*Incredibile.*"

"You did not know?" Lena asked.

"I had no clue," he said gravely.

Lena remained looking away.

"Vincenzo has set his sister's son above his own," Lena cried, "*my own.*"

Roberto fought to hide his tumultuous feelings. The thought that his brother was preparing to present the son of Giuseppe Agnello to the family in Sicily as his true heir tore at his heart.

That Louis was Francesca's son was of little consequence— this could not be allowed to happen.

For the honor of his father, Roberto swore silently that it would not.

At the same time, Roberto knew that a show of his vehemence would only distress Lena further.

Roberto calmed himself so he could attempt to comfort her.

"Lena, please, look at me."

Lena wiped her eyes and turned to face him.

"Your son Salvatore will take his proper place in the family, have no fear. My brother will be made to understand the grievous error of his deception," he said.

"How can you be certain?" she said, rising to her feet.

Roberto rose also, moved forward, and took her into his arms.

"I promise you," he said, feeling her strengthen the embrace, "trust me."

Roberto continued to soothe Lena's fears.

Eventually they moved into the kitchen for coffee and later Roberto escorted Lena to join her mother and the children—

and to post the photograph to New York.

Roberto had succeeded in fortifying her, yet as they walked down the hill to Columbus Avenue they both felt the awkwardness of the intimate moment in the study.

Roberto left Lena at the restaurant and headed for the warehouse at the piers.

When Roberto reached the warehouse, Benny Lucchese instantly recognized his friend's agitated condition.

"*Dio Mio*! What has happened?"

"Do you know of someone in New York who would kill for money?"

"There are men in New York who for a price would kill their own mothers. But what is this crazy talk of killing? Have you not already disposed of your enemy?"

"It is not finished. Giuseppe Agnello had a son. It cannot be settled until his heritage is broken."

"A child?"

"A child who my brother Vincenzo has blasphemously christened Louis Leone."

"Roberto, think what you are saying. You would wish death upon a young boy, the son of your sister? He is your blood."

"It is tainted blood, and will continue to poison the house of Leone for as long as the boy lives."

"Will you take some time to reconsider?"

"I am resolved. Will you help me or refuse?"

The dark intensity in Roberto's stare chilled even the ruthless Lucchese.

"*Si, certo*," Benito said. "Of course, I will help."

Benny Lucchese chose to call upon someone he knew and could trust.

He wired his cousin Lorenzo in Chicago.

The younger Lucchese was given clear instructions—no harm should come to Vincenzo Leone and there should be nothing to connect the attack on the boy to Benny or to Roberto. Vincenzo must never know that his own brother was behind the plot to murder the boy.

Lorenzo Lucchese was very eager to please his cousin—he had always hoped to be invited to join the thriving business in the West.

The Overland Limited via the Southern Pacific Railroad carried Vincenzo Leone and Louis to Chicago in just over three days, with connections to the Union Pacific at Ogden, Utah, and the Chicago and Northwestern Railroad at Omaha.

In Chicago, the two travelers boarded the New York Central Railroad at LaSalle Station for the last leg of the trip.

They would arrive at Grand Central Station in New York City some twenty hours later.

At LaSalle Station, Lorenzo Lucchese boarded the train.

Louis was very quiet for most of the journey. The boy, who would turn eight years old in three months, was still uncertain about the reason for the long ride and the separation from Lena and the other children.

Louis spent many hours staring out of the windows of the railroad car—surprised and awed by the absence of buildings and people, by the strange and often frightening landscape, the desert, mountains, and unrecognized wildlife.

Vincenzo on his part devoted hours to simply watching the boy's reactions, and being constantly reminded of how much he had grown to love his sister's son.

Watching both Vincenzo and Louis was Lorenzo Lucchese. A young man who, as many others in that lawless age, had come to place personal ambition above the sanctity of human life. As the train entered Grand Central Station, Lorenzo felt both the power and the weight of what he had agreed to do.

A trolley took Vincenzo and Louis from Grand Central Station, down Park Avenue, and across Twenty-Third Street to the Hotel Chelsea. The man and the boy settled into their temporary residence, and soon the exhausted child was asleep on one of the two large beds.

Vincenzo sat and watched Louis sleep.

For the next day and a half, with Louis at his side, Vincenzo took care of the business matters he had scheduled. Leone met with fellow importers and made provisions for an exchange of services, and in between stops explored the varied districts. He and the boy strolled through lower downtown's Little Italy, reminding them of the ever-growing ethnic San Francisco neighborhood where Vincenzo ran his businesses. Leone walked the wide-eyed boy across the Brooklyn Bridge, and pointed out Ellis Island and the Statue of Liberty. They stood a while to watch the construction of the thirty-two story Barclay Building in lower Manhattan. Vincenzo then took the boy to Saint Patrick's Cathedral, and both were astounded by its magnificence.

They ended the second day with a trip through Central Park in a horse drawn carriage, riding along the large lake and catching a glimpse of the huge Dakota Building through the bare trees to the west. At Columbus Circle, they hired a cab and continued downtown, passing Bryant Park and the large stone lions standing guard before the New York Public Library.

On their return to the hotel, Vincenzo caught sight of a sign above a small office on Fifth Avenue and Twenty-Fifth Street. It simply read *Alfredo Catalano, Attorney*, but those few words sent a jolt of panic through his body.

Leone's reaction was so violent it startled Louis, and compelled the driver to ask if everything was alright.

Vincenzo calmed himself and draped his arm around Louis' shoulder to reassure the boy.

The front desk clerk at the Chelsea greeted Vincenzo with a warm good evening and an envelope mailed from San Francisco, which had been delivered earlier in the day.

Leone placed the envelope in his jacket pocket—thankful that the photograph of his sister, Francesca, had arrived in time.

Once again, the boy was quickly asleep.

Vincenzo sat awake quietly, watching Louis and picturing in his mind the sign above the lawyer's door.

Lorenzo Lucchese slipped into the hotel lobby at daybreak while the desk clerk was busy seeing to the trash removal. He quickly moved to the stairwell and climbed to the first half-floor landing.

Lucchese carried two weapons. A two-foot lead pipe and a stiletto knife. Lorenzo's duty was to subdue Leone, but not fatally. Then, in a true display of Sicilian justice, he would cut the boy's throat.

Lorenzo had no qualms about taking the life of a young child. It was a culture unwavering in the conviction that a harmless boy would someday grow to become the enemy his father and grandfather had been. Lorenzo took a deep breath and continued up the stairs.

The knock on the door startled Vincenzo, who woke to find he had slept in the armchair beside Louis' bed. He rose slowly and moved toward the door.

"Yes?" he said, shaking off sleep.

"Signor Leone, *per favore.* I have news from your family."

Vincenzo hastily opened the door, anxious about what may have happened to bring this early messenger.

Lorenzo Lucchese stepped past Vincenzo and into the room before Leone could protest, and without warning the pipe came around from Lorenzo's back and knocked Vincenzo to the floor.

Leone lay stunned and unable to lift himself until he heard the boy screaming.

Responding to Louis' call, much like the large cat that had given the family its name, Leone was instantly on his feet. Vincenzo pounced on the back of the intruder as Lorenzo struggled to bring his knife up to the neck of the thrashing child. Leone wrestled the man to the floor and felt the blade cut deeply into his own abdomen.

As they fought for control of the stiletto, Vincenzo Leone could feel consciousness beginning to desert him. Suddenly, Lucchese went limp. In a pure act of blind courage, Louis had picked up the lead pipe and swung it into Lorenzo's head. Vincenzo used all the strength he could command to snatch the pipe from the boy's hands and use it to repeatedly strike Lucchese before the man could rise again.

Lucchese lay lifeless on the floor. Vincenzo looked up into the boy's eyes and then passed out, collapsing across the dead man's body.

Louis looked down from the bed in shock, unable to make a sound.

When Leone regained consciousness, the boy was sitting beside him holding his hand.

Louis had placed a wet towel across Vincenzo's forehead, to stay the bleeding from the blow Leone had suffered at the door.

The stomach knife wound was much more serious. Leone's shirt had turned reddish black by the expanding circle of blood.

Vincenzo knew he had no time to delay.

Leone quickly went through the dead man's pockets, pulling out a train ticket and a Western Union telegram. He glanced at the name on the documents and felt his heart sink. Vincenzo threw on his jacket, stuffed the papers into his pocket, grabbed the boy's travel bag, and rushed Louis out of the room and down to the street.

At the hotel entrance, he hurried the boy into a standing cab, directing the driver to Fifth Avenue and Twenty-Fifth Street. When they reached their destination he spoke to Louis, losing strength by the moment.

"Louis, enter that door and ask for Signor Catalano. Tell him you are Agnello, the lamb. He will understand, and he will protect you."

"Papa, please," cried Louis, unable to control his trembling.

Vincenzo Leone reached into his jacket and produced the envelope his wife had posted from San Francisco, together with the items he had taken from Lucchese's body. He handed them all to Louis and spoke again, this time in barely a whisper.

"Please, Louis. Do as I say. Take this—it is a photograph of your mother."

"Papa," the boy cried again.

"Go now, do not disobey me," Leone said with all of the force he could summon. "Remember, Catalano, like cat. And, Louis, never forget that I love you."

With that, he ushered the boy out of the cab and told the driver to hurry away.

Louis stood on the sidewalk and watched as the cab disappeared, tears clouding his eyes.

Louis lifted his suitcase, clutching the envelope and the documents in his other hand, and he walked away from the street and toward the door of Alfredo Catalano's office.

Finding the door locked, the boy curled up in the small vestibule with the suitcase—the papers held tightly against his chest.

The driver turned to the passenger in back of the cab.

Vincenzo Leone had slumped down in the seat and lay motionless.

Vincenzo's jacket had opened to reveal the blood, which now stained nearly all of his shirt and trousers. The driver instinctively headed east, in the direction of the hospital but, at the last minute, passed the entrance and continued to the river. He pulled over to an isolated spot and checked his passenger. The man was deceased. The driver removed the body and gently lay it down on the ground. He had experienced trouble with the police in the past and did not wish to be involved in the tragedy.

The driver made the sign of the cross, and drove off.

Vincenzo Leone carried no identification, having abandoned all of his belongings behind at the hotel.

He died not knowing his father had passed away in Sicily only a few days earlier.

When Alfredo Catalano arrived to his office he found the boy asleep, huddled in a corner against the door, the suitcase in front of him like a small protective wall.

Catalano knelt down and gently nudged the boy, who woke and looked fixedly at the man's face.

"Who are you, child?" asked Alfredo. "Where is your mother?"

The boy reached up, handed the envelope and the other papers to the puzzled man, slowly rose to his feet and took a posture of respect.

"I am Louis," he said.

"Louis?"

"I was to say *agnello* to the man inside, Mr. Cat, and he would protect me."

"I am that man, Catalano, will you come with me? I am a friend to your father."

Louis picked up his suitcase and prepared to follow.

Alfredo took the bag from the boy's grip, placed the papers inside his coat, took Louis' hand, and started back in the direction of his apartment.

Louis clung to Alfredo's arm as the two walked west, the boy constantly looking around him as if hoping to find something familiar.

Alfredo stopped in front of the tenement and went to his knees, eye to eye with the boy.

The lawyer placed his hands upon Louis' small shoulders and spoke softly to the bewildered child.

"Are you frightened, son?"

In answer, Louis threw both his arms around Alfredo's

neck and held fast.

"Be brave, *figlio*," said Catalano, embracing the boy. "You are safe now. You have come home."

Alfredo stood, lifted Louis up into his arms, and carried the boy into the house to meet the family.

THIRTEEN

New York. 1924.

In May, the Catalano family, along with the Bollas and their children, celebrated Louis' eighth birthday. In the three months since his separation from Vincenzo Leone, Louis had slowly come around to feeling secure in his new home. The boy interacted very well with Catalano's sons, Peter, ten, and Alfredo, nine, and with the three Bolla children as well. All the other children soon took Louis into their play and into their hearts.

Catalano and his wife Julia also came to quickly love the boy, and were jointly resolved to raise Louis as their own child if it were God's will. Alfredo clung to the slim hope that Giuseppe Agnello would one day reappear to claim his son.

Sergio and Sophia Bolla had confirmed that the woman in the photograph, found clutched in the abandoned child's hand, was Francesca Agnello. Catalano had placed the faded photograph into a simple wood frame and set it on the small table beside the bed they added for Louis in the room he shared with the other boys.

The other papers Louis had held were a complete mystery to Alfredo Catalano.

The name of Lorenzo Lucchese meant nothing to him.

The body of Vincenzo Leone had been discovered shortly after being abandoned by the cab driver, but the corpse remained unidentified.

The following morning, in a case the police considered unrelated, Lorenzo Lucchese was found dead in a room at the Hotel Chelsea.

It was Lucchese's body that then came to be identified as Vincenzo Leone, who had checked into the room three days earlier with a young boy.

Leone's belongings and the hotel clerk's hasty identification settled the matter.

The child was never found.

San Francisco.

News of Vincenzo's death reached his family some days later, and Roberto made arrangements to have his brother's body transported back to San Francisco. Roberto Leone and Benny Lucchese met the train and traveled with the casket to Russo's Funeral Parlor on Broadway. At the mortuary, the two men looked at the deceased. They were shocked by the terrible beating that had been inflicted upon the head and neck, rendering the dead man nearly unrecognizable.

But Benny and Roberto knew well who lay there.

"The coffin must remain sealed," said Roberto to the undertaker sternly. "His wife and children must not be allowed to see him in this condition."

And so it was that Lorenzo Lucchese had finally made the trip west he had so yearned for, only to be buried before a tombstone bearing the name of Vincenzo Leone.

Roberto Leone immediately took control of all of the Leone businesses.

Roberto retained the assistance of Theodore Harding to help operate the import enterprise, and Lena's cousin, Nino, carried on the management of the salumeria.

Lena's mother and aunt, Nino's mother, operated the restaurant together until Lena rejoined them following a three-month period of mourning.

Roberto and Benny Lucchese continued to prosper in the illegal alcohol trade.

Lena struggled to provide the children with a feeling of security. Rosa and Maria constantly cried for their father, and young Salvatore was forever asking for Louis.

Roberto was always near at hand, to comfort and console the widow and to distract the children. Lena came to depend on his strength and to respond to his attentiveness.

In May of 1925, on the occasion of Salvatore's fourth birthday, Roberto proposed marriage and Lena accepted.

A year later Lena gave birth to their first child, a daughter, Antonia.

A second girl, Roberta, was born in 1928.

New York. 1934.

In early November, United States Congressman Fiorello LaGuardia won a hard-fought campaign for the Office of Mayor of the City of New York.

LaGuardia had been helped immeasurably by the support of Franklin Roosevelt.

Two years earlier, President Roosevelt had won a landslide victory in the election against the incumbent, Herbert Hoover. Roosevelt did not forget that when he had asked for the support of New York's Tammany Hall Democrats, they had failed to deliver.

It was *get-even* time. Roosevelt retaliated by backing the Fusion Party candidate, LaGuardia, who defeated the Tammany bosses.

LaGuardia, who had held his congressional seat for five terms, was aided in his 1930 and 1932 bids for the House by a young Italian-American attorney in Manhattan.

LaGuardia urged the attorney to run for the seat he would be vacating.

With LaGuardia's support, and an endorsement from Roosevelt, Alfredo Catalano was elected to the House of Representatives from New York's Eighth Congressional District. The Catalano family celebrated the victory as they prepared for the holidays. It would be the first holiday season without Peter, Catalano's eldest son, who had been killed in an automobile accident just two weeks before his twentieth birthday.

The two other boys were now both attending college. Alfredo Jr. in his second year of studies at Columbia, and Louis in his first year at New York University—where LaGuardia and Catalano had both earned law degrees.

As Thanksgiving Day approached, Alfredo Catalano was determined it be a joyous occasion, that the tragedy of Peter's death be respectfully put behind them, and the household be well fortified for the periods of absence his new responsibilities in Washington, D.C., would require.

Alfredo was most concerned for Louis, who of late had become more and more inquisitive about his family history.

San Francisco.

After the death of Vincenzo Leone in 1924, the growth and prosperity of Leone Importing fell primarily upon the shoulders of Theodore Harding.

Throughout the remainder of the decade, Harding diversified and expanded the company's inventory, adding clothing, shoes, furniture, cookware, and tobacco to the initial concentration on food products. Harding had also established trading in a number of additional European countries including Spain, Portugal, and France, and negotiated contracts for the importing of coffee from South America.

Although never fond of Roberto Leone, Harding was fiercely loyal to Leone Importing and the memory of its founder, a dear and respected friend.

The Great Depression affected the lives of millions of Americans and transformed Harding's focus. As early as the summer of 1930, he began relegating responsibilities to others in the organization with particular attention to preparing Roberto Leone to manage.

Harding's goal was to resign his position with Leone Importing no later than the spring of 1932, and to pursue his increasing commitment to public service.

One of the final pieces of advice Harding had to offer Roberto Leone was to begin exploring markets for the importing of alcoholic beverages.

"The repeal of the Volstead Act is inevitable and imminent," Harding counseled. "It is not too soon to line up prospective suppliers."

Harding had no idea that Roberto, in partnership with Benny Lucchese, had a nine-year head start in establishing those connections.

In the fall of 1932, Harding vigorously campaigned in San Francisco and in Northern California in support of Franklin Roosevelt's first run for the White House.

Vincenzo Leone had wisely, if not prophetically, made specific provisions for the disbursement of his estate before leaving on his planned trip to New York and Sicily.

The bulk of his estate, including all real estate and the Leone Importing Company, would be passed to his wife, Lena.

Lena's parents would inherit one-half interest in the restaurant, Lena's mother having always been instrumental in its success and efficient operation.

Vincenzo's brother, Roberto, would earn equity in the importing company for continued service.

An escrow savings account would be established for each of the four children—Rosa, Maria, Salvatore, and Louis. The funds would become available to each heir at age twenty-one or, in the case of the girls, at the time of their marriage if it came earlier.

As reward for his diligence and loyalty, Theodore Harding would be granted a perpetual endowment equaling two percent of the import company's net profits per year following ten years of service.

Having reached tenure at the time of his resignation in 1932, Harding devoted his energies to social purposes while remaining comfortable financially.

In 1934, Harding waged his own successful battle for a seat in the U.S. House of Representatives.

In the eight years following Vincenzo's death, while Harding continued to build and strengthen Leone Importing, Roberto ran the shipping and delivery end of the business and oversaw operation of the delicatessen.

At the same time, Roberto remained a silent partner in L&L Supplies with Benny Lucchese, continuing to realize large revenues through the sale of illegal liquor.

By the end of 1933, Theodore Harding's prediction was proven correct. The Twenty-First Amendment was ratified in the number of states required to put into effect the repeal of the Volstead Act and the end of Prohibition.

Roberto Leone was forced, reluctantly or otherwise, to make some very consequential and dangerous decisions.

Benny Lucchese became a problem and the solution became increasingly clear.

L&L Supplies fronted as a wholesaler of building materials and did make profits as such, however certainly not the kind of profits Benny Lucchese was accustomed to and required. On the other hand, acting upon Harding's timely advice, Roberto Leone was in a position to benefit greatly in the newly legalized alcohol market due to the inroads already developed from the illegal trafficking.

Since Leone's involvement in L&L had always been hidden, and Benny Lucchese had never been vested in Leone Importing, Benny was left out in the cold.

Benny had made moves to ensure his continued prosperity, particularly in additional illegal operations including gambling and prostitution, but he was well aware that these activities were far riskier.

Prohibition had never been an overwhelming mandate of the American people and, with the exception of a handful of zealots in Lucchese's hometown of Chicago, law enforcement often looked the other way as long as dead bodies did not litter the streets.

Gambling and prostitution drew much more heat. Roberto had always distanced himself from Lucchese's forays into those arenas, and Benny himself understood the volume of business in gambling and prostitution necessary to equal the fortunes made in illegal liquor would be difficult if not impossible to sustain.

Benny was ambitious and resourceful—he had ideas and money-making schemes. All he needed was a hiding place—a structure within which he could implement his plans undercover, a seat of operation where no one would think to look. Lucchese needed to get inside of Leone Importing and therefore asked Roberto for a position in the company.

Roberto, seeing the intrinsic jeopardy, shut Lucchese out.

Roberto creatively worked to placate Lucchese, while remaining as invisible as possible.

Roberto assisted Benny in the establishment of three large saloons in San Francisco, including one at the bustling Fisherman's Wharf—and Leone promised to supply Benny with all of the liquor his bars could handle, at cost.

Roberto also provided Benny with a handsome monthly income through the leasing of the L&L warehouse by Leone Importing, which could be written off as a business expense, and he offered Lucchese a large lump sum for the supplies remaining in the warehouse.

Roberto Leone was attempting to buy-off Lucchese in ways that would bring little attention to himself, with the hope of getting Lucchese off his back and gradually out of his life.

For a while it seemed to work.

Lucchese's pockets were always full and Benny became involved in the nightly operations of his drinking establishments.

For years, the two young men had painted the town together— but since Roberto's marriage and fatherhood, Lucchese had taken on new friends, more available to share his revelry.

For weeks at a time, Benny and Roberto would not cross paths, which was fine with Roberto and no real hardship to Benny as long as the monthly allowances came.

Then one day when the two met for lunch, as they did less and less frequently, Benny made a comment that was unexpected, unexplainable, and threatening.

"I was out to the cemetery yesterday morning, to visit the grave of my cousin. It is a very impressive monument you have erected for your brother. Imagine how many would be surprised to learn it is poor Lorenzo who rests there. And, speaking of final resting places, how is your old friend Giuseppe Agnello doing beneath the warehouse floor?"

Benny's words, uttered so casually, stunned Roberto. A week later, when Leone was visited by two agents of the federal government, the shock turned to mortal fear.

The two agents, Burns of the Treasury Department and Sterling from the FBI, appeared at the front door of the Leone home on Russian Hill a few days before Thanksgiving. To his great relief, Roberto Leone was at the house alone when they arrived. Without disclosing the precise nature of their investigation, the two men queried Leone about his business relations with Benny Lucchese.

Roberto quickly decided, from the demeanor and approach of the agents, that he was not yet considered a suspect. That

Leone Importing had sold Italian tile and marble to L&L Supplies over the years was no secret, and not a crime.

Agents Burns and Sterling explained they were routinely questioning everyone who may have done business with Benny Lucchese, in confidence, and they expressed great regret for the imposition.

Roberto believed them.

He allowed that his late brother Vincenzo Leone had established a wholesale contract with Lucchese's company, which continued until L&L was dissolved.

He also volunteered that Leone Importing had arranged to lease the former L&L warehouse from Lucchese.

Asked if he was aware of any partners Benny Lucchese may have had in the building supply enterprise, Roberto said he had never met or had knowledge of any. The two agents departed after an agonizing forty-five minutes, expressing appreciation for Leone's cooperation and the assurance he would not be bothered further.

Roberto closed the door behind them and felt extremely fortunate. The feeling lasted all of two minutes.

It would only be a matter of time before the investigation of Lucchese landed on Benny's own doorstep.

And Roberto knew Benny would give up his former partner in a heartbeat if he thought it could save his own skin.

Roberto realized he would have to act swiftly, before Benny learned of the investigation, to protect himself and the honor of the family.

On Thanksgiving Day, 1934, as the Leone family sat at the dinner table, the sound of sirens screamed at them from Fisherman's Wharf.

By the time the firefighters brought the blaze under control, the former L&L Supplies Warehouse had burned almost completely to the ground.

The charred body found inside among the ashes was soon identified as that of Benito Lucchese, owner of the building.

An investigation determined that the fire was the work of an arsonist—most likely Lucchese himself.

It appeared as if the bulk of the inventory had been removed from the warehouse before the fire.

The supposition was Benny had hoped to collect insurance for the structure and market the valuable waterfront property.

Lucchese apparently fell victim to his own criminal scheme.

The unearthing of a second body, discovered beneath a portion of the floor, was not so easily explained.

The second victim had been killed by a gunshot wound to the head, possibly as long as a decade earlier. There was little remaining other than a male skeleton and severely deteriorated clothing.

It was by chance that the coroner, while reaching to pick up pieces of clothing that had been cut from the body at the morgue, caught sight of a small name tag sewn into the shirt collar.

However, no record of a man named Giuseppe Agnello having ever lived in the city of San Francisco could be found.

Among those questioned as to possible knowledge of the deceased were Roberto Leone and Theodore Harding.

At that time, Harding had never heard the name Giuseppe Agnello—and he could offer no assistance.

Nor would Roberto Leone.

FOURTEEN

Washington, District of Columbia. 1935.

The two men first met at an orientation for first term representatives to the 74th Congress of the United States in Washington, D.C., on the third of January, 1935. They took part in the selection of Joseph Byrns of Tennessee as Speaker of the House—Congressman Byrns having been strongly supported by the outgoing Speaker, Henry Rainey of Alabama, and former House Speaker John N. Garner, the current Vice President.

In light of their respective experiences, one having litigated many legal disputes at the Chelsea Docks in New York City and the other having ten years in the import business in San Francisco, both Congressmen were assigned to the House Committee on Interstate and Foreign Commerce chaired by Sam Rayburn of Texas.

The freshmen Representatives, Alfredo Catalano and Theodore Harding, became direct working associates and, in a few short weeks, became good friends.

On an afternoon in April, before a recess that would allow both men a short trip home for Easter, Catalano felt comfortable enough to broach a subject that had been haunting him since first hearing of Harding's business background.

Though not at ease enough to state the exact nature of his interest, Alfredo Catalano asked Harding about his term of office with Leone Importing.

Before too long, both men openly confided in one another.

Harding shared knowledge of his former employer and close friend, Vincenzo Leone, and Catalano related the story of Giuseppe Agnello and of the quest for Agnello's only child.

Catalano learned of Giuseppe's fate, and Harding learned of Louis' survival.

The destiny that had brought them together astounded both men, and much of what they communicated held dark implications.

And when the name Lucchese surfaced in each of their accounts, it forged a mutual commitment to attempt discovering the significance of these disturbing coincidences.

For the time being, however, the two men dismissed the subject and turned to talking of happily anticipated family reunions.

"I would very much like to meet Louis one day," said Harding. "I have fond memories of him as a child."

"I am sure he would be pleased to see you," Catalano said. "He has grown into a fine young man, and he hopes to practice the law."

"Will you tell him of Giuseppe Agnello's death?"

"He has a right to hear of it, though it was Vincenzo Leone who Louis actually came to know as a father."

"And you, of course. How is the young man known?" asked Harding. "As Leone or Catalano?"

"We have done our best. We decided from the day he first came to us that he would bear the name of his true father. His name is Louis Agnello," Alfredo said. "And how was the circumstance of Vincenzo Leone's passing explained back in California?"

"I felt that it was never explained satisfactorily. Vincenzo murdered in his hotel, the boy missing, and no more. Why do you think he delivered the boy to you?"

"I could only surmise at the time, and continue to believe to this day, that Leone felt the boy was in danger and was uncertain about who to turn to for help."

As the two men parted for the holiday, both understood what Leone's uncertainty tragically implied—that somehow Vincenzo could not trust the boy into the hands of his own brother Roberto, in the event of his death.

New York City.

Alfredo Catalano sat at the table with his family and their Easter guests, the Bollas, and watched as the women cleared the dishes in preparation for coffee and dessert.

Alfredo had spoken briefly with Sergio Bolla before the meal, sharing what he had learned of Giuseppe Agnello's fate.

Both men agreed Louis would need to be told, but neither was sure how it should be handled.

Alfredo would be returning to Washington the following morning, and he decided to delay no longer.

Alfredo invited Louis to walk with him to the river after dinner.

Over the years, Alfredo Catalano had related to Louis the history of the boy's family, as he knew it, at stages in the boy's life Alfredo had deemed appropriate. Louis learned of his parent's emigration to America, Giuseppe's involvement in the Great War, and Francesca's move to Philadelphia and the safety of her brother's home. Alfredo had been generous in his depiction of Vincenzo Leone. He did not condone Leone's decision to keep Louis from his real father, but he believed Vincenzo loved the boy as his own. Alfredo had no real proof that Leone was trying to conceal the boy—Vincenzo may not have known how to contact Giuseppe Agnello or may have thought him lost in the war. Although Leone did not immediately respond to Catalano's letter, he had deposited the boy at Alfredo's doorstep. Alfredo had chosen to give Leone the benefit of the doubt, particularly when discussing Vincenzo with Louis.

After all, Leone had been the only father the boy knew for

the first eight years of his life, and Louis had loved the man.

Alfredo had decided to give Louis his rightful name, Agnello, but not at the expense of slandering the name of Leone. The suspicions concerning Roberto Leone were quite a different story, but not one Catalano felt informed enough about to place on Louis' shoulders. At least not on that Easter Sunday afternoon.

As they walked along the Hudson riverfront, Alfredo was careful to keep conjecture out of his narrative, and out of his responses to Louis' many questions.

"What was this place, where my father's body was found?"

"It was a warehouse belonging to a man named Lucchese, who died in the fire that uncovered your father's body," said Catalano.

"And you say my father had traveled to San Francisco to locate me?"

"Yes. It was all he wished for."

"And what would have brought him to this warehouse?"

"We cannot be certain," said Catalano. "Lucchese is known to have purchased certain goods from Leone Importing. Perhaps Giuseppe had been misdirected there by someone he spoke to at the shipping docks."

"But you say he had the address of the house where I lived."

"Yes. He may have found no one at home and ventured to the wharf to search for Vincenzo. Leone Importing had a facility of its own nearby."

"And why would my father have been shot?"

"Again, Louis, we do not know and we may never know. It is possible he was taken for a trespasser and his death was then concealed for fear of the repercussions."

"Do you think it possible Vincenzo Leone was somehow involved?"

There was the question Catalano had dreaded. Alfredo could do nothing but be honest with the young man.

"I sincerely believe Vincenzo had no knowledge of Giuseppe's fate. I also believe Vincenzo, in bringing you to my door, was attempting to return you to your father."

"Thank you," Louis said.

Louis was silent as they walked back to the house. The weight of what he had learned bore down on him.

The thought of having lost two fathers, both lost violently, was overwhelming.

Louis still had nightmarish memories of the horrible struggle in the hotel room years earlier.

Louis turned to the man who walked by his side. It was the strength and goodness of Alfredo Catalano, who had taken Louis into his family and into his heart, that helped ease the turmoil Louis was feeling.

All of the tumultuous and dangerous thoughts

He tried to focus on the miracle that had given him the great fortune of not one but three loving fathers.

"Thank you," he said again.

San Francisco.

Across the continent, Theodore Harding and his family shared Easter dinner with the Leones and the Territos. Harding's wife had accepted the invitation from Lena, and Harding could not refuse. Roberto Leone had boasted for weeks about having a United States Congressman for a holiday guest. Harding was less than enthusiastic, and he was uncomfortable throughout the afternoon. Two days earlier, Harding had collected evidence that, though not conclusive, had disturbed him greatly.

Harding had been privy to findings in the investigation into Giuseppe Agnello's death, through a friend in the San Francisco Police Department.

It led Theodore to three men, who he spoke with on the

Friday and Saturday before Easter.

Harding documented the information he learned from these men, not entirely sure what he would do with the knowledge.

The manager of the hotel where Giuseppe Agnello had boarded on the night he arrived in San Francisco had come forward after seeing Agnello's name in a short news report.

Gino Mancini had been searching for something in the hotel storage room, a large area that held everything from broken lamps and excess furniture to luggage left behind at the hotel and never claimed. He came across the suitcase abandoned by Giuseppe Agnello and carried it to the nearest police station. As was customary in such cases, Mancini had tagged the unclaimed baggage with the name of the guest and the date on which it had been deserted. The date on the tag was the fourth of July, 1923.

"It was strange," said Mancini, when Harding visited him at the hotel. "I was searching for a light fixture to replace one that had become irreparable in the first-floor corridor. It was beneath a tall pile of boxes filled with assorted hardware, partially hidden by a large rug, where I spotted the suitcase. I was surprised to find a piece of luggage that had sat there for more than eleven years. We normally hold these types of items no more than six months, and then donate them to charity. I moved the suitcase aside just for that purpose. When I noticed the name, it stirred up a memory. I only remember this man, who I spoke to very briefly more than a decade ago, because of something he said which I found amusing. He stated that his name was Agnello and he was hoping to locate a man named Leone, lamb and lion, do you see? It remained in my mind. After replacing the fixture, I took lunch and, looking through the newspaper, came across the very name again in regard to the terrible fire at the wharf last Thanksgiving."

"Can you remember anything else he may have mentioned?"

"We exchanged only a few words on that July fourth morning. As I told the police, I did recommend to Agnello the diner next door when he mentioned he was hungry."

Ralph Bianco was the owner of the diner adjacent to the hotel.

Harding had been there many times, and Ralph was pleased to see the Congressman walk in.

"I do remember the man, and I will tell you why," said Bianco. "He had asked for directions to Vincenzo Leone's home, saying he was an old friend. I said he could walk up Union Street to Hyde. The next morning, Signor Leone came in. God rest his soul. He had breakfast here often, with the salumeria soon to open just across the avenue. I asked him if his friend had found him at home, and he did not understand what I meant. Leone insisted no one had visited, and he was expecting no one. I tried to describe the man to him, but it did not help, and the man had not given me his name. I thought it odd, for the man seemed very anxious to see Signor Leone."

"You found it odd enough to recollect after so many years?" Harding asked.

"There was something else. Months later, shortly after Christmas, I remember the holiday decorations were still displayed in these windows, Leone came in to see me. He appeared agitated. He inquired about the man who had asked directions to his home the past July. I could tell him no more than I had told him then, or that I can tell you now. But it was his insistence that impressed me, and which has kept the incident in my memory."

Shortly following Christmas day in 1923, Harding realized, was just after he had delivered to Vincenzo the letter sent by Alfredo Catalano from New York.

It was a great relief to Theodore Harding to hear what he believed was evidence that Leone had never seen Giuseppe Agnello on that July morning.

For some reason, Giuseppe had never reached Vincenzo Leone's door.

Harding thanked Bianco and took the walk Agnello would

have taken from the diner up to Russian Hill.

As Harding approached Hyde Street, a man unexpectedly came up from behind.

The man's appearance was so sudden that Harding stopped short and stepped aside.

The man stopped also and looked at Theodore as if he couldn't speak.

Finally, he sighed deeply and addressed Harding.

"Please forgive me, Congressman, for coming upon you so rudely. My name is William Nash, and I live in this house," he said, indicating the large Victorian adjacent to where they were standing. "I have followed you from Bianco's diner."

"It is good to meet you, Mr. Nash," Harding replied cautiously.

"I could not resolve whether or not to disturb you, and I am afraid my abrupt approach has startled you. I am a great admirer and I voted for you in the election."

"Thank you. It is quite all right, I overreacted."

"I heard your discourse with Mr. Bianco, not meaning to eavesdrop. I could not help myself, for you spoke of a man I clearly recall. The gentleman from New York City, Giuseppe Agnello."

"What do you know of Giuseppe Agnello, Mr. Nash?" asked Harding.

"It was the Fourth of July, a windy morning up here on the hill, and I was having difficulty rigging the American flag. Agnello stopped and offered assistance. We spoke briefly as he helped me raise the flag. He told me he was looking for the home of Vincenzo Leone, and I directed him to turn the corner at Hyde Street. He then asked me if I knew the boy, Louis. I told him I knew the boy well, he was a playmate of my own son, James. He asked me what kind of boy Louis was, which I thought strange, but I nevertheless assured him Louis Leone was a fine boy. He thanked me, though it was I who had reason to be thankful for his help."

Nash paused, as if trying to find the proper words to continue.

"And here is the thing that has remained with me since that day so long ago," said Nash. "The man had tears in his eyes as he bid me farewell and moved on toward the Leone home."

"And you never saw him again?"

"In fact, I did, several minutes later. I thought to follow and catch up with him, to invite him to visit me again sometime, as a gesture of gratitude to a stranger to the city. When I turned the corner, I saw him walking with Leone down Hyde Street toward the wharf."

"He was with Vincenzo?" Harding said, with great alarm.

"No, Signor Agnello was with the younger brother, Roberto Leone."

Theodore was about to ask William Nash if he knew of the second body found in the warehouse fire the past November, and if he had mentioned his meeting with Agnello to anyone else. In the end, he did not ask. Instead Harding asked Nash, as he had asked Bianco at the diner and Mancini at the hotel, to document his account as a personal favor. All three men agreed, in deference to the well-respected Congressman. By Saturday evening, Harding had three affidavits. He was still uncertain what he would do with the information or what, if anything, it confirmed about the death of Giuseppe Agnello.

He was certain of one thing.

He would relate all he had learned to his friend, Congressman Catalano, once he returned to Washington.

For the time being, he would not take his findings to the police.

That Roberto Leone was the last person known to have seen Giuseppe Agnello alive was knowledge of great consequence, and Harding needed to be clear in his own mind about what he felt it suggested.

With these grave considerations, which he could not even share with his wife, Harding sat uncomfortably at the dinner table with Roberto Leone on that Easter Sunday.

Harding excused himself late in the afternoon, following dinner, claiming he needed to speak to a group of assemblymen before returning to Washington the next day.

He left his wife and children at the Leone home, promising he would return as soon as possible.

Harding felt compelled to do something which he knew was both unethical and risky.

He visited the office of Leone Importing where he had worked for so many years. He reluctantly admitted himself to the office but, once past the threshold, he went straight to work.

First, he went to the accounting books, those he had personally kept involving purchases and those Roberto had overseen in regard to deliveries.

Harding soon found a pattern when comparing both sets of ledgers.

Though at no additional cost to Leone Importing, more cargo was listed in the record of items delivered from overseas than had actually been ordered by the company.

Harding finally discovered the discrepancies were with regard to dealings with L&L Supplies. L&L had taken delivery of products fairly purchased from Leone Importing, such as Italian tile and marble, but had also taken delivery of items shipped in the name of Leone Importing that did not appear on any bills of lading. Lucchese was receiving deliveries, coming through customs under the auspices of Leone Importing, which were totally unaccounted for.

Someone inside Leone Importing, though not stealing from the company per se, was clearly using the shelter of the company to smuggle undocumented goods into the country, in partnership with Lucchese.

Theodore seriously doubted Vincenzo had knowledge of this dishonesty. And, since it had continued well after Vincenzo's death, he could only conclude Roberto Leone was involved.

No one else had the means to arrange such a deception.

Harding determined these unaccounted deliveries had ceased more than a year before, in 1933.

He went back in the ledgers to discover when they had begun and found records going back to 1923, not long after Roberto had arrived from Italy.

Finally, to his greatest distress, Harding stumbled upon a document that seemed to confirm his most terrible fears.

Tucked inside a ledger, Harding discovered a copy of the birth certificate of Louis Agnello. That it was an official copy, issued by the New York City Health Department, made it horribly evident to Harding that the document had come to San Francisco with Giuseppe Agnello from New York and had then somehow fallen into the hands of Roberto Leone.

Harding carefully removed a few representative pages from the ledgers, which would demonstrate the discrepancies he had uncovered.

He sat at his old desk and hand wrote a declaration of what these papers were and how he had come by them, and also a statement of where he had obtained the birth certificate.

Harding would add these documents to the three affidavits and carry them to Washington the next morning.

He left the office and returned to the Leone home.

Soon after, Harding again sat at the dining table over coffee, impatiently talking with Roberto Leone and Lena's father about his experiences in the Capitol.

The documents he had confiscated lay hidden in the inside pocket of his suit jacket, pressed against his wildly beating heart.

Insisting he needed to prepare for his long journey back east, he collected his wife and two children and bid the Leones and Territos a good evening.

Harding slept poorly that night.

Early the next morning, his family saw him to the railroad station.

He waved to them from the window of the train.

In a brown leather briefcase on Harding's lap were the affidavits, and all of the documents Harding had taken from the Leone Importing office, protected by a wrapping of heavy plastic.

Alfredo Catalano arrived back in Washington at the beginning of the week.

Congress would officially reconvene on Wednesday. The Commerce Committee had scheduled a special session for Tuesday afternoon, to review and finalize a presentation they would be giving to the entire body the following morning.

Alfredo was anxious to hear what Theodore Harding may have learned during his trip home to California.

As Catalano and the other committee members arrived at the meeting, they found Chairman Rayburn pacing aimlessly.

Rayburn did not acknowledge anyone's presence with as much as a look, gazing only at the floor as he walked the perimeter of the room.

When everyone had arrived, Rayburn asked that they all be seated and he stood solemnly before them.

"I have very tragic news," he began. "Please wait until I have completed my statement before asking any questions, though actually I do not know any more than what I am about to tell you now. Last night, a train traveling out of New York City, destined for Washington, was derailed due to a badly damaged section of railroad track. It is not yet certain how the damage occurred. It is currently being investigated by the authorities. Speculation is that it may have been an act of senseless vandalism, or perhaps an attempt to acquire materials for resale. We are living in desperate times. In any event, the accident took the lives of nineteen passengers, among them our colleague Theodore Harding."

After a few moments of stunned silence, followed by a

short respectful discussion, the Chairman suggested the committee address the work at hand.

Throughout the meeting, Catalano sat dazed.

The loss overwhelmed him.

A fine man lost to Congress, a father and husband lost to his family, and an admired new friend lost to Catalano himself.

And lost also, the knowledge Theodore Harding may have uncovered in San Francisco.

Two ten-year-old boys walked along the train tracks in southern New Jersey on their way home from school on a Friday afternoon in 1935.

They hoped to explore the wreckage of the train that had derailed earlier that week.

Before they could get near to where workmen were busy cleaning up the area, a police officer stopped them and diverted the boys away from the tracks.

Cutting across a small meadow, one of the boys came upon a brown leather briefcase lying in the tall weeds.

He quickly looked around, scooped up the heavy case, and ran toward a nearby cluster of trees—his schoolmate following.

The boys sat on the ground excitedly looking at their prize.

"What do you think is in it?"

"Maybe a million dollars."

"Should we look inside?"

Without answering, the boy who had found it reached to open the latch on the briefcase. He had no success getting it open.

"It's locked," he said. "We need something to break it with. Let's hide it here and come back in the morning, I'll bring my father's tools."

"I can't come tomorrow. My grandparents are still visiting, since Easter, and I won't be able to get away."

"We'll bury it, and come back Monday after school."

The boys burrowed a large hole in the ground, placed the briefcase deep within it, covered it with the excavated earth, and leveled the ground.

"Do you think someone will find it?"

"No, I can hardly see where we digged."

"Let's go, we're late."

Heavy rains had fallen all weekend. When the two boys returned on Monday afternoon, armed with hammer and chisel, they failed to find where they had buried their treasure.

FIFTEEN

In January of 1939, William Sebold walked into the American Consulate at Cologne, Germany, to replace a lost passport in order to return to the United States. He had left Germany in 1921, after having served in the German Army during World War I, and he had spent years working in industrial and aircraft plants throughout the United States and Mexico.

Sebold became a naturalized American citizen in 1936.

He returned to Germany in 1939 to visit his mother. On his arrival in Hamburg, he was approached by a member of the Gestapo who told Sebold he would be contacted in the near future. Sebold continued on to his mother's home in Mulheim and took employment there.

In September, Sebold was picked up and interrogated by the Gestapo in regard to military equipment and aircraft in America, and strongly persuaded to cooperate with the Reich or risk reprisals against his family in Germany.

Sebold was sent back to Hamburg where he was trained in methods of gathering and transmitting information from the United States to Germany, which he was to employ upon his return to New York. He was also given a list of contacts in America, men and women already set in place for purposes of espionage.

When Sebold walked into the Consulate at Cologne for a new passport, he confessed his predicament and indicated his desire to cooperate with the United States as a double agent.

Sebold returned to New York City in February, 1940, under

the assumed name of Harry Sawyer. During the next eighteen months, he helped the FBI build cases against thirty-three Nazi German spies operating in New York.

Nineteen of the accused pleaded guilty, and the remaining fourteen were brought to trial in September, 1941, at the Federal District Court in Brooklyn.

Louis Agnello. New York City. 1941-1947.

On the prosecuting team at the spy trials was a recent graduate of New York University Law School. He had landed a prize position with the Justice Department due to glowing recommendations from the Mayor of New York, the President of the United States, and a popular New York Congressman named Alfredo Catalano, the young man's adoptive father. Fresh out of school and part of the largest spy trial in U.S. history, Louis Agnello's future looked very bright.

The espionage trial continued for more than three months, culminating in the conviction of all thirty-three defendants on the thirteenth of December.

Six days earlier, Japanese aircraft had attacked the United States Naval Base at Pearl Harbor in Hawaii.

On January 2, 1942, sentences were handed out in the espionage case, more than three hundred total years in prison terms.

In March, Louis joined the United States Navy. Fifteen months later, he was heading to the Mediterranean to join the Allied troops under the command of General Eisenhower.

They were paving the way to an invasion of Italy, through his ancestral home of Sicily.

Home from his military service in early 1945, Louis returned to work with the Justice Department in New York.

Louis married Dolores Bolla, who he had known since childhood, the youngest daughter of Sergio and Sophia Bolla who had been friends to his father, Giuseppe.

They moved into a house in Brooklyn, not far from Coney Island.

In 1946, a son, Joseph, was born.

A second son, Vito, was born the following year.

Richard Harding. San Francisco. 1942-1951.

During late 1942 and well into 1943, another young attorney, Richard Harding, was involved in a civil liberties case—a class action suit against the state of California.

Thousands of Japanese-Americans, a majority of whom were American citizens by birth, were being interned in large relocation camps throughout the state and the Pacific Northwest, simply because of their ethnic background.

Thirty-one-year-old Harding was a graduate of Stanford Law School, husband of attorney Jane Adams Harding, and son of late U.S. Congressman Theodore Harding. Richard accepted a position as an Assistant District Attorney in San Francisco in 1949.

His wife, Jane, continued working part time as a civil rights attorney while raising their two children, Jack, two, and Rachel, one.

Salvatore Leone. San Francisco. 1943-1948.

Not very far from the San Francisco courtroom where Richard Harding pleaded the case for the release of relocation camp prisoners, twenty-two-year-old Salvatore Leone worked with his uncle at the offices of Leone Importing.

His uncle *and* stepfather, Roberto Leone.

Salvatore, a graduate of the University of California at Berkeley with a degree in business administration, was training for his ultimate position as chief executive of the large corporation founded by his late father, Vincenzo.

The entry of United States into World War II had put a stop to legal trade with Italy.

However, through contacts made in neutral countries like Switzerland, established through his years smuggling illegal liquor and duty-free imports into the country, Roberto Leone was able to undermine trade restrictions.

Salvatore was unaware of his uncle's questionable arrangements, and the company continued to flourish throughout the war years.

Salvatore Leone married Josephine Silveri, a niece of his step-sister Rosa's husband, in 1947.

Their first child, Bruno, was born the following year.

SIXTEEN

In late 1949, Louis Agnello was appointed lead federal prosecutor in a case against Mann Enterprises, a New York importing company charged with illegal shipping practices. The indicted owner of the company, Phillip Mann, approached the Justice Department with a deal.

In return for immunity consideration, Mann was willing to divulge information about a San Francisco based importer guilty not only of illegal liquor smuggling during the years of prohibition, but also of illegal trade during the wartime trade embargo. When Agnello learned that Leone Importing was the business in question, Louis became interested in Mann's testimony.

Alfredo Catalano suggested that Louis contact San Francisco District Attorney Richard Harding.

Agnello and Harding met for the first time in Denver in early 1950 to discuss a cooperative effort to investigate the allegations and explore the possibility of building a case against Leone Importing.

It was a very difficult decision to make. Agnello had been raised by the founder of the company, and Harding's father had spent years working for the company. They decided they would look further into the case, unofficially.

Agnello returned to New York and prosecuted Phillip Mann to the fullest, claiming disinterest in Mann's plea bargain.

Harding returned to San Francisco and he began a slow, systematic investigation—as comprehensively as time apart from his work and family obligations allowed.

Alfredo Catalano had suggested Harding dig into the background of Benito Lucchese and L&L Supplies.

It was not until the summer of 1952 that Harding and Agnello felt they had adequate evidence to bring charges against Roberto Leone, and possibly Salvatore Leone, for federal crimes.

The two men met again, this time in San Francisco, to discuss the merits of the case, to determine the likelihood of a conviction and—most importantly—to take a hard look at their willingness to proceed.

Louis, armed with his suspicion that Roberto Leone was involved in his father's murder, won the argument.

The trial commenced in early November 1952, in San Francisco.

Federal prosecutors had been given all of the evidence collected by Agnello, New York District Attorney Jim Baldwin, and Richard Harding.

Included was sworn testimony by parties involved in the unloading of illegal liquor at the docks during the twenties, cargo entering the country under the auspices of Leone Importing and subsequently delivered to the warehouse of L&L Supplies.

Also in evidence was the sworn affidavit of Phillip Mann, who had been promised an early prison release in exchange for his cooperation.

The jury came in with a verdict in January.

Roberto Leone was found guilty of federal crimes and sentenced to fifteen years in prison.

Leone Importing was fined one hundred fifty thousand dollars.

The deaths of Giuseppe Agnello, Vincenzo Leone, and Benito Lucchese were never introduced.

With no direct evidence implicating Salvatore Leone, federal prosecutors had omitted him from the indictment.

Roberto Leone was unaware of the involvement of Louis Agnello and Richard Harding in the case against him, but swore he would seek revenge upon those who had helped put him in prison. First on his list was Phillip Mann. From within the walls of Alcatraz, Leone plotted with his associates outside. Mann would be hunted and mercilessly killed.

And before Mann took his last breath, he would be made to disclose the identities of the authorities in New York who had procured his damning testimony.

Salvatore Leone was left with the responsibility of running the company and raising the funds to pay the government fine. He was also burdened with what would be an ongoing, five-year federal monitoring of the company to guard against further criminal practices. Although not personally implicated in wrongdoing, Salvatore and his family lost respect within the community.

Salvatore visited his uncle in prison regularly, and Roberto never missed the opportunity to feed Salvatore's hatred for those responsible.

Nino Territo had worked at the Salumeria Leone since he was eighteen years old.

After Vincenzo Leone's death, as Roberto took less time and interest in the delicatessen, Nino took on the bulk of the responsibilities. In 1947, among the many gifts bestowed upon Salvatore Leone by Roberto and Lena on the occasion of his marriage, was full title to the salumeria. Shortly afterwards, Salvatore approached his mother with a request.

"I would like to give the store to your cousin, Nino," Salvatore said. "He has served faithfully for twenty-five years and he deserves to be rewarded."

"It is yours to do as you wish," said Lena, inwardly pleased at the fortune of her cousin and proud of her son's generous decision.

Nino's two sons grew up in the delicatessen. Both boys worked as assistants to their father throughout their teens and the oldest, Tony, had come on to work full time after high school. The gift from Salvatore gave Nino Territo something he could pass on to his sons, and Tony wanted nothing more than to carry on the business. But Nino's younger son, Frankie, had other ambitions—dreams that would not be satisfied by a simple life as a grocery clerk.

Frankie Territo was a friend and a cousin of Salvatore Leone, and they had been close since childhood. Frankie spent much time in the Leone home growing up and was very aware of the difference in lifestyles of the Leones and his own family. And Frankie was in awe of Roberto Leone, a man who carried himself with such power, a man he perceived as so much grander in stature than his own father. While his brother Tony threw himself fully and gladly into work at the Salumeria Leone, Frankie threw himself at Roberto Leone's feet.

And when Roberto needed a confidant, after the timely death of Benito Lucchese, Frankie Territo was conveniently at hand.

It was Frankie, not Salvatore, who Roberto turned to for assistance in any illegal undertakings. Out of respect for his wife, Leone was reluctant to involve her son, Salvatore, in any dangerous or compromising activity.

Salvatore remained clean, and Frankie Territo did the dirty work.

And it was Frankie who Roberto called upon to handle the matter of Phillip Mann.

San Francisco and New York. 1955.

Frankie Territo visited Roberto at the island prison.

After nearly three years of searching, Mann had been found. Mann had been released in exchange for his testimony against Roberto Leone and was fearful of reprisal. With the help of the Justice Department, Mann was relocated to Albany, New York.

Roberto had discovered Mann's exact whereabouts.

Roberto's instructions to his protégé were clear.

Frankie was to go to Albany, carefully choose the opportunity to capture Mann, and obtain the names of those who had bought his testimony—with the threat of death if he refused. Once Frankie had gained the information, he was to kill his captive and return to report the news to Roberto.

Frankie arrived in Albany at the beginning of October. He checked into a downtown hotel near the small novelty shop where Mann had set up business.

Frankie spent two days watching Mann's movements and scouting out a location for their ultimate confrontation.

On the third day, Frankie Territo came up behind Mann as the informer was entering his automobile after closing the shop.

Frankie, armed with an untraceable revolver, forced Mann to drive to an isolated factory area just outside of downtown. There, Frankie urged Mann to divulge the identities of his confessors.

The terrified shopkeeper gave up the names of federal prosecutor Louis Agnello and New York District Attorney Jim Baldwin without hesitation.

Frankie shot Mann twice in the head, then left the car, gun, and body behind.

Territo hiked back to the hotel, slept soundly, and was up at dawn to board the early bus to New York City. Frankie arrived in New York to learn the next train west would not depart for six hours. He hastily made up his mind—he would bring better news back to Roberto Leone than his *padrone* could have hoped for.

Frankie found his way to the District Courts Building where he would lay in ambush for Agnello and Baldwin.

. . .

The two boys were up at sunrise and they bounded down the stairs with the excitement usually reserved for Christmas morning. They found their father at the kitchen table, hot coffee and the morning newspaper close at hand.

Their mother stood over the gas range, frying potatoes and onions.

"Boys, you could have taken advantage of the day off from school and stayed in bed a little longer," said Louis Agnello.

"We don't want to be late, Papa," said Vito.

"The game doesn't start until one, we have plenty of time. Go wash up, your mother is about to add the eggs for the frittata."

The boys ran off and Louis moved to the counter beside his wife to cut the fresh bread, still warm from the corner bakery.

"They'll drive you mad until it's time to leave," Dolores said, smiling.

"I'm just as anxious as they are," admitted Louis.

"You had better find something to keep all of you busy for the next five hours."

"You've been complaining for some time the living room needs paint."

"Don't do me any favors. That's all we need around here, two would-be homerun sluggers with brushes in their hands."

"Actually, I was thinking of taking them to Basilio's when he opens, to buy them each a new glove—and from there over to the park to throw a ball around."

"That's a wonderful idea. And they can show off the new mitts when they visit their cousins on Sunday."

"Dolores, would you mind very much if I didn't go with you to your sister's?"

"Not at all, I understand. You have important work to do on Sunday."

"I do?" asked Louis, not remembering if he had spoken of

other plans.

"Yes. With me and the children out of your hair, you should be able to get the living room painted in no time," Dolores said, trying to hold back her laughter.

The look he gave her made it impossible, and soon they were both laughing aloud.

"What's so funny?" asked Joey, when the boys came back into the room.

"Your mother is a comedienne."

"Like Lucy?" said Vito.

"I was thinking more like Alice," said Louis.

"To the moon," both boys said in unison, giggling wildly.

"Sit down and eat your breakfast before it gets cold," said their father. "I hope old man Basilio doesn't oversleep this morning."

At the mention of Basilio's name, the boys looked at each other and then at their father with joy.

"He has the new Jackie Robinson model in the window," cried Joey.

"Let's hope he has another like it inside the store," said Louis.

At noon, the two boys sat beside their father in the front seat of the 1951 Studebaker sedan, heading east out Avenue U toward Bedford Avenue.

They each held a brand-new baseball glove in their laps, clutching the mitts as if they were matching Hope Diamonds.

Vito constantly brought the glove up to his face to smell the leather. Louis parked on Montgomery Street and they walked to the ball field.

Louis held the bag of sandwiches Dolores had prepared and a jug of grape Kool-Aid.

The boys carried the new gloves, each pounding a small fist into the pocket of their mitts in rhythm with their steps.

Ebbets Field stood gloriously before them.

It was the third game of the 1955 World Series, and the Brooklyn Dodgers were down two games to none.

But the Dodgers were at their home field now and the Agnellos would be there to cheer them on.

Johnny Podres, pitching for Brooklyn on his twenty-third birthday, held the New York Yankees to seven hits and, although one of those hits was a long homerun blast by Mickey Mantle, the Dodgers prevailed, winning 8-3. A hard-hit foul line drive off the bat of Jackie Robinson sailed just inches above Vito's extended glove where they sat on the third base line. An older man a few rows back managed to catch the ball and walked it over to where the boy sat. Seeing there were two boys, he wisely handed the prize to Louis—leaving it to the boys' father to play Solomon with the souvenir.

Joey and Vito were so excited, they forgot how much they both hated to share.

On their way home, Louis enlightened the boys regarding the proper way to break in their new baseball gloves. He had purchased a baseball for each of them from Basilio's, and he carefully explained how to tie the ball into the mitt overnight to form a good pocket.

The boys ran past their mother at the door to get directly to business.

But Louis was stopped dead in his tracks at the door. He knew the moment he saw his wife that something was terribly wrong.

"It's Jim Baldwin," she said. "He's been killed. The police have his assailant down at Grand Street Station."

Louis Agnello kissed his wife, placed the souvenir baseball into her hand, and walked quickly back to the Studebaker.

Frankie Territo had gone first to the Federal Court Building to seek out Agnello. When he discovered that the prosecutor was not at work that day, he crossed the street to the District Court. Territo found Baldwin's office and walked in.

Frankie apologized for coming into the wrong office by mistake, lingering long enough to take a good look at the DA. He patiently waited in the hall.

Less than an hour later, Baldwin left his office and entered the men's room. Frankie followed. At the sink, he asked Baldwin if he thought the Dodgers could catch the Yanks, repeating something he had heard discussed on the bus from Albany, and having no real idea what it was about. As Jim Baldwin turned to answer, Frankie plunged the knife into his stomach. Territo pushed the lawyer down to the floor, used his knees to pin Baldwin's arms, and worked quickly with the blade. Baldwin did not struggle long.

A police officer who had noticed Territo lingering in the hallway, and saw Frankie later go into the restroom behind Jim Baldwin, was curious enough to follow. He was not in time to save Baldwin's life, but he took the killer into custody and, with help, got Territo down to Grand Street Station. It was in an interrogation room at the police station where Frankie got the chance to come face to face with Louis Agnello.

Louis, with the aid of two persistent detectives, discovered who had sent the assassin. The name Roberto Leone had come back to haunt him again. In an ill-conceived attempt to protect Roberto, Territo claimed he had only been sent to find Mann and discover who had taken Mann's testimony against his boss. Frankie swore the decision to kill Mann, and to come after the two attorneys, was his alone. Frankie insisted Roberto Leone had never even heard the names Agnello and Baldwin in connection to Phillip Mann. Louis believed that at least the last part of Frankie's statement could well be true, and understood immediately the importance of making certain it remained that way.

Agnello saw to it that Territo would be held without bail, and not given the opportunity to make contact with anyone on the outside.

Louis would deal with the consequences of depriving Frankie Territo of his constitutional rights when the time came.

Louis' ultimate goal was to make a plea deal with Territo that would help Frankie forget the infringement of his rights and at the same time see to it that Roberto Leone remained on Alcatraz Island for the rest of his life.

As it turned out, Frankie Territo never had the chance to give Louis' name to Leone—or to help Agnello indict Leone.

The following morning, during the transfer from the police station to the arraignment at the courthouse, Frankie tried to overtake one of his guards and was mortally wounded in the attempt.

Louis stood over Territo's body and pleaded with the man to admit to Leone's guilt and save his soul. Frankie Territo whispered that he would die before he ever uttered a damning word against his *padrone*.

And then he died.

Two days later, Sunday afternoon, Louis was at home alone.

Painting the living room.

Agnello thought about Roberto Leone, and about how for the second time in his life he had come close to being killed at Leone's command.

And he felt certain it would not be the last time.

SEVENTEEN

For a quarter century, Leone Importing had been the largest importer of Western European goods in all of California and one of the largest family-run businesses in America. After the war, things were different.

The global conflict had made the planet smaller. Tens of thousands of soldiers who returned after the war brought back new knowledge of the old world. Contacts were made, opportunities were realized, and more and more competition arose for the markets Leone had cornered for so many years. By the early fifties, Leone Importing Company, although still able to support a large extended family, was becoming less and less influential beyond the San Francisco Bay area. When Roberto Leone was sent away to prison in 1953, his stepson, Salvatore, was left to run a business that would necessarily become more legitimate and far less lucrative.

Along with the criminal conviction of Roberto Leone came a large fine against Leone Importing and close scrutiny of their practices.

The hundred-fifty-thousand-dollar fine took a huge bite out of the family coffers. The scandal damaged the family reputation.

Smaller businesses were also being launched throughout the country and in the predominantly Italian-American North Beach neighborhood.

Restaurants surfaced all along Columbus Avenue and the cross streets, vying for business that had been monopolized by

Ristorante Naro for decades. Naro still did very well, but the
rising costs and the need for more competitive pricing affected
profits. The restaurant continued to be operated by the women
of the family. Lena Leone was the undisputed matriarch after
the death of her mother and Lena's two grown daughters, Antonia and Roberta, helped to bring the business into the postwar age.

The country, in general, had changed profoundly in the
fourteen years Roberto Leone was confined in prison. The
Eisenhower years had ended, a Catholic president had been
elected and assassinated, an unpopular war raged in Southeast
Asia. Families had become smaller, automobiles had become
larger, music had become louder, dress had become less respectful, television had captured the leisure time and the minds
of the population.

Roberto Leone had little evidence of these momentous
changes. He had spent ten years at Alcatraz and, when the
island prison was shut down in 1963 after the escape of Frank
Morris, another four years at San Quentin. The news Roberto
did receive was concentrated on family and family business,
and only served to fuel his bitterness and his hatred for the
Agnellos. During his incarceration, Roberto's mother had
passed away in Sicily. Leone had learned of her illness, but
was helplessly unable to visit or send comfort. What he
learned of the family finances also distressed and angered him.
He sat in his prison cell dwelling upon the power and riches
the family had once controlled.

His children had grown to adulthood and had started
families of their own.

Roberto Leone's grandchildren were strangers to him.

Leone could have counted his days in anticipation of a
joyous reunion with his wife, children, and grandchildren. Or
with hopes of reestablishing the former grandeur of the Leone
family enterprise. Instead, Roberto spent his waking hours
thinking only of the vendetta he had sworn against the Agnellos,

the perennial enemy.

As the day of Roberto's release approached, he reaffirmed his pledge.

The descendants of Giuseppe Agnello would pay for the sins against the Leones.

San Francisco. 1967.

On a chilly morning in March, Salvatore Leone sat at the desk in his office putting together a very large and essential order of goods required for the upcoming Easter season.

His wife, Josephine, and seventeen-year-old daughter, Sofia, were at home preparing foods for the salumeria.

The delicatessen was still operated by the family of Nino Territo, Lena's cousin. Nino was semi-retired. His son, Anthony, and Tony's son, handled the day-to-day operation. Nino's younger son, Frankie, had been killed by police in New York City a dozen years earlier following an unexplained act of violence against a city district attorney.

Salvatore's step-sisters, Antonia and Roberta, worked in the kitchen of Ristorante Naro, preparing dishes for the lunch menu.

Along Market Street in downtown San Francisco, scores of college students marched with signs and sang songs, protesting the Vietnam War.

At the terminal nearby, Lena Leone stood waiting for the bus that would bring her husband from the San Quentin Federal Penitentiary.

Beside Lena stood a handsome nineteen-year-old boy, who resembled his father, Salvatore, and his true grandfather, Vincenzo Leone.

The boy had never known Vincenzo Leone, and had not seen Roberto Leone for fourteen years.

When Bruno Leone was five years old, he had cried inconsolably when Roberto was taken away from the family.

The young man stood quietly at his grandmother's side, both nervous and excited.

Nonno Roberto, the man he loved and knew as grandfather, was at last returning.

Roberto Leone stepped off the bus and went immediately to his wife. As Leone held Lena in his arms, his eyes met those of the young man. Roberto could see in Bruno's eyes the same yearning and ambition he had felt at this very age upon coming to this strange and awe-inspiring new land. Roberto stepped away from his wife and he stood before the boy. He opened his arms wide. Bruno moved to him and was taken into Roberto's strong embrace. Roberto held the boy firmly, feeling as if he held the future salvation and vindication of the *familia* Leone in his arms.

"Bruno," Roberto said. "*Figlio mio*, take me home."

New York City.

On the fourth of July, 1967, Louis Agnello sat on the front porch of his Brooklyn home with his sons. The family had assembled for a holiday dinner, commemorating American independence and celebrating Vito Agnello's return from a two-year tour of duty in Vietnam.

Louis' wife, Dolores, and Joseph's fiancée cleared the dinner dishes and prepared coffee and dessert.

Louis, Vito, and Joseph sat watching the young children of neighbors, carefully supervised by parents, partaking in the traditional fireworks display on the street.

Louis watched Vito closely, worried that the noise of the small explosions might distress the twenty-year-old so recently back from combat.

To Agnello's great relief, Vito appeared calm, seeming to appreciate the familiarity of the festivities.

After the Mann and Leone trials in the early fifties, which followed the German spy trials that had made national headlines, Louis had risen quickly in his legal career. Many influential Democratic Party leaders were urging the fifty-one-year-old federal prosecutor to pursue politics. Louis' adoptive father, Alfredo Catalano, had served many years in the House of Representatives.

Louis was considered a rising political star. Discussions behind closed doors included talk of Agnello as a candidate for the House, the Senate, or for Brooklyn Borough President.

But Louis had other aspirations.

He possessed a general dislike for party politics and a strong dedication and love for the law. His ambition was to serve as a federal judge, and his prospects were good. As Agnello sat with his grown sons on that July fourth evening, Louis was confident he would sit at the bench of a federal court before he retired.

Louis knew much less about the hopes and dreams of his son, Vito.

Joseph had avoided military service due to a back injury sustained in childhood. Joe had gone directly from high school to work in a neighborhood restaurant. He loved the restaurant business and he took to it quickly and successfully.

Joseph spoke of opening a restaurant of his own one day. Joe's fiancée, Maryann, was a lovely and supportive young woman. The couple had met and dated in high school and planned to be married the following year.

Louis and Dolores were confident that together, Maryann and Joseph would achieve their goals.

Vito was more an enigma to his father. Vito had been quiet and pensive since his return, and spoke little of his future plans. Louis was reluctant to press the young man. The family had always been close and communicative. Louis assured himself that Vito would share his thoughts and his feelings with them when he was ready.

Dolores and Maryann joined the three men on the porch, bringing with them coffee and Italian pastries. The family watched as the neighborhood children lit sparklers, Roman candles, and firecrackers.

"It seems like yesterday we were the kids putting on the show out in the street," said Joe.

"It's good to be home," Vito Agnello said, taking his father's hand.

EIGHTEEN

San Francisco. 1972.

Roberto Leone was moved to San Quentin when Alcatraz was shut down in 1963. He served fourteen years of a fifteen-year sentence and was released on parole in 1967. The same year Vito Agnello returned from Vietnam.

As Roberto adjusted to life outside of San Quentin, Bruno Leone was always at his side. Bruno's father, Salvatore, was working constantly to keep the import business viable. Bruno's mother, Josephine, and his sister, Sofia, worked diligently preparing foods for the salumeria.

Bruno was at a very impressionable age, and the person who made the greatest impression upon him was Roberto Leone.

What impressed Roberto Leone was the great increase in the taxation on goods and income since he had been sent to prison. Leone saw his brother's son, Salvatore, work like a slave only to give a huge portion of the profit back to the government. He saw the politicians in Washington use the Leone family's hard-earned income to support those who were too lazy to work for themselves—and to support a war in a country he had never heard of. Roberto Leone set his mind to finding a solution to this unacceptable situation.

Less than five years after his release from prison, Roberto had set up a statewide distribution of tobacco and alcohol that was smuggled into the country without tariff. He used the resources of Leone Importing in much the same way as he and

Benny Lucchese had used them years earlier. Salvatore had kept the business legitimate for nearly two decades, and the importing company was no longer closely watched. Roberto systematically set up his network without Salvatore's knowledge.

And at Roberto's right hand, through all of the planning and implementation, was Salvatore's son, Bruno.

Bruno was married in 1971. Roberto gave the newlyweds a house on Russian Hill, close to his own, as a wedding gift.

Bruno's first child, Vincent, was born a year later.

New York. 1972.

Shortly after returning from service in Vietnam, Vito Agnello joined the New York City Police Department. While still at the Police Academy he met Donna Fazio—a friend of his brother Joseph's fiancée, Maryann.

Joseph and Maryann were married in 1968. A daughter, Patricia, was born a year later. Also, that year, Joseph and Maryann opened Giuseppe's Restaurant on Kings Highway in Brooklyn.

In early 1969, Vito and Donna were married. Before year's end, their first son, Joseph, was born. In 1970, their second son, John, was born.

Vito worked out of a police precinct near their Brooklyn apartment, and took classes in criminal investigation at Brooklyn College.

In 1971, Louis Agnello was appointed to the bench of a federal court in New York.

With the help of Louis's political connections and the strong recommendations of Vito's college professors, Vito Agnello was accepted for employment by the U.S. Department of the Treasury later the same year.

After six months training in Washington, D.C., Vito began working with the newly established Department of Alcohol,

Tobacco and Firearms out of their Brooklyn Field Office.

In 1972, Vito Agnello was able to purchase a home for his family next to the house on the Brooklyn street where his parents lived.

San Francisco. 1977.

The home of Hungry Lion Foods was a two-story building on Terry Avenue. It sat at the mouth of the narrow China Basin inlet, across the Third Street Bridge below the South Beach Marina. Roberto Leone had purchased the property in the late twenties, and it had been used at times to store excess contraband when the inventory of illegal alcohol was too large for the L&L Supplies warehouse on the wharf to handle. Now, fifty years later, Roberto Leone was back in business.

The building was two floors of open space with load-in doors facing a dock on the waterway. Along the west wall on the second story were a small office and an apartment. Cases of cigarettes and cigars, crates of imported Scotch and Irish whiskey, domestic and imported wines and liqueurs were stacked high in the open areas. The goods came in by boat and went out by truck to retailers throughout California, Oregon, Washington, Arizona and, most recently, Nevada.

It was these newly established markets in Lake Tahoe and Reno that attracted the attention of the Falco family in New York.

Charlie Falco had been brought up in Brooklyn. After returning from the Korean War, Falco married and started a family. Now Falco and his two sons, Ferdinand and Dominic, operated an illegal business much like the one Roberto and Bruno Leone ran on the West Coast.

Falco had long wanted to expand his market to Las Vegas. He had the casino connections necessary to move great quantities of goods, but he lacked safe means of transportation.

When Falco discovered alcoholic beverages and tobacco were reaching Nevada cities through California, he determined that cooperation would take him much further than competition.

He pictured an operation spanning the entire continent.

Charlie Falco decided to pay a visit to Roberto Leone.

A meeting between the two families was arranged.

On the day Charlie and Dominic Falco arrived in San Francisco, Sammy Orso was sent to meet them at the airport.

Sammy Orso was an eighteen-year-old totally devoted to Roberto Leone.

Orphaned at thirteen, Orso had pan-handled, robbed, and scammed on the city streets to survive. When the sixteen-year-old attempted to mug a sixty-year-old man in a North Beach alley, the older man had convinced the boy it was a bad idea. Then that man, Roberto Leone, had taken the boy and fed him a large meal at the Ristorante Naro.

Sammy became another in a long line of young men who were taken in, literally bewitched, by Roberto Leone's relentless determination and charisma.

Roberto gave Sammy work overlooking the warehouse.

Leone built a small apartment for Orso on the upper floor of the building, complete with a kitchen and bathroom facilities. Leone used Sammy as a live-in security guard and driver.

Orso picked up the Falcos and drove them out to the Hungry Lion warehouse, where Roberto and Bruno Leone waited to meet them. Roberto would have preferred the sit-down to take place at the Naro, but needed to keep the meeting away from the eyes and ears of Salvatore Leone.

Orso escorted the visitors to the warehouse office and left the four men to speak privately. There was no argument that both families would profit greatly by combining their resources in supply, markets, and transport.

The Leones would gain an important inroad to Las Vegas. The Falcos would acquire the means of shipment they lacked.

Charlie and Roberto were both smart businessmen, and it

did not take long to iron out an arrangement that was agreeable and beneficial to both sides.

Though Roberto Leone had taken no action since his release from prison, he was always imagining he would finally settle with the Agnellos.

And for years, he had filled Bruno's head with a strong hatred for the enemy.

It was Bruno who brought the subject up once the business discussions were completed.

"Are you familiar with the family of Louis Agnello?" Bruno asked Charlie Falco.

"Very familiar," said Falco. "Why do you ask?"

Bruno explained his interest, and his desire to see the Agnello family suffer.

"My good friend," said Charlie Falco, turning to address Roberto. "Louis Agnello is a thorn in our side, as is his son, Vito—but they are discomforts we have learned to live with, and must live with, at least for the time being. Vito Agnello is a federal agent and his father, Louis, is a federal judge. We avoid attracting their attention at all costs. Any action against them would severely threaten the plans we have discussed here today. Perhaps, in time, we may be in a position to safely retaliate. But I must warn you, Roberto. If you intend to pursue your vendetta, the Falco family cannot support you. And, more than that, we would be sadly forced to do what is necessary to prevent such a threat to our interests."

Bruno was about to protest, but Roberto silenced him with a raised hand.

"We will wait," said Roberto. "Bruno, please, bring a bottle of our finest scotch. Let us all drink to our new partnership."

San Francisco police detectives Carl Taylor and Jack Harding sat in an unmarked car on Illinois Street watching the building.

A large sign above the entrance identified the warehouse as

Hungry Lion Foods.

The two men were well into their second thermos of coffee.

"Remind me why we've been sitting here for two hours on our day off," Taylor asked.

"A favor for a friend."

"Anyone I know?"

"I didn't twist your arm, Carl. I simply asked if you would care to come along."

"Correct me if I'm wrong, but I'm guessing you wouldn't have asked if it weren't important."

"You're right."

"So, to return to the original question."

"My friend is an ATF agent out of New York City, Vito Agnello. He asked if I could watch Charlie Falco's movements while he was here in San Francisco. I thought I wouldn't mind a little company and, since all you do on your days off is get into trouble, I invited you along."

"Thank God."

"Thank God, I invited you?"

"Thank God, they're coming out."

Charlie and Dominic Falco walked out of the building alone.

The young man who had driven them from the airport opened the back door of the late model Cadillac and the two men climbed in.

"That kid looks familiar," Taylor said, as Jack started their car.

Harding and Taylor followed the other vehicle back to the airport.

The Falcos were dropped off for a flight back to New York.

"Whatever the reason for their visit, Carl, it definitely wasn't to see the sights."

"Should we follow the driver?"

"No, let's go back to the station. I want to see what we can find out about Hungry Lion Foods and I need to call Vito Agnello. Then I need to pick up a birthday gift for my daughter.

Martina will turn five years old tomorrow."

"Five, unbelievable," said Carl. "It seems like only yesterday."

"Not quite."

Back at the station they did some research.

Hungry Lion Foods was identified as a wholesale food distribution and catering company owned by Lena Territo. The name was not familiar to either Taylor or Harding. Carl continued to insist he had seen the driver before, but still couldn't put a name to the face. Jack thanked Carl for coming along for the ride and, when Taylor left to salvage what was left of his day off, Harding phoned New York.

Jack reached Vito Agnello at home.

"They made only one stop, a warehouse south of the Embarcadero," said Harding. "Why are they in your sights?"

"Since they legalized gambling in Atlantic City last year, we've been routinely looking at all businesses that supply the casinos. Falco has been distributing slot machines in Nevada for years and has a corner on the market in New Jersey. We are trying to determine if he's dealing with anything else. We suspect there is illegal tobacco and alcohol going in, but we can't find the source. What can you tell me about who Falco met with out there?"

"Not much at the moment, but I can look deeper. I can tell you the warehouse is allegedly the home of a food supply and catering company owned by a Lena Territo. The name on the building is Hungry Lion Foods. Do those names mean anything to you?"

"Nothing," said Vito.

"I'll keep digging."

"Thanks, I appreciate your help, Jack."

"No problem, but I'm curious. Don't you guys have agents out here?"

"Too much red tape. I discovered only yesterday that Falco was going out to California. By the time I could get the ATF office out there in motion, we would have missed the surveillance."

"Sounds like the SFPD. Lucky, I had the day off. I'll call you if I learn anything more."

"I'm taking my vacation, I'll been gone for a week. My two sons have been glued to the television set every Saturday morning watching *Bonanza* and *Roy Rogers* reruns, so I decided to take the family out to visit Hank and Katy Sims' place in Wyoming to see some live cowboys."

"Happy trails," said Jack Harding.

Over dinner, the two boys babbled excitedly about the upcoming trip to Wyoming. Joey asking about Uncle Hank's horses. John asking about wild Indians. Vito trying to explain that Iron Mountain wasn't actually made of iron.

Donna sitting back, enjoying the show.

After dinner, Vito walked next door to talk with his father.

"How's Mom feeling?"

"She's resting, son. She's not well."

"Is there anything I can do?" Vito asked, following Louis back to the kitchen.

"Pray. Have you had coffee?"

"I'll have coffee."

The two men sat at the kitchen table over espresso.

"I suppose the boys are very excited about the trip," said Louis.

"That's an understatement. They're up in their room pawing over a map of the United States, trying to figure out how many inches it is to Wyoming."

"I've been thinking about Colorado," said Louis.

"Colorado?"

"I was there years ago, to meet Richard Harding about the Roberto Leone prosecution. I thought it would be a good place to retire."

"Retire?"

"Vito, I'm almost sixty-two. I can retire anytime I like. I

think it would do your mother good to make a change. The doctors tell me a drier climate would be helpful."

"Jesus, Pop, I can't picture you living anywhere but New York. Have you spoken with Mom about it?"

"I'm planning to."

"It won't be an easy task trying to drag mom away from her children and her grandchildren. And you won't find good Italian bread out there."

"Let's talk of something else."

"I spoke with Jack Harding today."

"How are they?"

"Good. His daughter, Martina, will be five years old tomorrow. Dad, does the name Lena Territo mean anything to you?"

"San Francisco?"

"Yes."

"That is the name of Roberto Leone's wife, who was Vincenzo Leone's wife. And, it was a Territo from San Francisco who murdered Jim Baldwin. What have you learned from Jack Harding?"

"I'm not certain yet, but it looks as if the Leones may be stepping outside the law again. A business, said to be owned by Lena Territo, was visited today by Charlie Falco and his son, Dominic. Jack is looking into it."

"There may well be more than one Lena Territo in San Francisco."

"Hungry Lion Foods?"

"Lion," Louis said, sadly. "It's been so many years, I had myself believing I would never hear the name Leone again. And praying Roberto Leone would never hear our name again."

"I have to follow it up, Pop, I have no choice. I'm my father's son."

"Be very careful, Vito."

NINETEEN

In February 1978, a Philadelphia police officer purchased a package of cigarettes at the bar of an Atlantic City hotel. As he tapped the pack against his palm, he noticed there was no tax stamp on the bottom.

He telephoned the Department of Alcohol, Tobacco, and Firearms in Washington.

A team of ATF agents out of Trenton, New Jersey, began an around-the-clock surveillance.

Three days later, they observed a delivery of cigarettes and alcohol to the hotel. Warrant in hand, the agents impounded the truck and arrested the driver. After two hours of interrogation and an offer of immunity, the driver gave up Charlie Falco and provided the location of Falco's warehouse in Long Island City in Queens.

At the hotel, bargains were also made. In return for leniency for the owners, Falco was not to be alerted that the shipment had been confiscated. The hotel would provide payment for the goods and the driver would return to deliver payment to Falco.

The case was handed over to Vito Agnello and Harry Stone of the ATF's Brooklyn Field Office.

Vito Agnello wanted to be careful about how they would proceed—do everything by the book.

Fortunately, he had a father who knew the book well.

Louis and Vito went over every contingency. Before making a move on Falco, the government had all the proper documentation in place—evidence, affidavits, search and arrest warrants.

Two weeks after the failed delivery, Agnello and Stone led a team of ATF agents and New York City police in a raid on the Falco warehouse. Falco and his sons, Ferdinand and Dominic, were taken into custody.

Charlie Falco's chief concern was his two sons. He insisted they were not involved.

Agents Agnello and Stone insisted they were not convinced.

To protect his sons from prosecution, Charlie Falco offered to name his business partner—the man operating distribution of contraband goods in the western states and Las Vegas. Vito Agnello took the proposition to his father.

"We both know who Falco's partner is," Vito said, when he visited Louis. "Falco's testimony can put Roberto Leone away for good."

"Is Salvatore Leone involved?" asked Louis.

"We don't know."

"He was like a younger brother to me."

"We don't know," Vito repeated.

"Son, whatever is decided, you must do everything you can to keep your name quiet."

"I think I can do that."

"Putting Roberto Leone away for good will not keep you and your family safe from terrible danger if it is discovered the Agnellos have come back to haunt the Leones."

"They are criminals and murderers," said Vito.

"Yes," said Louis Agnello, "and you must never forget that."

Charlie Falco was quickly convicted and sentenced to fifteen years in Attica.

The company operated by Falco and his sons was heavily fined and prohibited from doing any commerce with gambling casinos for five years.

Falco's sons were forced to sell off their inventory of slot machines to a competitor to pay the fines. Ferdinand and Dominic were each placed on two-year probation—they were out of jail but also out of business.

Casinos in New Jersey and Nevada were also penalized, and additional evidence was gathered to support an indictment of Roberto Leone. With this evidence, and with the damning testimony of Charlie Falco, the government was building a strong case against Leone.

It was Dominic Falco who alerted Bruno Leone about the situation and named Vito Agnello as a prominent figure in the investigation and inevitable indictment.

The Leones quickly suspended all transport in and out of the Hungry Lion warehouse, but they could do little about the large inventory on hand. Knowing they were being watched, they set out to destroy the illegal goods. Burning cases of cigars inside the warehouse itself, draining bottles, removing labels, crushing glass. The action did little to solve their dilemma and the effort infuriated Roberto Leone. Although it hardly seemed possible, his hatred for the Agnellos intensified.

Roberto realized the danger to Bruno. He demanded Bruno stay away from the warehouse and return to work with Salvatore. Roberto was confident Salvatore would not be implicated and wanted to insure the same for Salvatore's son.

Bruno protested but, as always, finally submitted to Roberto's will.

Bruno swore vengeance upon the Agnellos.

Roberto asked Bruno to hold off until the current situation was resolved. All Roberto wanted his protégé to do was to hide behind Salvatore, take Sammy Orso with him to Leone Importing, and never forget Nonno Roberto who loved him like a son.

Bruno vowed he would never forget.

. . .

The trial of Roberto Leone in San Francisco went as rapidly as that of Charlie Falco in New York.

Leone, as Falco had done before him, pleaded guilty to all charges taking full responsibility.

Protecting Bruno, as Falco had protected his own sons.

Roberto was sentenced to twenty-five years in prison in 1979. He was seventy-six years old.

Bruno went to work with his father, Salvatore, taking Sammy Orso along as instructed.

Bruno soon came to learn his father had little sympathy for Roberto, even though Roberto was both uncle and stepfather to Salvatore.

Again, Roberto had disgraced the family name.

Although Bruno resented his father's position, he held his tongue and did as Roberto wished. He worked diligently for Salvatore and never let it be known that he had been involved in the Hungry Lion activity.

And Bruno never missed a weekly visit to San Quentin.

Although Salvatore Leone and Leone Importing were not implicated in the Hungry Lion case, once again the scandal surrounding Roberto Leone damaged Salvatore's reputation and hurt business. And once again it was Roberto who took it upon himself to rescue the family fortune.

Salvatore Leone's daughter, Sofia, Bruno's younger sister, had traveled to Italy during the summer of 1972.

In Milan, Sofia had met a young man, Giorgio Facella. Giorgio's father, Luciano Facella, was a highly successful clothing designer. After returning to San Francisco, Sofia corresponded with Giorgio by mail. Several months later, Giorgio traveled to California to visit Sofia and meet her family.

Josephine Leone was charmed by the handsome young man who had come from so far to court her daughter.

Salvatore Leone, though protective of his youngest child,

could not help but be impressed by Facella and his family's reputation.

Giorgio Facella made his intentions clear to Sofia's parents—he wished to marry the woman he loved.

During Facella's two-week visit, Salvatore Leone came to accept that his daughter was ready to start a life and family of her own. He gave the young couple his blessings and plans for a wedding were discussed. First, as tradition dictated, the Leone and the Facella families would arrange to meet.

Luciano Facella had for some time wished to find new outlets for his clothing. It was decided that Giorgio's parents would go to California, where they could meet the parents of their son's intended bride and where Facella could also explore markets. In the spring of 1973, Luciano and Nina Facella joined their son Giorgio on a visit to San Francisco.

The families discussed arrangements for the marriage, both families wanting to host the event. It was finally decided that two ceremonies would take place—the first in San Francisco, followed by another in Milan. Dates were agreed upon for the coming autumn.

At the same time, Luciano and Salvatore discussed the possibilities of a partnership. There was no reason why Leone Importing could not get into the clothing business—they had in fact been importing shoes from Italy since the days of Theodore Harding. It would be a tremendous opportunity for the young couple. Giorgio could move to San Francisco to establish a retail outlet for the clothing, while Leone Importing could handle wholesale distribution of the line throughout the country. It would bring new life to Leone's struggling business and create greater visibility of Facella designs. Salvatore and Luciano saw the union of their two children as a marriage of both romance and enterprise. It was a time when Americans were beginning to find imported European clothing extremely appealing. Leone and Facella could be at the forefront of a fashion revolution.

While the fathers talked commerce, the women talked ceremony. They sat around a large table at the Leone family restaurant, Naro. Bruno's wife, Connie, held her one-year-old son, Vincent, on her lap. The mothers of the betrothed couple were determined that the wedding ceremonies and the festivities after would be the fall social events of both San Francisco and Milano.

Nina Facella promised that Sofia's gown would be the talk of both towns.

At the same time, Bruno Leone was showing Giorgio Facella around the city that would soon be his new home. The two gregarious twenty-five-year-old men had taken an instant liking to each other. Bruno had become wealthy through his collaboration with Roberto Leone. With a large home on Russian Hill, a healthy young son, and money to burn, Bruno was a model of what Giorgio aspired to be in his new surroundings.

When Bruno proudly introduced Giorgio to his Nonno Roberto, Facella immediately saw the elder Leone as a strong and much more influential role model—and Roberto found in young Facella the possibility of another devoted ally. When Roberto was sent back to San Quentin in 1979, he decided it was the right time to test Giorgio's devotion.

The early years of the Leone and Facella partnership had been successful, but by the late seventies the circumstances had changed.

Giorgio's clothing shop in North Beach remained popular and lucrative, but outside the San Francisco Bay Area, sales of Facella designs had dropped.

As Salvatore and Luciano had predicted, Italian fashion had become a rage in America. But there was more and more competition, and New York City remained the center of fashion commerce. On top of that, the trial and conviction of Roberto Leone had once again injured the respectability of Leone Importing. Sitting in his jail cell, Roberto Leone again realized that the way to increase profits was to somehow get around the heavy government taxation on imported goods.

And the means to do so sat before him each week, when Bruno Leone and Giorgio Facella came to visit San Quentin.

The destruction of the contraband goods at the Hungry Lion warehouse had left the building in shambles, and the continued government scrutiny rendered the site useless. Roberto arranged from prison to have the building razed and the property sold. The site would years later become the location of a new ballpark for the San Francisco Giants.

Roberto had Bruno and Sammy Orso search for a similar warehouse on the Oakland docks. On the east side of the San Francisco Bay, they could more effectively avoid the eyes of the authorities.

The new facility would become the receiving and distribution point for European designer clothing illegally smuggled into the country.

Throughout 1979 and early 1980, Roberto outlined his criminal plans with Bruno and Giorgio during their weekly visits to San Quentin.

Sammy Orso was included in their discussions, as was Dominic Falco from New York.

Sammy Orso would serve as live-in security at the Oakland warehouse, as he had at Hungry Lion.

Bruno Leone would set up the Western markets for distribution, concentrating on San Francisco, Los Angeles, and Las Vegas.

Dominic Falco would do the same in New York City, Philadelphia, and Boston.

Giorgio Facella, during his frequent business trips to Europe to buy for his North Beach shop, would find suppliers in Italy and France.

By the spring of 1981, the business was taking in at least a hundred thousand dollars every month, tariff free, under the noses of Salvatore Leone and Luciano Facella without their knowledge.

From his prison cell, Roberto Leone had once again come to the rescue of his family business and had ensured the continued prosperity of his young and ambitious protégés.

New York City. 1981.

Dominic Falco walked a tightrope.

It was Dominic who had alerted the Leones about the ATF investigation.

Charlie Falco had testified against Roberto Leone to deal clemency for his sons, Dominic and Ferdinand.

Dominic knew that even if Roberto Leone appreciated Charlie Falco's motivation, the fact remained Charlie had sold Leone out.

Dominic decided warning Leone could assuage any animosity the Leones may have held for the Falcos.

Bruno and Roberto discussed the Falcos often during prison visits.

Roberto understood Charlie Falco's testimony was not motivated by any desire to hurt the Leones but was rather a father's attempt to protect his children. Roberto considered the decision commendable—in spite of the harm it did him personally.

At the same time, Leone knew his family could take advantage of Dominic Falco's willingness to do penance.

Dominic Falco was not eager to become involved in the latest venture suggested by Bruno Leone. Falco and his brother, though not indicted with their father, were being watched closely by the authorities. Dominic had no desire to join his father at Attica penitentiary.

But Dominic did not have a way to say no to Leone.

Dominic agreed to join in partnership with Bruno Leone and Giorgio Facella, to set up markets for the illegally imported European clothing on the East Coast. Dominic asked that

Leone allow him to proceed cautiously, wait until the government interest waned, then build up business slowly and systematically.

Roberto advised Bruno to accept the terms.

By spring 1981, Dominic Falco had arranged just enough marketing contracts to satisfy Leone while managing to stay clear of law enforcement.

In time, Dominic felt confident enough to assist his brother, Ferdinand, in launching and operating an exclusive clothing shop in New York City. Falcon on Fifth Avenue, specializing in gentlemen's business and formal attire imported from Italy, Spain, and France, opened its doors to the public in the summer of 1981.

On hand for the gala opening ceremonies were Bruno Leone, Giorgio Facella, and Sammy Orso.

In an unmarked car across the avenue, Vito Agnello and Harry Stone sat and watched.

During the month that followed the opening of Falcon on Fifth Avenue, ATF agents Agnello and Stone diligently observed the clothing shop and the activities of Ferdinand and Dominic Falco.

Agnello and Stone had located the Falco warehouse on the Brooklyn waterfront and watched the steady arrival and distribution of clothing. The investigation revealed that the Falcos were again violating laws of international tariff. Although clothing was not specifically a case for the ATF, the crime did fall under the jurisdiction of the Treasury Department. A task force was created combining the resources of Treasury, the Department of Justice, and the New York City Police Department. Trucks leaving the Falco warehouse were tailed to destinations in Boston, Miami, and Philadelphia. Evidence was collected and documented in preparation for a coordinated offensive.

At the same time, San Francisco federal officials had been alerted about the possible involvement of Bruno Leone and Giorgio Facella. Treasury and FBI agents began twenty-four-hour surveillance of Facella's clothing store in North Beach. With the aid of the San Francisco Police Department, including Detective Jack Harding, authorities were led to the Oakland warehouse where Leone and Facella handled distribution, and from there the agents followed deliveries to Las Vegas, Beverly Hills, and San Diego.

As on the East Coast, law enforcement agencies in San Francisco were carefully gathering the evidence needed to shut down Leone's illegal activity.

In late September 1981, representatives of Treasury, Justice, the New York and San Francisco police departments, and state authorities from Florida, Nevada, Massachusetts, and Pennsylvania met in Washington, D.C.

The meetings resulted in strategies for a synchronized attack on all businesses taking delivery from Falco or Leone, the Oakland and Brooklyn warehouses, and the clothing shops in Manhattan and North Beach.

The date set for the massive crackdown was scheduled for the Friday before Thanksgiving.

In the six weeks that followed the meetings, all necessary warrants were put into place.

After returning from Washington, Vito Agnello, as he had done so many times before, walked to his father's house to speak with Louis about Roberto Leone.

TWENTY

Louis Agnello had served ten years as a federal judge, the last four years on the Court of International Trade.

Agnello's wife, Dolores, had been ill for some time.

A respiratory ailment combined with chronic allergies had left her weak and often bedridden. Doctors had strongly recommended relocating to a drier climate, preferably the Southwest. Louis Agnello favored Colorado over New Mexico or Arizona and had been trying for two years to sell the idea to his wife. Dolores wasn't buying—she refused to leave her children and grandchildren in New York. Louis turned sixty-five in the spring of 1981 and talked more often about retiring.

By the end of that summer, Dolores had taken a turn for the worse and it seemed a move would be mandatory if she were to survive.

Agnello decided he would wait until the holidays were past. Louis would make the announcement to his sons, Joseph and Vito, after Thanksgiving and Christmas.

In late September, Vito came to his father with the news that a massive offensive against the Falcos was planned for the week before Thanksgiving.

As the senior member of the International Trade Court in the New York District, Louis would definitely be hearing the case.

"I wanted to hold off telling you until after the New Year, son," Louis said. "I'm stepping down from the bench and moving your mother to Denver. I need to spend more time with her, and need to do what is necessary to give us that time."

"Pop, you have to wait," said Vito. "There are four states involved. This will be your most important case since the German spy trials. The evidence is overwhelming. The trials will move quickly. I promise we'll be able to move you and Mom to Colorado by summer."

"I don't think we can wait, son."

"The government is going after the Leones also. Bruno Leone, certainly under the supervision of Roberto Leone, is neck deep in these federal crimes."

"I need time to consider, and I need to speak with your mother," Louis said. "And you, Vito, need to control this obsession you have to destroy Roberto Leone."

"Leone killed my grandfather and tried to murder you, twice."

"Your vehemence troubles me greatly, son. It is blind hatred that has perpetuated the violence among the Leone and Agnello families for a hundred years. What will it take to end the vengeance?"

"I don't know," said Vito.

"I pray you do not instill this hatred in your young sons, Vito. Now leave me, please. I need to go up and speak with your mother."

On the twentieth of November, 1981, joint law enforcement teams waited for the command to move.

Nearly two hundred officers in eight cities stood ready.

The order to converge on the designated targets came from Washington at 9:15 a.m.

It was 6:15 on the West Coast.

Twenty-seven retail businesses and four warehouses were raided simultaneously.

Seventy-three men and women were taken into custody, including six U.S. Customs employees.

Dominic and Ferdinand Falco were arrested in New York,

and Giorgio Facella was picked up in San Francisco.

Bruno Leone was not located.

Arraignments and indictments followed during November and December. Facella was extradited to Italy, where the authorities hoped Giorgio's trial testimony would help to destroy the European end of the operation.

The search continued for Bruno Leone.

The trial of Dominic and Ferdinand Falco began in late February at the Federal Court of International Trade, Judge Louis Agnello presiding.

The New York trial, and the trials in Massachusetts, Pennsylvania, and Florida, led to seventeen federal convictions and twenty-one convictions in state and local jurisdictions.

After nearly two months of testimony, Dominic and Ferdinand Falco were each sentenced to eight years imprisonment.

In March, Bruno Leone came out of hiding. He agreed to turn himself in to authorities if he would be allowed to visit Roberto Leone at San Quentin.

Roberto had suffered a massive heart attack in his cell, and he was in critical condition at the prison hospital.

Bruno was permitted to visit Roberto before being taken in for booking and arraignment.

Bruno pleaded that he be allowed to speak to Roberto in private. He sat handcuffed at Roberto's bedside. Two federal marshals stood guard across the hospital ward.

Bruno tenderly kissed Roberto's forehead.

"Nonno," Bruno whispered.

Roberto opened his eyes and tried to speak.

"Please, don't try to talk. I spoke to my cousin, Carlo Silveri in New York. It was Louis Agnello, and his son Vito, who attacked our family once again. We are planning retaliation. I wanted you to know."

"*Figlio, mio,*" Roberto said weakly. "Come near."

Bruno leaned in closer to Roberto, bringing his ear to the old man's lips.

"Kill them all," Roberto said.

"I swear it to you," Bruno promised.

Bruno squeezed Roberto's hand as the marshals walked over to inform him his visiting time was over.

In the hall, Salvatore Leone sat on a bench consoling his mother.

Lena rose when she saw her grandson, and asked permission to embrace Bruno.

Lena held on to Bruno for just a moment. Then, without a word, she moved quickly into the ward to be with her husband.

Bruno turned to his father. Salvatore looked deeply into his son's eyes, and neither man could find words.

The marshals escorted Bruno Leone away.

He was charged and arraigned later that afternoon.

Roberto Leone died the following day.

Bruno was released on bail, waiting for what looked to be a Grand Jury indictment.

His father put up the bond.

Carlo Silveri traveled from New York for Roberto Leone's funeral. After the burial, Bruno and his cousin Carlo arranged to meet privately.

Carlo was the son of Salvatore's older step-sister, Rosa. He was a grandson of Vincenzo Leone.

Silveri had moved to New York from San Francisco after the Vietnam War. During his youth, Carlo had also been greatly influenced by his great-uncle Roberto.

Silveri had been involved in the smuggling business with the Leones and the Falcos since the seventies, serving as a Leone family representative in the East, and also participated in the clothing operation.

Carlo had avoided prosecution on both counts, but was enraged by the course of events.

He wanted very much to help Bruno deal out punishment to the Agnellos.

The two men met at the house of Bruno's grandmother,

Lena, where the entire family had come to congregate after leaving the cemetery.

Bruno led Carlo into the room that sixty years earlier had been the study of Vincenzo Leone.

"What have you learned?" Bruno asked his cousin.

"All three families live in Brooklyn. Louis and Vito Agnello are neighbors. The older son, Joseph, lives in a home nearby. Vito works out of an ATF field office in Brooklyn, Louis sits on the bench at the federal courthouse in lower Manhattan, and Joseph operates a restaurant in the neighborhood where they all live."

"Are there grandchildren?"

"Three. Vito has two sons, and Joseph a daughter."

"The boys must be killed, also. If they grow to manhood, they will seek revenge."

"I understand."

"We must strike at a time when they are all gathered together," said Bruno.

"Easter is near," suggested Carlo.

Bruno liked the sound of it.

The total destruction of the Agnellos on the day of the Resurrection.

"I will not be allowed to leave California," Bruno said.

"I have the men I will need in New York, and I will join them personally on this mission."

"Good. Let us pray we can do this at Easter, for the memory of Nonno Roberto."

Young Vincent barged into the room. The ten-year-old ran excitedly to his father.

Bruno scooped Vincent up into his arms, and the three left the room to join the others.

PART THREE

SOCIOLOGY

*Murder is unique in that it abolishes the party it injures,
so that society has to take the place of the victim and on
his behalf demand atonement or grant forgiveness.
It is the one crime in which society has a direct interest.*

—W.H. Auden

TWENTY ONE

April 11, 1982. Brooklyn.

Easter Sunday.

Opening day of the stickball season.

Games would be played every Sunday through the summer, following the early Mass at Saints Simon and Jude.

The field was the concrete schoolyard of Public School 97 in Gravesend.

The strike zone, a filled-in chalk box on the wall of the handball court.

Batting statistics would be recorded throughout the season.

A tradition handed down from father to sons.

From Vito Agnello to Joseph and John.

Joey was an altar boy. He had just turned thirteen and he would soon receive Confirmation. He stood up near the parish priest with two other boys, there to assist with Communion. His father and mother, Vito and Donna, and his younger brother, Johnny, sat in the gallery. With them sat Vito's brother, Joseph, with his wife, Maryann, and their daughter, Patricia.

And sitting between Vito and his brother sat their father, Louis.

Louis' wife, Dolores, was not feeling well and had stayed at home.

. . .

The family waited on the steps of the church until Joey joined them after completing his altar boy duties.

Joey and Johnny were in a rush to get home. Get out of their Sunday best and into jeans and long-sleeve pullover shirts, pick up the stickball bat cut from an old broom handle and wrapped in tape at one end for a sure grip, grab a few Spalding rubber balls, and join their friends for the short walk to the schoolyard.

Patricia asked if she could go along and though the boys weren't happy with the prospect of having a *girl* at the ball game they knew their father, Vito, would not accept no for an answer.

Joseph and Maryann were headed for their restaurant, Giuseppe's, to begin preparing the Easter feast.

Donna would go along with them to help.

Vito decided to accompany his father back to Louis' home and look in on his mother.

"Dinner at one," Joseph said, as the group broke up. "Don't be late."

Carlo Silveri recruited Baldassare "Baldy" Amato, Cesare Bonventre, and Frankie Atanasio for the move against the Agnello family on Easter Sunday.

The three had been left out in the cold when their boss, Carmine Galante, was gunned down after lunch at an Italian-American restaurant in Bushwick, Brooklyn, in July, 1979.

Galante—who had seized control of the Bonanno family after Joseph Bonanno was exiled by the other *families* and Bonanno's successor, Philip Rastelli, was imprisoned—had made too many enemies due to unsanctioned trafficking in heroin. Genovese family boss Frank Tieri obtained permission from the Mafia Commission to hit Galante.

Amato and Bonventre were Galante's bodyguards, and sat at the table where Galante was killed. Although they survived the assault, the successful assassination did not look good on their bodyguard résumés.

Carlo Silveri and his three henchmen had staked out the houses since early that Easter morning.

Amato and Bonventre had watched from a car across from the home where Joseph Agnello lived with his wife, Maryann, and their daughter, Patricia. Silveri and Atanasio watched the home of Vito, his wife, and two boys—and Louis Agnello's home next door. The two teams followed the groups leaving the three homes to where they all converged at the church.

When the family broke up after Mass, Carlo Silveri had sent Amato and Bonventre to follow Joe Agnello, his wife, and sister-in-law—while Atanasio and Silveri followed Vito, Louis, and the children.

The children were in and out of Vito's house quickly and headed for the schoolyard.

Vito and his father entered the house next door.

Vito and Louis found Dolores in the kitchen breaking eggs into a bowl of ricotta cheese for her legendary Easter cheesecake.

"Mom, I was going to pick up a cheesecake at Carmine's Bakery," Vito said. "You should be resting."

"Don't be foolish. I'm fine and my cake is better than Carmine's. There is fresh coffee. Drink, watch, and learn something."

Suddenly the color went out of her face and she put both hands on the counter to steady herself. Vito rushed to his mother and led her to a chair at the kitchen table.

"What is it, Mom?"

"I felt faint for a moment. I'll be fine."

"Are you having trouble breathing?" Louis asked.

The look on his wife's face answered his question.

"We're taking you to Coney Island Hospital. Vito, bring

the car around."

"I'm sorry," Dolores said. "I don't want to ruin Easter dinner."

"Now *you* are being foolish," Louis said.

Silveri and Atanasio had watched the two boys and the girl run out and join their friends.

Silveri then decided to strike immediately—hit Louis and Vito who were their primary targets—but just as he and Atanasio were about to climb out of the vehicle Vito Agnello rushed out, jumped into the automobile parked in the driveway, and moved the car to the front of the house.

Moments later, Louis led his wife to the vehicle and they pulled away.

"Fuck," Silveri said. "Follow them."

Suddenly, Amato's car came up alongside.

"The others went to the restaurant on Kings Highway," Amato said. "A sign in the window says the place is closed."

"Then I'm sure they will all meet there for Easter dinner," Silveri said. "Go back. We'll follow behind."

"What about the two young boys?" Atanasio asked, as they drove over to Giuseppe's Ristorante.

"We will act according to the wishes of my cousin, Bruno Leone," Carlo said. "Kill them all."

At the restaurant, Joe, Maryann, and Donna were busy at work.

Donna checked the leg of lamb in the oven, Maryann put the finishing touches on the lasagna, and Joe grated the pecorino Romano cheese before going down to the cellar to choose a few special bottles of Chianti.

Across Kings Highway, Silveri, Atanasio, Amato, and Bonventre sat in Carlo's 1981 Coup de Ville waiting for the other Agnellos to arrive.

. . .

Johnny Agnello smashed the red rubber ball clear across the schoolyard into the playground. It was an automatic home run, scoring three, and giving his team a 4-2 victory in the final inning.

Joey was a hero as well. His double with two out in the last inning had brought his brother to the plate.

Patricia cheered her cousins like a fanatic at Shea Stadium.

The twelve rings of the church bell at St. Mary's announced noon.

"We should start heading for the restaurant," Joey said, twenty minutes later, after they had recorded all of the vital statistics of their first win.

"I need to pick up the Italian bread," Patricia said.

"You go on ahead," John said to his brother. "I'll go with Patty. Tell Uncle Joe we're on the way."

At the hospital, Louis and Vito sat in the waiting room while Dolores was in an examination room for tests.

The nurse had steadied Dolores' breathing with oxygen.

"What is it, Dad?" Vito asked, when Louis began pacing nervously.

"I know what they will say. Your mother needs to be moved to a drier climate. We need to leave New York and move to some desert in Arizona or New Mexico."

"You're nearly sixty-six, it's time you retired. You could go to Denver."

"No, the doctors claim the altitude would not be good for her breathing. And your mother will fight hand and foot to not be separated from her children and grandchildren. Call your brother, let him know where we are."

Vito went to the nurses' station to use the phone and returned to his father to report there had been no answer at the restaurant.

"Go ahead then," Louis said. "We will be alright here."

"Call me as soon as they're done with the tests."

"I will. Go. Save some of Maryann's lasagna for us. And pick up the cheesecake at Carmine's."

The four men watching Giuseppe's restaurant saw the boy, Joey Agnello, enter the front door.

"Where are all the others?" Atanasio said.

"I don't know. Surely on the way," Silveri answered. "Baldy, Cesare, go now. Take care of those inside and wait in ambush. When the others come we'll follow them in and finish the job."

When Vito Agnello turned onto Kings Highway from West Sixth Street, he saw the two men rushing toward the restaurant entrance.

They were carrying handguns.

Vito pulled to the curb, jumped from the car, and ran into the newsstand adjacent to the subway station.

"Vito, happy Easter."

"Geno, call nine-one-one, report a ten-double-zero, officer down, give my name and the location of Giuseppe's."

Without another word, Vito pulled out his service weapon and rushed across Kings Highway.

Silveri and Atanasio left the Cadillac and followed Agnello.

A bullet missed Vito by inches and shattered the front window of the restaurant.

He ducked behind a parked car and fired at the two assailants.

His first shot knocked Atanasio to the ground. The next three sent Silveri in retreat.

Vito heard shots coming from inside the restaurant and he

ran up to and through the front door. He saw Amato moving toward him and shot twice.

Amato went down.

Vito rushed further into the restaurant and shot Bonventre in the back as the man was heading for the rear door. He heard the sirens of at least two police cars screaming to the location. Vito made sure the two men were dead and then found his family.

His brother Joseph, Joe's wife, Maryann, his own wife, Donna, and his son, Joey.

All killed.

When the police officers burst in they found Vito Agnello holding his wife and son in his arms.

Vito Agnello got a good look at the man who escaped during the gunfight outside the restaurant. He identified Carlo Silveri from mug shots, and fingerprints in the vehicle Silveri had been forced to abandon confirmed his identity. A massive manhunt was mounted throughout the city, extending into the tri-state area.

Silveri could not be found.

San Francisco. April. 1982.

Silveri made it to San Francisco, evading the net, and called his cousin Bruno Leone from a downtown hotel. Bruno set up a meeting at a diner in the Fillmore District. Although Leone was displeased by Carlo's failure to end the lives of Louis and Vito Agnello, Bruno greeted Silveri warmly with praise and appreciation. Leone's greatest concerns were to avoid being connected to the events in Brooklyn and deciding how and when to take care of the unfinished business.

And Silveri had another piece of information Bruno could

not permit to become known. The name of the New York ATF agent who had been bought by Leone, with a great deal of money and threats to his family, and had given Silveri all of the information on the residences of the Agnellos in Brooklyn.

Leone felt certain the hunt for Silveri would eventually reach San Francisco. Silveri would need to remain out of sight until things cooled down. Carlo was not to let anyone know he was in California, not even his mother or his Uncle Salvatore.

Bruno had access to a house in Santa Rosa, untraceable to the Leones, where Silveri could safely stay hidden for the time being.

Salvatore Leone ran the import business as his father Vincenzo had—legitimately.

Leone Importing, after nearly sixty years, still dealt primarily in foodstuffs legally imported from Italy and other Western European countries.

Bruno Leone, on the other hand, operated as his Great-Uncle Roberto Leone had—smuggling alcohol, tobacco, clothing, and other illegal contraband, often using Leone Importing's facilities without Salvatore's knowledge—in the same way Roberto had deceived his brother Vincenzo from the time he had partnered with Benny Lucchese in the twenties.

And Bruno held a similar disrespect for his father, Salvatore, as Roberto had for his brother, Vincenzo—a disrespect for their puritanical attitudes, their unwillingness to go outside the law and the government that drained ambitious businesses with excessive tariffs and taxation.

However, despite their differences, Salvatore and Bruno Leone did have a common passion—a hatred for the Agnello family and a wish to finish them.

Bruno's hatred was fueled by the toxic council of his hero, Roberto.

And Salvatore still believed, after more than forty years,

the untruth his Uncle Roberto told him on his eighteenth birthday—that the Agnellos were responsible for the death of his father, Vincenzo.

A week after that fatal Easter Sunday, Carlo Silveri's mother became worried.

Her son hadn't called, and she couldn't reach him.

Rosa Silveri went to her step-brother, Salvatore, with her concern.

Knowing Carlo was close to his cousin, Salvatore asked Bruno if he had heard from Carlo.

Bruno assured his father he had not.

Bruno Leone knew Carlo's mother would not let it rest, and he was not confident in Carlo's ability to remain incommunicado.

Bruno's lack of faith was well founded.

Before the month was out, Carlo contacted his mother. He told Rosa he could not come down to San Francisco, and asked that she come up to see him in Santa Rosa.

When the hunt for Carlo Silveri was exhausted in the east, Vito Agnello reached out to his friend, SFPD Detective Jack Harding, with the hope Silveri would turn up and be spotted in San Francisco.

Carlo had not been sighted, but Harding secured permission to tap Rosa Silveri's phone.

When the call from her fugitive son was reported, Jack Harding and his partner, Carl Taylor, raced up to Santa Clara.

When Harding and Taylor arrived, they were presented with a standoff. Carlo Silveri refused to surrender and instead began firing at the detectives. Silveri was killed in the exchange and with him went the hope of implicating Bruno Leone in the Brooklyn murders.

The SFPD, FBI, and ATF did however begin vigilant surveillance of Bruno Leone—which caused him to curb his illegal activities and put his plans of going after the Agnellos once again on hold.

In 1987, Bruno Leone felt it was time.

He had been trying for nearly five years, unsuccessfully, to discover the whereabouts of Louis Agnello.

He decided dealing with the old man would have to wait, but he could take care of the son and the grandson now.

Leone recruited two of his most trusted New York City associates to assassinate Vito and John Agnello.

TWENTY TWO

Brooklyn, 1987.

The massacre five years earlier had left Vito Agnello a widower—alone to care for his only remaining son.

The events of that Easter Sunday had left Patricia Agnello an orphan, and Vito took her into his home to live with him and John.

Vito's mother, Dolores, passed away shortly after her son and grandson were killed. She had given up her fight to survive her illness.

Following the loss of his wife and his oldest son—and moving his father, Louis, to Denver—Vito spent a great deal of time teaching his son John and his niece Patricia how to handle firearms. Vito had little doubt that sooner or later Bruno Leone would stage another assassination attempt.

Even after five years, Vito could not put his guard down.

Vic Campo and Dan Cirelli had been watching Vito Agnello's house for hours, waiting until both father and son were at home.

Finally, after Vito arrived home, Campo and Cirelli made their move.

Together, the two men easily kicked in the front door. Vito had been preparing dinner. He grabbed the gun he had set on the table in the kitchen and moved to the doorway. Vito's first shot struck Vic Campo in the forehead. The man was dead before he hit the floor. His second shot hit Cirelli in the shoulder, but not before Cirelli had put two bullets into Vito's stomach.

When he heard the first shot, John seized the gun from his bedside table and rushed from his bedroom. He first spotted the body on the floor, then the second man standing over his father.

John fired four times into Cirelli's back, and the man went down.

John made sure both intruders were dead, then he rushed to his father.

"I'll call for an ambulance. I'll be right back."

Vito grabbed John's arm—which still held the weapon.

"It's too late, John. You can't be here when the police arrive. There's cash in the top drawer of my dresser. Take only the money, a few changes of clothing, and the gun. Use only ground transportation. Take the subway to Forty-Second Street in Manhattan and then take the first bus out of the Port Authority Bus Terminal heading west."

"To Grandfather?"

"No, John. Listen carefully. Stay away from your grandfather. You will go to Hank Sims. First get to Cheyenne, Wyoming, then to Iron Mountain. Ask for Hank in the town and he will be called to come for you. You'll be safe with Hank and Katy. I love you, son."

Those were the last words John heard from his father.

John threw some clothes, the cash, and the weapon into a small gym bag.

He also gathered a few photographs of his mother, his father, and his brother Joey.

Two days later, John made it to Iron Mountain, Wyoming. He walked into a diner and asked how he could find Hank Sims.

John was told to wait, and he was brought food.

Twenty minutes later, a tall man who John knew by sight

walked into the diner.

"Johnny?" the man said, coming to the table where John sat.

"Yes."

"Do you know who I am?"

"Yes. Hank. My father's friend."

"And your father?" Hank asked.

John shook his head.

"Come with me, son," Hank Sims said.

They left the diner, climbed into Hank's truck, and drove to the Sims' ranch outside of town.

John Agnello would remain in Wyoming for the next four years.

John Agnello had not completed high school—and he never would.

John watched as, one by one, the Sims' children—Hank and Katy's two sons and their daughter, Amy—went off to attend universities in other parts of the state and other parts of the country.

John's university, his institution of learning, was the ranch.

From Hank, he learned about horses—riding, grooming, husbandry—and was introduced to hunting and woodworking.

From Katy, he learned about the intricacies of automobile mechanics—and a thing or two about cooking.

And John was a voracious reader, he possessed a passion for the written word inherited from his mother. He regularly borrowed books from Hank and Katy's well-stocked bookcases.

History. Philosophy. Biographies. And the great classics of literature—Hugo, Dickens, Tolstoy, Melville, Cervantes.

Although he was less than three hours away from his grandfather, and longed to see Louis, John honored his father's wish that he would not.

John was sure his father had good reason, as he was certain the trouble with the Leones was far from over.

TWENTY THREE

Vincent Leone. San Francisco. 1991.

In 1987, Bruno Leone was pleased that Vito Agnello had been killed in Brooklyn—but he was far from satisfied.

The son, John, had not been discovered at the scene—the young man had simply *disappeared.*

And, after years of searching, Bruno was no closer to discovering the location of Louis Agnello.

In the fall of 1988, while John Agnello was under the hood of a pickup truck being instructed by Katy Sims on how to install a carburetor, Bruno's son Vincent was preparing to begin studies at the University of California in Berkeley.

Before Vincent began college, Bruno had another of his many talks with his son. For as long as Vincent could understand such things, his father had continually fueled the boy's hatred for the Agnellos.

"When you graduate, Vincent, you will have a prominent position in our business," Bruno promised. "But never forget the Agnellos will always attempt to destroy all we have built unless we destroy them first."

Bruno had orchestrated two deadly attacks on the Agnello family, in 1982 and 1987, and both times had escaped culpability. He had been very careful in his illegal dealings since the second attack, and the heat he was getting from all of the law enforcement agencies had gradually cooled.

Business was going well, and his son was solidly behind him.

In 1991, Vincent Leone was preparing for a commencement ceremony, where he would be graduating with honors. At the same time, John Agnello, who had just turned twenty-one, was preparing to see the world.

John Agnello. Wyoming. 1991.

Vito Agnello and Hank Sims had served together in Vietnam and had developed a strong friendship—they were as close as brothers. They had also become friends with others who had shared their war experience—some who had not made it home. One of those former comrades who *had* come back, Charlie Porter, studied graphic design after the war and had developed many useful skills—some of which would be useful in helping John Agnello fulfill his wish to travel abroad.

With a number of documents, some official and others expertly forged, Charlie Porter supplied John with an Italian passport identifying him as Giovanni Vota—Vota having been John's maternal grandfather's surname.

While Bruno Leone watched his son, Vincent, graduate university in Berkeley—Hank Sims was seeing John off at Stapleton Airport in Denver.

Destination Rome, Italy.

Lincoln Bonner. Colorado. 1991.

At the same time John was off to Rome, Lincoln found himself in the sort of trouble he would need serious help getting clear of.

And the only person he could turn to for serious help was his father, Frank.

After completing his junior year at the University of Colorado at Denver, and having just turned twenty-one, Lincoln took a summer job bartending at a restaurant downtown.

Don Leonard was ten years older than Lincoln and was a regular at the restaurant—often arriving for dinner with an attractive young woman on his arm.

When Leonard came alone, he sat at the bar.

After a while, he and Lincoln became more and more familiar.

One evening, as the restaurant was about to close, Leonard sat at the bar while Lincoln cleared and washed glasses.

"Ever take a drink yourself?" Leonard asked.

"Not while I'm working."

"That's commendable. How about *after* work? Can I buy you a drink?"

"Sure."

"Tonight?"

"Sure. I won't get out of here for another thirty or forty minutes."

"Do you know the Skylark on Broadway?"

"Yes."

"I'll meet you there," Leonard said. "What do I owe you for the drinks?"

"Six dollars."

"Keep the change," Leonard said, dropping a twenty on the bar. "See you in a while."

Lincoln found Leonard alone at a booth in the rear of the Skylark Bar and joined him.

"What are you drinking?" Leonard asked.

"Beer is fine."

"Coors okay?"

"Sure"

Leonard waved a waitress over to the booth.

"Molly, bring us a pitcher of Coors and a couple of shots of tequila."

"I'll pass on the tequila," Lincoln said, as Molly turned for the bar. "I don't do very well with it."

"No problem, I can handle both shots. How is work?"

"Okay. It's a summer job, money for school expenses."

"How's that going?"

"How is what going?"

"Are you making any money?"

"It's not too bad. Some good nights, some not so good. If everyone tipped the way you do, I would be doing a lot better."

"Could you use an extra few hundred dollars a week?"

"I'm not exactly sure what you're asking."

"I can pay you at least two hundred dollars for each time I give you a package and you pass it on to someone else. One, occasionally two a week."

"What's in the package?"

"I won't say. But I can tell you that you won't be breaking any laws."

"Can I think about it?"

"Yes, but not for very long. I have two other students working with me and I need a third as soon as possible. The others, Thomas and Susan, have been making good money with no problems. If you need testimonials to help you decide, you can talk with them," Leonard said, handing Lincoln a slip of paper with names and phone numbers as Molly brought their drinks.

"Are you sure you won't try a shot of tequila?"

"I guess one won't kill me," Lincoln said.

Lincoln called Thomas, if that was his real name.

"When Don Leonard approached me, I didn't actually believe there was nothing illegal about what he was asking me to do, but I really needed money so I took a chance. I've been making a thousand dollars a month for the past six months with no trouble," Thomas said.

. . .

The next evening, Leonard approached Lincoln at the bar.

"Are you in?"

"Okay."

Leonard handed him a small package wrapped in plain brown paper and asked Lincoln to put it into his pocket. It was clearly a box, approximately the size of one that might hold a pair of earrings.

"Do you get much call for Glenlivet with orange juice?" Leonard asked.

"Never. Who would mix orange juice with aged single-malt scotch?"

"In the next hour or so, someone will come up to the bar and ask for Glenlivet and orange juice. Hand over the package and you're done."

"That's it?"

"That's it," Leonard said. "I'll see you again soon."

With that, Don Leonard casually placed two one-hundred-dollar bills on the bar.

Throughout the summer, at least once a week, Leonard handed Lincoln a package and two hundred dollars at the bar and someone ordering a Glenlivet and orange juice took the package away.

There were never any problems.

However, as the fall semester approached, Lincoln decided it was time to stop pushing his luck.

When Leonard came into the restaurant again, Lincoln told him he was ready to discontinue their arrangement.

"When is your next day off?" Leonard asked.

"Tuesday."

"Do you know the College Inn on Eighth Avenue?"

"Yes."

"Meet me at the College Inn at nine, Tuesday night," Leonard said, "and we'll talk about it."

Then Leonard placed a package and two hundred dollars on the bar and quickly left.

The following morning was Sunday.

It was the Labor Day weekend and Lincoln would be starting classes on Wednesday. He received a phone call from Thomas.

"Have you been approached by the police?" Thomas asked.

"No. What's going on?"

"I got a call from Susan. Two detectives came to talk with her at the bar where she works, asking if she knew a man named Leonard Donaldson. She said she didn't. They said she had been seen talking with him at the bar, and she said she spoke with many people at the bar but didn't know them all by name. They said she could be in a great deal of trouble, and they could help her out. The detectives left her a business card.

"She said she told Leonard about the detectives that night when he came in. He told her not to worry, to not say a thing. Don asked her to meet him after work. She told me she would let me know what happened after she met with him.

"She never called, and I haven't been able to reach her. That was two days ago. And I haven't had a visit from Leonard. I'm really worried, and I'm frightened."

"I'm supposed to meet him Tuesday night," Lincoln said. "I'll try to find out what's going on and I'll call you."

"Be careful," Thomas said.

Monday morning Lincoln saw it on the local TV news. Susan Oliver, a University of Denver student, left her job at a bar near campus and failed to return home. Police were looking at her disappearance as a possible case of foul play.

Susan's parents had flown in from New York City and had held a press conference, begging anyone who knew of her whereabouts to come forward.

Lincoln called Thomas a few times on Monday, but could not reach him.

Finally, Lincoln called his father.

Lincoln's mother had passed away when he was ten years old. From that time, it had been only Lincoln and his father.

Cheyenne Wells is on the plains in eastern Colorado, not far from the Kansas border, 180 miles from Denver.

Early Tuesday, Frank Bonner made the drive from Cheyenne Wells to Denver in less than three hours.

Lincoln told his father everything, except what was in the small wrapped packages.

Lincoln had no idea.

"Do you think this man is dangerous?" Frank asked. "Do you fear your life is in danger?"

"I do."

"And you're meeting him at nine?"

"Yes."

"I'll follow you to the meeting place and wait outside. Tell him again that you want out, but let him convince you to reconsider. Excuse yourself to go to the restroom and come out to see me. Meanwhile, keep trying to reach Thomas."

"What are you thinking?" Lincoln asked.

"I'm thinking I could use lunch."

Lincoln and Frank arrived at the College Inn just before nine. They parked both vehicles in the lot behind the bar.

"Do you see his car?" Frank asked.

"There," Lincoln said, pointing out a red Camaro.

"You know what to do?"

"Go back to the restrooms and come out the back door here."

"Make sure you don't come out together," Frank said.

. . .

Lincoln joined Leonard at a booth near the front door.

"Have you been visited by the police?" were the first words Leonard said.

"No."

"Good. If they come into the restaurant, you've never heard of me."

"Last night was my last night there. School begins tomorrow."

"Better. We'll find another place to do business."

"I would really like to stop doing business," Lincoln said.

"I'm afraid that's not possible. I need you, and I need to find more help."

"What about Susan and Thomas?"

"Susan and Thomas are not your problem, Lincoln. Are you going to be *my* problem? I would not recommend it. As they say, if you are not with me, you are against me. Are you with me?"

"Yes."

"Great, let's drink to it."

"I'll take a beer and a shot of tequila," Lincoln said.

"My man."

"I need to use the restroom. I'll be right back."

"Okay. Then I'll tell you where to meet me tomorrow night. Somewhere less public."

The restrooms were in back, near the rear door. Lincoln went out to his father in the parking lot.

"He very clearly threatened me," Lincoln said. "He wants to meet me tomorrow night at a *less public* place. Susan is still missing and I haven't been able to reach Thomas. I think he's done something to both of them, and I think I'm next."

"We don't have much time, he'll be expecting you back. Do you have somewhere you can go, now, where there will be others?"

"There's a party, a last bash before school starts again.

There should be a good turnout."

"Go straight there, and don't leave until everyone else has. Whatever happens, son, you must say you never had anything to do with this man."

"What do you mean, whatever happens?"

"I mean exactly what I said. You deny knowing him or knowing anything about him *no matter what happens.* I need you to swear it to me."

"Dad?"

"Promise me, Lincoln."

"Okay."

"Good. Now go. I love you, son."

Lincoln drove off.

Frank waited.

Leonard Donaldson, a.k.a. Don Leonard, waited more than five minutes before going back to the restrooms to find out what was taking Lincoln so long. When he couldn't find Lincoln in the men's room, he went out the back door to the parking lot.

Donaldson spotted the stranger sitting the hood of the red Camaro.

"Get the fuck off the car, old man," he said.

"Is this your car, Leonard?"

"Yes, it's my fucking car."

Frank Bonner took two steps, raised his weapon, and shot Donaldson twice in the chest.

Immediately, a few people came out of the rear door of the bar.

"Everyone, back inside," Frank said, still holding the gun.

They all retreated.

When he felt sure no one was coming out again, Frank placed the gun, in plain sight, beside the body and listened for the sirens.

When the squad car pulled into the parking lot, Frank went to his knees and raised both arms in the air. Two police officers moved up to him, one with his weapon drawn, and Frank was handcuffed.

"What happened here?"

"I had just arrived and was getting out of my truck when he came out the back door pulling a girl with him. He slapped her twice across the face. Hard. I told him to stop. He said something like, *mind your own business, old man,* and he slapped her again. I reached into the truck and took my gun from the glove box. I approached them and told him again to stop. He let the go of the girl and reached behind his back. I thought he was going for a weapon and I shot him twice."

"Just like that?"

"Just like that."

"Where's the girl?"

"She ran off."

"And if he didn't have a weapon?"

"Doesn't matter to me," Frank said. "It was more about protecting the girl than protecting myself."

The officers locked him in the back seat of the squad car. One stayed with the vehicle, the other went into the bar.

Ten minutes later he was back.

"No one in the bar saw the victim with a woman," the officer said to Frank.

"I don't know what else to tell you," Frank said.

Lincoln Bonner could have testified—provided a reason for his father's actions.

It may have resulted in a lesser charge, a lighter sentence.

But Frank wouldn't allow it. He was protecting Lincoln from a criminal record as much as he was protecting his son from Donaldson.

Susan and Thomas were never found.

PART FOUR

DESCENDANTS

There is no escape—
we pay for the violence of our ancestors.

—Frank Herbert

TWENTY FOUR

Vincent.

Bruno Leone was haunted by two obsessions.

Locating and finally ending the lives of Louis and John Agnello—and re-establishing the network Roberto Leone had built in the east, from Florida to Massachusetts, that had been decimated by the coordinated raids by ATF and FBI agents in November 1981.

After the raids, Roberto Leone had insisted from his jail cell that Bruno had no part in the illegal importing and sales. Prosecutors lacked the needed evidence and Bruno escaped conviction after a lengthy trial.

In 1985, following three years of caution after the death of Roberto Leone and the Easter Sunday attack, Bruno began to reach out to those he, and Roberto before him, had done business with in New York and New Jersey.

And Bruno had an important friend—James "Jimmy Brown" Failla.

Failla was capo under Paul Castellano, who became boss of the Gambino family after Carmine Gambino's death. Roberto Leone had done business with Jimmy Failla in the late seventies and early eighties.

Bruno reached out—inviting Failla to visit San Francisco with hope of setting up a meeting with Castellano to discuss business. Leone could offer the Gambino family a wealth of smuggled alcohol, tobacco, food delicacies, clothing, and shoes for the *family's* outlets in New York and Atlantic City.

Failla liked what he heard and said he would bring it to Castellano.

In December, Jimmy Failla called Bruno from New York. Castellano was interested in meeting with Leone to consider Bruno's proposition. They would meet at a restaurant in Manhattan on the sixteenth. Bruno flew to New York City and met with Failla. Later, the two rode together to Sparks Steak House on Forty-Sixth Street.

From inside the restaurant, they heard the gunfire.

When the shooting ended, Paul Castellano and his newly appointed underboss, Tommy Bilotti, were dead.

When the news reached Failla at their table, he rushed Bruno through the kitchen and out the rear exit of the restaurant.

"Who?" Leone asked.

"It had to be John Gotti."

"What happens now?"

"If Gotti didn't have a go-ahead from the commission, and I doubt he did, there will be trouble. It could be a while before I know where I stand. I suggest you leave the city. I'll be in touch when I can."

Bruno hailed a cab, stopped at his hotel for his bags, and went directly to the airport.

After power struggles throughout 1986, which included a failed attempt to murder Gotti with a car bomb in April, a truce was agreed upon between the Gambino and Lucchese families, and Gotti solidified his position as Gambino Boss. Jimmy Failla was able, in time, to work his way back into Gotti's good graces.

Once Failla was confident he was on solid ground, he approached Gotti with the idea that they could increase revenues through an arrangement with Bruno Leone of San Francisco. Gotti was not interested.

Failla called Bruno Leone with the news.

Leone then shifted his focus to the Agnellos, again with the help of the New York ATF agent he had in his pocket—arranging the hit that would result in the death of Vito Agnello and send John Agnello into hiding with Hank and Katy Sims in Wyoming in 1987.

In 1991, John Gotti's underboss Sammy Gravano agreed to turn state's evidence against The Teflon Don.

Gotti was indicted on five counts of murder, including the assassinations of Castellano and Bilotti.

The trial began in February 1992, and Gravano's testimony was enough to convince a jury to convict. Gotti was sentenced to life imprisonment without the possibility of parole on June 23, and he eventually surrendered to federal authorities on December 14.

Vincent.

In 1993, Vincent Leone earned an MBA from Stanford University.

Vinnie immediately went to work with his father, Bruno, now possessing the best tools available for *cooking the books.*

Bruno's father, Salvatore, had just turned seventy-two. For several years he had been gradually turning the operation of Leone Importing over to his son. Salvatore *wanted* to believe Bruno had not been involved in the unlawful activities of Roberto Leone. By 1993, Bruno had total control and it became much easier for him, with his son Vincent's help, to hide the illegal smuggling beneath the legitimate imports. Bruno was making a great deal of money, and with it came influence, power, and friends in high places. Police, judges, customs agents—any number of city, state, and federal bureaucrats who would turn a blind eye for the right price. There was every reason for Bruno Leone to be a satisfied man, but he was continually plagued with the same nagging desire—to find Louis and John Agnello and wipe out the last of that hated family.

But all attempts to locate the old man and his grandson had failed.

Meanwhile, in New York, with John Gotti in prison, Peter Gotti had taken the reins of the Gambino family—and his chief advisor was Jimmy Failla.

Failla's call to Bruno temporarily put the Agnellos out of Bruno Leone's mind.

"Peter would like to talk business," Failla said.

Vincent Leone began to restructure all of Leone Importing transactions. He hid their purchases and sales beneath a maze of dummy corporations. It would take a genius to connect the sale of illegal imports to Leone. Profits increased and risks decreased. Once all was in place, Vincent told his father they were now ready to go to New York to present a business proposition to Jimmy Failla and Peter Gotti.

The four men met at Umberto's Clam House on Mulberry Street, where Joey Gallo had been assassinated twenty-one years earlier.

Bruno let his son do the talking.

"We can supply you with whatever you can use from our inventory at costs we are certain will increase your profits considerably," Vincent began. "You will be supplied with bills of sale for all purchases, protecting you from criminal charges. If you are questioned about the purchases, all you need to do is produce the bills of sale. The sellers named will not be located and you, of course, will insist you had no knowledge about how those sellers obtained the goods. It will be nearly impossible to trace those goods back to *our* family even if someone in your organization, for any reason, decided to name us as the source. How you choose to distribute the merchandise is not our concern. All we guarantee is that you will receive what you request quickly, if paid for in advance at the prearranged price."

"How soon can we begin?" Peter Gotti asked.

"Now," Bruno Leone said.

Over the next several years, Leone Importing experienced the greatest profits in its history.

In 1996, in celebration of Salvatore Leone's seventy-fifth birthday, a gathering of family and friends assembled at the house on Russian Hill.

Salvatore still lived in the house where he grew up, the mansion of his father, Vincenzo.

The house where Louis Agnello had grown up.

He and his wife, Josephine, shared the large home with his step-sister Rosa and her husband, Thomas Silveri. Josephine was Thomas' niece.

After Vincenzo Leone's death in New York in 1924, his second wife, Lena, continued living in the house with Vincenzo's two daughters and their own son, Salvatore. When Lena married Vincenzo's younger brother, Roberto, he joined the household.

Roberto died in prison in 1982. Lena passed away three years later, and Salvatore inherited the mansion.

Both the Ristorante Naro and the Salumeria Leone, just down the hill on Columbus Avenue, were still thriving businesses after more than seventy years—managed by Vincenzo's grandchildren and great-grandchildren.

Following the colossal feast, as dessert was being prepared by Josephine and Rosa, Salvatore approached his grandson.

"Can we talk, Vincent?"

"Of course."

"Come with me to my father's study," Salvatore said.

The two men sat facing each other across the large desk, the same desk where Vincenzo Leone had read the letter from the New York lawyer, Catalano, inquiring about Giuseppe Agnello—which led to the events Salvatore had never learned the truth about.

Vincent broke the silence.

"Is there something troubling you, Grandfather?"

"My father was an honest man, Vincent, a generous man. He built a business that became respected throughout San Francisco and the entire country. Our restaurant and the salumeria are city landmarks. My father took pride in the fact that he adhered to the laws and the rules of the country that gave him and his family a new beginning, free from the poverty and the troubles of the old country. His brother, Roberto, rest in peace, threatened to tear down all my father had built. My father was unaware of Roberto's unlawful activities—or chose not to believe. I am aware of how much Bruno admired and wished to be like Roberto. Roberto paid dearly for his actions. I fear a similar fate for you and your father. Tell me, Vincent, that my fears are unfounded."

Although Vincent respected and honored Bruno's wishes, he had much more affection for his grandfather. It was difficult for him to lie and as he did he made a vow, to himself, that as soon as possible what he was about to tell Salvatore would come to be the truth.

"Do not worry, Grandfather. With my help, my father is running Leone Importing as your father would wish it to be."

"That is good to hear. It is the best birthday present I could hope for. Let's get back to the others before all the cannoli are gone."

And that is exactly what Vincent did—he kept his vow to transform Leone Importing into a legitimate enterprise.

Without the knowledge of his father, Bruno.

It took nearly four years.

First, they would need to lower the cost of goods that

could be bought *legally* from vendors in Europe. Vincent found they could do this by ensuring longer term contracts and increasing the volume of purchases to bargain for discounts—which was no problem since business was booming.

Second, they would need to begin importing merchandise that more reflected the demands of the nineties—adding electronics, computers, cell phones, and video game equipment to their traditional imports of clothing, alcohol, and ethnic foods to their inventory.

Next, Vincent calculated the expenses incurred doing business on the *black market*—factoring in the risks involved—including the dangers of exorbitant fines and criminal charges.

The profits would surely decrease in the legalized system, but not as much as Vincent had imagined.

All he needed to do now was to make up the difference.

Vincent studied every tax and tariff code in the books, exhaustively, and identified every tax break and loophole available to Leone Importing—provided, within the laws, by international, federal, state, and local governments.

Finally, in the spring of 2000, Vincent had the details worked out and was ready to present it all to his father.

"You are saying our profits will suffer," Bruno said, after Vincent had explained everything as clearly and simply as possible.

"For a while," Vincent admitted, "but in the long run, without the payoffs, which continue to become costlier, and free from the present risks, we will be in a better position to considerably increase the variety of products we import and to explore new markets for those more profitable goods. In a very short time, Father, we could possibly be generating as much revenue, if not even more, than we do now."

"And why go through all of this trouble for the *possibility* of greater profits?"

"Because it is safer. Because it is *good business.* Because it honors the wishes of your father and his father before him," Vincent said, as he handed a printed document to Bruno.

"What is this?"

"Our new invoice form, which can be used for *all* of our business dealings going forward. Take a look at the heading. Leone Importing. San Francisco, California. Established 1918. We can now proudly display the Leone name for all time."

"I approve, son. I am proud of you—of your abilities and your hard work. And I am deeply moved by all your efforts to honor the name of our ancestors. Now, I have great news for you, also. I have received word that John Agnello has reappeared—in New York City. He is being watched constantly—in the hope he will lead us to his grandfather, Louis, and we can finally end both of their lives. Be assured, Vincent, this news will please my father greatly. The final destruction of the Agnellos will do as much as you have done to honor and bring pride to the Leone name."

TWENTY FIVE

John.

In 1991, when John Agnello reached Rome, he had experienced little of history beyond what could be read about in books or seen in photographs.

He had spent the past four years in southern Wyoming, where the oldest monuments had been created by nature—not by the hands of man.

Even growing up in New York City, the oldest building John could recall seeing was St. Paul's Chapel at Trinity Church in Manhattan, not much more than two hundred years old.

Here, he was experiencing art and architecture that dated back five hundred to more than two thousand years. The Roman Forum, the Coliseum, Saint Peter's Basilica and Michelangelo's *Pieta*, The Sistine Chapel. John was awestruck, everywhere he turned was a journey through the past—he fell in love with the *Eternal City*. It was nearly a month before he could tear himself away. Finally, he moved on to Florence, feeling it was time he began to study the language—and knowing he would surely return to Rome again.

John discovered a language school in the Santo Spirito neighborhood, in the Oltrarno District, just across the Ponte Vecchio. He took a room in a small pensione catering to students. He met young men and women who had come from England, Portugal, Spain, France, Germany, Switzerland, and from as far away as Russia and Japan to study the Italian language. And he began to learn about the world.

When he was proficient enough in basic conversation, John obtained a job as a waiter in a restaurant, Osteria San Spirito, on the piazza near the school and his lodging.

After two years of study, and with money put away from his work at the Osteria, John decided it was time to explore more of Italy and more of the continent. John was very well liked by the restaurant's owner, Giancarlo Falconi. Falconi told John he was always welcome to come back to work any time he became weary of the road—an offer John took advantage of from time to time during his years in Europe.

John also found work in other cities, when he wished to spend longer periods in one place or needed to replenish his pocketbook. His Italian passport made moving around easy, and getting work was not a problem.

In Venice, he captained a gondola and lived in a building that was built before Columbus sailed for the New World.

In the north, he worked as a gardener at a mansion overlooking Lake Como, where composer Igor Stravinsky had created musical works while he vacationed from Milan or Venice.

John travelled throughout Italy—from north to south and sea to sea from the Mediterranean to the Adriatic. Parma, Milan, Assisi, Genoa, Bologna, Pisa, Naples, Sorrento, and the Amalfi Coast.

Then he visited the great cities of Europe—Amsterdam, Paris, Athens, London, Dublin, Berlin, Vienna, Budapest, Prague, and Warsaw. He crossed the Adriatic to the former Yugoslavia—to Montenegro, Slovenia, Croatia and Bosnia— not very long after the bloody civil wars that had divided Yugoslavia into seven separate nations.

Occasionally, John would return to Florence for a while. He had found a good friend in Giuseppe Falconi, son of the owner of Osteria San Spirito. Joey, as his new friend liked to be called, reminded John of his brother Joey, who he had lost years before. The two young men shared many adventures, and Joey was a perfect guide for all of the wonders of Tuscany.

The new millennium was quickly approaching and, after nearly nine years abroad, John began thinking about returning home to see his last surviving relatives—his grandfather, Louis, and his cousin, Patricia.

But John decided he would first visit Sicily—the home of his earliest ancestors.

He visited the ruins of Pompeii, Mt. Vesuvius looming innocently in the distance. Artifacts and building foundations, preserved longer than two thousand years beneath volcanic ash until excavated in the eighteenth and nineteenth centuries.

John continued to Naples, visiting the National Archeological Museum, which housed the real treasures of the Pompeii excavations.

He then booked passage on a Naples to Sicily ferry for the eleven-hour trip to Palermo.

After several days in Palermo, John rented a car and headed east—planning to drive around the entire island along its coasts.

His travels told a different history than that of the Italian mainland.

For centuries, foreigners had invaded the island, conquering and in turn being conquered.

Phoenicians, Greeks, Romans, Byzantines, Arabs, Normans, Spaniards.

John made stops in Cefalù, Capo d'Orlando, and Messina before reaching Taormina, which had remained a Greek stronghold long into the tenth century. He spent time in Catania before moving on to Syracuse, where the Byzantines had moved their capital from Constantinople in the seventh century. Rounding the southern tip of the island at Portopalo di Capo,

John continued on, passing through Pozzallo and Gela, until stopping overnight in Licata.

Looking out over the Port of Licata the next morning, John recalled the story—told to him by his father—of the first and the last time his grandfather had travelled to the land of his forefathers.

Louis.

In early 1942, following the Japanese attack on Pearl Harbor, Louis Agnello enlisted in the United States Navy. He did his training at San Diego and was stationed there.

It was his first time in California since childhood.

Louis fully expected to be sent to the Pacific Theatre, to help chase the Japanese all the way back to Tokyo—but he never got the call. Instead, he spent nearly a year at a desk, writing up reports based on communications coming in from places he would never see—Guam, Midway, Guadalcanal.

Louis sometimes wondered if being the adopted son of a United States Congressman delayed his deployment for the safety of a desk job.

Finally, in early 1943, his orders came—but instead of boarding a ship bound for the Philippine Sea, he was sent to Norfolk, Virginia.

Soon after, Louis was on a ship at last, the USS *Shubrick*—a Greaves-class destroyer built in Norfolk the year before—but that ship was heading east, across the Atlantic, setting out for North Africa on June 8.

It was called Operation Husky.

The planning had been going on since the Casablanca Conference of American and British commanders in January.

General Dwight Eisenhower was appointed Commander-in-Chief of the Allied Expeditionary Force, with British General Harold Alexander his second-in-command. British Admiral

Andrew Cunningham was appointed Naval Force Commander.

The British were advocating the invasion of Sicily. The Americans were opposed at first, but were then convinced that the result of driving the Italians and Germans out of Sicily would be the opening the Mediterranean, which had been under the control of the Axis since 1941.

In a meeting on May 2, it was agreed the invasion would be aimed at the southeastern ports in the Gulf of Gela as opposed to the original plans that had centered on Palermo in the north.

In June, the USS *Shubrick,* Ensign Louis Agnello aboard, was headed for the Gulf of Gela.

Operation Husky was launched on July 9, 1943.

It would be the largest amphibious operation of World War II in terms of the size of the landing zone and the number of divisions put ashore on the first day.

And the *Shubrick* was in the thick of it.

From her position in the Gulf, during what came to be known as the Battle of Gela, the *Shubrick* engaged enemy shore batteries and broke up an enemy tank concentration.

Then the *Shubrick* retired to protect the transports offshore.

On July 11 and 12, she shot down two aircraft.

Once the enemy had retreated from the beaches, Louis accompanied a shore party delivering rations and medical supplies to Licata and stepped for the first time on Sicilian soil.

Although Allied casualties were not as great as those of the enemy, there was a considerable loss of American and British lives during the engagement.

The land forces suffered most. The killed, wounded, captured or missing from the U.S. Seventh Army and British Eighth Army exceeded twenty thousand.

The number of U.S. Navy personnel killed or wounded was close to eleven hundred.

Louis witnessed death all around him.

The success of the Sicilian invasion was instrumental in the fall of Italian Dictator Benito Mussolini, who was arrested and imprisoned on July 25.

The new Italian government signed an Armistice with the Allies in early September, and declared war on Nazi Germany in October.

The *Shubrick* escorted the Cruiser *Savannah* to Palermo where, on August 4, she was hit amidships by a five hundred-pound bomb, killing nine and wounding twenty, and leaving the ship without power.

After completion of repairs in New York, January 1944, *Shubrick* made two convoy runs to Europe and back before joining the Normandy bombardment group in Belfast. After escorting the battleship *Nevada* and five Navy cruisers to the Normandy beaches, *Shubrick* took her own fire support station. At five-fifty on June 6, she opened fire on her preassigned targets. She continued her fire as the troops landed, then checked her fire to avoid hitting friendly forces.

In August, *Shubrick* sailed from Malta with four escort carriers and five other destroyers to provide air cover for the landings in southern France.

Louis completed his tour of active duty in early 1945, while the *Shubrick* was being overhauled in the United States. He missed the ship's next mission to join the Pacific Fleet. The *Shubrick* received four Battle Stars for her service in World War II.

Louis came back from his war experience a changed man—and it was a change for the good. He learned something about the blessing of being alive—and the responsibility that gift demanded. And the nightmares stopped, the nightmares that had haunted Louis for twenty years, of a hotel room in New York where an eight-year-old boy and the only father he knew had battled for their survival—where Vincenzo Leone fought to save Giuseppe Agnello's son.

The lion had sacrificed his life to protect the lamb.

Louis Agnello returned to Brooklyn and, for the first time in his life, he imagined a family of his own.

John.

From Licata, John continued on to Agrigento, and found himself only twenty-eight kilometers from the hometown of his great-grandfather.

John left Agrigento mid-afternoon and he arrived in Naro less than thirty minutes later. He checked into a small hotel in the center of town and walked to Piazza Giuseppe Garibaldi. In Centro Turistico, a welcoming gentleman, Arturo Grimaldi, provided John with a map of the city, and he highlighted the places John wished to visit the following day to begin his research—Comune di Naro, the town hall, and the public library, Biblioteca Comunale Feliciana. Arturo also recommended a restaurant on the Piazza. John asked Grimaldi if he knew of any Agnellos or Leones in the town, families that had lived in and around the town at the turn of the century. Arturo did not.

"Over the course of time, with the hardships of life here, the two world wars, and the advances in science and technology, many of our young people left this area to seek broader horizons—to the larger cities in Sicily and on the mainland, to other parts of Europe and to America. You may have little if any luck in finding remains of Naro families who resided here one hundred years ago. I hope I have not been discouraging, but you seem like a young man who appreciates honesty."

"I do," John said, "and I thank you for that and for your help."

After dinner, and a casual walk through the Old Town, John returned to his hotel room. He read for a while—Giuseppe di

Lampedusa's *The Leopard*—and before long decided it was time to get some sleep.

John spent several hours in both the town hall and library the following morning and, as Grimaldi had sadly predicted, the trail was cold. He did find the names of Agnello and Leone in census records, but none that were directly descended from his family. It seemed as if that lineage disappeared from the hills of Naro once all of the children of the patriarchs Salvatore Leone and Luigi Agnello left for America. He did discover, from the many photographs he viewed of the town from the late eighteen hundreds and the early nineteen hundreds, possible reasons why the generation of his great-grandparents felt compelled to leave Naro—it had been a rocky, arid land, unsuitable for farming or industry.

Although he wasn't sure what he expected to find, John was disappointed.

He had hoped for a good story, something *romantic* to offset the tragic stories that had cursed the two families in the New World.

As John came out of the town hall, Arturo Grimaldi was coming up the stairs toward him.

"I was hoping to find you here," Arturo said. "I would be pleased if you would join us for lunch."

"Us?"

"There is someone I would like you to meet. Come, it is only a short walk from here."

"Your English is very good," John said, as they walked.

"I studied in college. It was difficult to learn, in many instances it is a very illogical language. Your Italian is not bad."

"I studied in Florence," John said. "Who will we be meeting, Arturo?"

"My Uncle Giacomo. He is nearly ninety years old. He lives alone and can take care of himself very well, but I like to look in on him often. I visited last night and mentioned the names you asked about. I recalled them easily, Agnello and Leone, lamb and lion. He has many stories, but one that will be of particular interest to you. Fortunately, he also speaks English well, which he learned during his years in the United States when in his late twenties. If not, I would need to be translating Sicilian to Italian for you."

The house was on a steep street. John followed Arturo to the door, up stone steps that looked ancient. They entered the house and walked straight back to the kitchen. The old man was standing at the stove putting finishing touches on their meal—pasta with capers, olives, fresh tomatoes, and basil.

"Please sit," Giacomo said in English. "Arturo, please open the bottle of wine."

Arturo and John sat at the table.

As Arturo uncorked the Chianti, his uncle brought over bowls of pasta, grated pecorino Romano cheese, a fresh salad of tomatoes and cucumbers in balsamic vinegar and olive oil, and a warm loaf of bread from the bakery at the bottom of the hill.

Giacomo joined them at the table as Arturo poured the wine.

"*Saluti,*" the old man said. "*Mangiamo.*"

It was not until they had finished the meal, and Giacomo had set out the coffee and biscotti, that the old man began.

"Arturo told me you asked about Agnello and Leone. I was born in 1910. My oldest brother, Antonio, Arturo's father, was fifteen years my senior—he the first and I the last of nine children. When I was in school we read *Romeo and Juliet*. It affected me deeply, and I talked with Antonio about it. He was thirty years old at the time, had been to America and back, and recently married. He told me a story which rivaled the drama of Shakespeare. These were Antonio's words, '*I had a very close friend, Giuseppe Agnello. Giuseppe had fallen madly in love with a beautiful girl, Francesca Leone. The Agnellos and Leones were bitter enemies, but the two lovers would not be deterred. They were secretly married and, to honor Giuseppe's wishes, I stood up for him at the ceremony. Soon after, they went to America. I tried to find Giuseppe when I travelled to New York years later, with no luck. I often think of Giuseppe and I pray they found peace in their new home.'* Now," Giacomo said, "I would like to know of your interest in the Agnellos and Leones."

"Giuseppe Agnello was my great-grandfather, and Francesca Leone was my great-grandmother."

"So, they had children."

"One child, my grandfather, Louis."

"Did Giuseppe and Francesca find happiness in America?"

"Sadly, no. The Leones and the Agnellos have continued to battle to this day. And, I'm not certain my grandfather ever heard the story you have told me today."

"That is very sad," the old man said. "Is your grandfather still alive?"

"I'm not sure."

"That is sadder, yet," Giacomo said. "You must find him if he lives, and share with him the love story of his parents."

The three men sat together, drinking wine through the afternoon and far into the evening, talking of the past and the future.

The next morning, John resumed his trip around the island, travelling west now and continuing along the coast.

John made overnight stops at Marsala, Trapani, and Castellammare del Golfo before finally arriving back in Palermo.

From Palermo he flew to Rome, wanting to spend some more time in the city that had captured his heart and his imagination.

Two weeks later he boarded a flight to New York City.

It was his thirtieth birthday.

. . .

John Agnello faced a difficult decision—whether or not to seek out his grandfather, Louis, and his cousin, Patricia.

John clearly remembered his father's final words. Vito had warned John against going to Louis—obviously believing both would be safer apart.

But John had also been moved by his evening with Giacomo Grimaldi in Naro—the old man's insistence that John be reunited with his only remaining family.

John had been forced to leave Brooklyn when he was seventeen, not yet out of high school.

John had seen little of New York City beyond the borders of his own neighborhood. The city did not have as long a history as those he had visited in Europe—Rome, Athens, Paris, London—but there was much in New York to discover.

John decided he would spend some time exploring while he struggled with the decision about searching for his grandfather.

He took a room, by the week, at the St. George Hotel in Brooklyn Heights and became a sightseer. Ellis Island, where his ancestors had been processed for entry to America—and the Statue of Liberty that had welcomed them. The Cathedral of St. John the Divine, one of the five largest church buildings in the world—a list that included the Milan Cathedral and St. Peter's Basilica, which he had visited in Italy. The Empire State Building, once considered the Eighth Wonder of the World—and the Twin Towers, impressively overlooking the Upper Bay.

In Brooklyn, John took the subway to Coney Island—where he had spent many summer days in his youth. He purchased a hotdog at Nathan's, finding that the price had increased considerably. He was tempted to visit the street where he grew up, to see the friends of his parents who were the parents of his closest friends—but John was dissuaded by the possible danger of word getting around of his presence in

New York. He did visit L&B Spumoni Gardens in the old neighborhood—a slice of the Sicilian square pizza and a tart lemon Italian ice transporting him back to happier times.

John felt a strong need to see *someone* from his past, and chose the one person he felt it was safe to contact. He knew where Harry Stone, his father's partner in the ATF, lived—so he went to Harry's home in Bay Ridge.

John rang the doorbell and a few moments later Stone opened the door.

"Can I help you?" he asked.

"I'm John, John Agnello, Vito's son."

"Johnny? My God. Please, come in."

John most wanted to hear stories of his father—and Harry Stone had many.

They sat for hours exchanging memories.

"I should be going," John said, when afternoon had turned to evening.

"What are your plans?"

"I'm thinking of going to Denver."

"Colorado?"

"Colorado."

"Soon?"

"Fairly soon."

"Do you need a place to stay while you're here?"

"No, I'm paid up at the St. George Hotel for several more days."

"If there's anything you need while you're here in New York, don't hesitate to call on me," Harry said. "Anything."

"Thank you."

Harry escorted John to the front door, gave him a parting embrace, and watched John walk away toward Eighty-Sixth Street and the subway station.

Then, Stone returned inside and he immediately phoned

Bruno Leone in San Francisco.

Bruno thanked Stone for all his years of service and loyalty to the Leone family—and told Harry to expect a very handsome reward.

Leone called upon Sammy Orso to make all of the arrangements.

"John Agnello is in Brooklyn. The St. George Hotel. I want two of our best men in New York to sit on him around the clock, watch his every move and report every move to us. Agnello is not to be interfered with under any circumstance. I have reason to suspect he may travel to Colorado, so I want two of our best men from here to get to Denver immediately and be prepared for further instructions. I believe John Agnello is going to lead us directly to his grandfather."

Two days later, John climbed into a taxicab in front of the hotel.

Two men in a late model Cadillac followed the cab to LaGuardia Airport.

TWENTY SIX

Martina.

Theodore Harding had been Vincenzo Leone's closest and most loyal friend and confidant—and most able business associate.

Theodore had always respected Vincenzo for his honesty and his fair and legitimate business practices, but doubted Roberto was as dedicated or interested in carrying on his brother's legacy.

Harding ultimately turned to politics. He was elected to the House of Representatives and began serving in January, 1935—and met a Congressman from New York, Alfredo Catalano. Harding lost his life in a railroad accident in New Jersey soon after. Although Harding and Catalano were acquainted for a very short time, their meeting led to a collaboration between the Harding and Agnello families that would last for many years.

Theodore's son, Richard, became an Assistant District Attorney in San Francisco, and had worked with Louis Agnello.

Richard's son, Jack, became a San Francisco police detective, and had worked with Vito Agnello.

Jack Harding's daughter, Martina, had always been a tough kid.

It came with the territory.

Martina grew up in the inner-city. Her father was a police officer in a neighborhood that had little fondness for cops. Her mother was a Russian immigrant at a time in America when Russians were the feared and hated enemy.

Martina loved her mother's accent. By the time she was eight years old she could mimic it perfectly, and later used it in undercover police work.

She could hit a baseball as far as any boy her age. The boys began to call her Marty. It stuck—and she liked it.

Marty met Vito Agnello when she was nine. He had come to dinner at their home. He and Marty's father were working on something that had to do with Jack's job.

Martina remembered Agnello as soft-spoken and funny, with an accent almost as foreign as her mother's. He told her he had two sons near her age, and he was sure they would love to someday meet a charming young lady like herself.

It made her smile—she particularly liked the *young lady* part.

When Vito's wife, his oldest son, and his older brother were murdered in Brooklyn less than six months later, Martina's father did not talk about it—but she could sense something terrible had happened.

In 1987, not long before her sixteenth birthday, Marty found her father sitting at the kitchen table. Jack was clearly upset.

"Dad, what's wrong?" she asked.

"I've just received horrible news. Our friend Vito Agnello was killed in New York, yesterday."

"I'm so sorry. What about his son?"

"I don't know. There's no news of his whereabouts—or if he's alive."

Martina pulled a chair up to her father, and she took his hands in hers.

Martina excelled in high school, graduating near the top of her class and earning a full scholarship to the University of San Francisco.

Marty had developed a strong interest in the law, specifically criminal law, inspired by her grandfather and her father. She thought she might follow in the footsteps of one or the other—as a criminal prosecutor or an enforcer of the law.

At USF, Martina majored in urban studies, with a minor in criminal justice.

Again, she graduated with honors and was accepted into the University of California Davis School of Law *and* into the Graduate Program in Criminal Justice at California State University, Long Beach.

She decided on Long Beach.

In 1994, she earned an MS in Criminology and Criminal Justice and went directly into the San Francisco Police Academy.

In 1998, in record time for a woman in the Department, Martina Harding earned a detective's shield.

Two years later, after dinner with her parents, Marty's father walked her out to her car.

"I have good news and bad news," Jack told his daughter. "John Agnello turned up in Denver a few days ago, and managed to be arrested and charged with manslaughter the same day. He may be facing up to five years in prison."

"And the good news?"

"The good news is it may keep him safe from the Leones for another five years."

TWENTY SEVEN

Sammy Orso received word from his men in New York that John Agnello had boarded a plane out of LaGuardia Airport. Orso contacted the two-man team he had already placed in Denver, gave them all the information they needed—airline, flight number, and arrival time—and a description of their target.

"You are to follow him," Orso reminded them, "make no moves against him. We expect him to lead us to his grandfather. When you are certain the two men are together, call Bruno Leone for instructions."

John. 2000.

When John landed in Denver he carried only a small bag, holding a few changes of clothing. John's only identification were an Italian passport and an Italian driver's license, both in the name Giovanni Vota. He also had a phone number, committed to memory, that he had never used. John found a public telephone and dialed the number.

A woman answered.

"Hello?'

"Patricia?"

"Who is this?"

"Your cousin. John."

"My God, Johnny, where are you?"

"At Denver International Airport, East Terminal."

"Do you have a cell phone?"

"No."

"Okay. I'll pick you up outside the terminal on the baggage claim level. Give me thirty minutes or so. You can tell me all about it when I get there."

"Don't tell Louis I'm here. I want to surprise him."

"Let's hope you don't surprise him into a heart attack," Patricia said.

As John stood waiting, he had the feeling he was being watched. A man outside of the exit nearest to where John stood kept taking quick glances his way. Soon, a car pulled up and the driver seemed to make eye contact with the first man— but neither moved.

Paranoid, John thought.

Patricia had lived with John and her Uncle Vito from the time her parents were killed in 1982—until she went off to college in 1986.

John and Patricia had not seen each other since John went into hiding in Wyoming after his father's death but, when she arrived at the airport, she recognized John immediately.

Patricia jumped out of her car, rushed to John, and she gave him a long embrace.

"Wow. You're a grown man."

"And look at you."

"Let's go home," she said.

They climbed into her car. As she pulled away, John saw the man he felt was watching him move to and enter the car that had parked close by. As they headed west toward the city, John had no doubt they were being tailed.

"We're being followed."

"Are you sure?" Patricia asked.

"Positive."

"What do they want?"

"I am guessing they want to kill me, but they're after Louis as well."

"What should we do? Should we stay away from the house?"

"They'll stay glued to me until I lead them to Grandfather. Is he there now?"

"Yes."

"Is there a gun at the house?"

"John."

"Is there a gun at the house, Patricia?" he repeated.

"Yes."

"Then, that's where we'll go."

John followed Patricia to the front door. He noticed a mail-box near the door on the front porch. They went inside.

Orso's men parked their car up the street and watched them enter the house. They needed confirmation that Louis Agnello was also there, but they weren't sure how to find out.

Louis had not seen his grandson since John was a boy of twelve, but John looked a lot like his father. Louis looked at John when they came into the house, and he seemed confused.

"Who is this?" he asked Patricia.

"It's John, Vito's son."

Louis' eyes lit up. John took his grandfather into his arms.

"Grandfather, I would love to sit with you, drink coffee, and talk about the years we have been apart—but we are in danger. Patty, please get the weapon. Grandfather, I need you to go out, fetch the mail, and come right back. Then I need you and Patricia to go out the back door and get as far away from here as possible. You will need to move to a different house, the safety of this location has been compromised. And, if I'm arrested, don't try to see me."

"I don't understand," Louis said, as Patricia handed John the gun.

"Please trust me," John said.

Louis stepped out to the porch, took the mail, and returned inside.

"Now leave, quickly, please."

John gave them both an embrace and ushered them out the back door.

And he waited.

Bruno Leone answered the phone after the first ring, and received the news he had been hoping for.

"They're all in the house. John Agnello, the woman, and the old man. What do you want us to do?"

"Kill them all," Leone said.

They came in fast and hard.

John fired at the first man who came through the door, hitting him twice in the chest. He went down. The second man returned fire, missing his mark, and John's third shot struck him in the shoulder. One dead, the second out of the battle. John tore cords off the window curtains, hogtied the wounded man, and called the Englewood Police reporting a home invasion. John collected the weapons of both men and set them on the front porch, along with the gun he had used. He sat on the porch steps and he waited for the police to arrive.

"My name is John Agnello. There are two men inside," John said, once he was handcuffed. "One dead, the other incapacitated. They were sent here to kill me. I acted in self-defense."

"Sent by who?"

"Bruno Leone, from San Francisco. I'm sure the two in the house have long arrest records—may even be wanted for other felonies, including murder. The one still breathing may be willing to corroborate my story in exchange for leniency. All of the weapons are there on the porch."

. . .

As John had predicted, both of the would-be assassins had impressive criminal records.

The survivor, Al Batali, was a fugitive wanted in California for the murder of a Customs agent.

There was enough evidence against Batali to insure a conviction, but he had evaded capture for more than four years.

Faced with a possible death sentence, Batali agreed to testify against the man who hired him to kill the agent and had also sent him to kill the Agnellos—in return for a reduction of his sentence to life imprisonment.

Batali's testimony was enough to convict Bruno Leone of conspiracy to commit murder and send Bruno to San Quentin, where he had so often gone to visit his mentor, Roberto Leone.

Bruno Leone's sentence was twenty to thirty years.

John Agnello was charged with voluntary manslaughter. His attorney, paid by an anonymous benefactor, had John plead self-defense. A bargain was struck between the prosecution and defense.

The prosecution agreed to accept a plea of guilty to involuntary manslaughter with mitigating circumstance.

John was sentenced to five years at the Arapahoe County State Correctional Facility.

TWENTY EIGHT

John. Colorado. 2000.

Less than one week into his prison sentence, John Agnello was in the prison yard when a man a head taller, and at least seventy pounds heavier, approached him and came very close. John stood his ground.

"You are a very good looking young man."

"I've always considered myself average, with regard to looks, and I'm not that young anymore," John said.

"You'll do."

"Do for what?"

"I'll surprise you. Soon."

"Max."

Max turned. The man who had called his name joined them. John estimated the man was in his mid-sixties.

"Frank," Max said.

"I see you've met my friend," Frank said.

"Your friend?"

"My good friend."

"Well, we haven't really been properly introduced."

John, who had remained quiet, picked up the ball.

"John Agnello," he said.

Max looked from John to Frank and walked away without another word.

"Max is a nasty fellow, but he won't bother you again."

"John Agnello," John repeated, extending his hand.

"Frank Bonner," the older man said, accepting a handshake.

"Why?" John asked.

"Why what?"

"Why help a total stranger? From what I hear, people in prison last much longer minding their own business."

"Being helpful *is* my business. We'll talk again," Frank said, and he walked away across the yard.

Vinnie. California. 2001.

Vinnie Leone tried to get out to San Quentin once a week to visit his father, Bruno.

He didn't enjoy the visits.

The place itself made him feel very uneasy, and all his father ever talked about was the Agnellos.

"I've sent Sammy Orso out to Denver a few times. We can't find the old man, Louis. He disappeared again. We bought a guard at the prison, to keep an eye on John Agnello, to let us know if his grandfather or his cousin show up there. He's had no visitors at all. I looked into putting out a contract to have him killed in the joint, maybe the old man would come out for the funeral, but Agnello is protected by a lifer who no one wants to mess with."

"We know where John Agnello is, and he isn't going anywhere for another four years," Vinnie said. "And the old man will surface eventually."

"And I'm not going anywhere for at least twenty years," Bruno Leone said. "I want them both dead."

Vinnie left the prison and decided he needed to talk with his grandfather.

He found Salvatore on the back porch of the house on Russian Hill.

"You saw your father?"

"He's not doing very well."

"Who could, in a place like that," Salvatore said.

"He continues to be obsessed with the Agnellos."

"Bruno was more passionate in his love for my Uncle Roberto than in his love for me. And Roberto's hatred for the Agnellos was fierce."

"I need to know something, Grandfather."

"What is it, Vincent?"

"Do you carry such hatred for the Agnellos?"

"The Agnellos helped put both Roberto and Bruno in prison—but Bruno and Roberto brought it upon themselves. They violated the law and also soiled our family name. I understood that those who were compelled to punish them for their crimes, including the Agnellos, were simply doing their jobs. When I was eighteen years old, I learned the Agnellos were responsible for the death of my father—and for *that* they must answer. But we can only wait, Vincent. In four years, John Agnello will be released. I am confident he will lead us to his grandfather."

"And then?" Vincent asked.

"And then, you will do everything in your power to bring them both to me."

Salvatore looked out to the Golden Gate and sighed.

"I used to love this house. It was so very peaceful. Now, listen, you can hear the noise from Columbus Avenue. And I have always loved walking, but the hills are becoming more and more difficult for me. I am feeling very old."

"How would you like walking on the beach instead, with the only sounds coming from the waves against the shore?"

"It sounds lovely, Vincent."

"I've looked at a beautiful house for sale on Stinson Beach. I'll purchase it for you and Grandmother. And I promise, as soon as I can, I will bring Louis and John Agnello to you there."

Louis. New Mexico. 2002.

After the attack that put John Agnello in prison, Louis and Patricia relocated to Albuquerque.

Patricia found a teaching position easily. Louis was unhappy there.

"I can't even spell the name," he complained, "and it's dry as a bone. I grew up on two oceans. I need to be close to water."

"I don't see us close to an ocean in the near future."

"A lake then. And I want to be closer to John."

"You know we can't see John," Patricia said.

"Yes. I know. But I need at least to be nearby."

"Okay, but you'll have to give me time to work it out."

"Hopefully, I won't melt before you work it out."

A few months later, after several trips back to Denver, Patricia rented a house on Sloan's Lake.

Hank. Colorado. 2003.

Charlie Porter had business in Denver. Charlie called Hank Sims, they had served together in the army. They arranged to meet in Fort Collins.

They talked first about what was new since their last reunion five years earlier.

Their work, wives, children.

The tragedy at Columbine High School in 1999, where a good friend of Hank's had lost a grandson.

The 2000 presidential elections, and the role Charlie's home state had played in its outcome.

The horror of September 11, 2001.

Then, as they often did, they talked about Vietnam.

"It's a different world, Charlie. I grew up exactly where I live now, where my father and his father lived before me. When I enlisted—straight out of high school—I had never been south of Denver, east of Omaha, north of Casper, or west of the Great Divide. I didn't know Paris, France, from Paris, Texas. I had never seen a body of water larger than Horsetooth Reservoir right here in Fort Collins. I remember when we met at boot camp. You told me you were from Miami, and all I could picture was how close that was to Cuba," Hank recalled. "And Vito, with his South Brooklyn accent. I could hardly understand a word he said at first. At the end of the day, though, I'm glad I came back to my isolated mountain. It's a little too unpredictable for me anywhere else."

"What became of Vito's son? Did he make it to Europe and back?"

"John did make it to Europe. He's not quite back yet."

Lincoln. Colorado. 2004.

Lincoln Bonner visited his father at least once a week.

Lincoln always brought a book, something new for Frank to read.

"I have a good friend here," Frank said. "He is near your age. He was in Europe for years, and his stories take me to places I had always wished to see. I believe you and he would get along. John is scheduled to be released in less than a year. I will miss his company. He may need help when he gets out."

"You know I'll do whatever I can for any friend of yours," Lincoln said.

Martina. San Francisco. 2005.

After pressing her father and his superiors for nearly a year, Martina Harding was finally given her first undercover assignment.

A popular nightclub in the Mission District was suspected

of being a drug-trafficking exchange point. It was not known if the management was involved.

Martina was called in to a meeting with her father and Captain Lopez.

"They're looking for a bartender," Lopez said. "We can equip you with letters of recommendation and arrange a crash course in mixology, but we can't give you the job. Getting hired will be up to you."

"I can get the job."

"Okay. Go for it."

A week later, Martina was behind the bar.

A month later, Martina and her father Jack were back in Lopez's office.

"You both know how much I wanted this," Marty said, "but if there's anything illegal going on in that place, I'm not seeing it from where I stand behind the bar."

"Do you think you need more time?" Lopez asked.

"I really think it's a dead end."

"Jack?"

"At the risk of sounding biased, my daughter has very good instincts."

"Okay. We'll pull you out."

"I would rather not just walk out. I'd like to give two weeks' notice. I don't want to burn my bridges. I might need a *real* recommendation one of these days. I'll tell them I found another job, one with benefits."

"All right."

"Speaking of *benefits*, I have vacation time coming which I thought I might like to take. Maybe two weeks from now."

"You're a chip off the old block," Lopez said, "put in a request form."

. . .

Marty had two more shifts remaining at the nightclub. A man sat down at the bar. He wore a suit that was clearly custom made and had movie star good looks.

"What's your pleasure?"

"At this moment, it's looking at you."

"I bet you say that to all the girls."

"Only some. Do you have single-malt scotch?"

"How old?"

He reached into his pocket, pulled out his wallet, and opened it to show her his driver's license.

"Am I old enough?"

"I was referring to the scotch. I have twelve, fifteen, and eighteen-year-old single-malt," Marty said, glancing at his ID.

"Eighteen sounds perfect," he said.

He sat at the bar for more than an hour, and they talked.

"I'd like to see you again," he said, handing her a credit card to pay for his drinks. "Maybe we could have dinner sometime."

"Maybe. But after tomorrow night, I'm done here."

"Tomorrow, then?"

"I'll be done working by eight. Come by then, if you like, and I'll let you know if I'm hungry."

"I'll be here. Is it proper to leave a tip for someone you just asked out to dinner?"

"It's fine with me," Marty said.

He left a twenty on the bar before he left.

The next morning, Marty called her father. She asked if they could meet for lunch.

"The assignment may not have been a total bust after all," she said.

"What do you mean? Did you learn something?"

"No. But you'll never guess who asked me out to dinner."

"Barry Bonds?"

"Cute. Try Vincent Leone."

"*That* Vincent Leone?"

"The very one. I saw his ID, and he used a business credit card. Leone Importing. Isn't he still a big-time person of interest?"

"Not any longer."

"Oh?"

"The police and the feds had been shadowing his family for decades. Roberto Leone was put away at San Quentin, twice, in 1953 and 1979. He died there in 1982. Apparently, around the mid-nineties, Vincent Leone, who by the way holds an MBA from Stanford, began to clean house—because by the time his father, Bruno, was incarcerated in 2000, Leone Importing appeared to be totally legitimate. Then, following nine-eleven, the Feds turned to what they considered more pressing concerns, and the SFPD was left alone to keep tabs on the Leones. Bruno Leone died last year, and the department pretty much let it go."

"What about John Agnello?"

"What about him?"

"Doesn't he get out of prison soon?"

"And?"

"And, do you think Bruno Leone's death ended the threat to John and his grandfather?"

"That I'm not sure about."

"It might be good to be sure."

"That's not something Vincent Leone is going to talk about over dinner."

"Do you remember what you said to me on the day I graduated from the Academy? And you said it was maybe the most important thing you could tell me about the job."

"I said, *police work is full of surprises and you never know.*"

"I think I'll take Vincent Leone up on his invitation to dinner. You never know, maybe he'll surprise us."

. . .

The next evening when Vincent Leone pulled up in front of the nightclub, Martina was waiting outside the door.

"I'm hungry," she said.

"Nice dress."

"It was my last day. I thought I'd clean up a bit," she said, getting into the car. "And I didn't know where you would take me for dinner."

"Do you know the Ristorante Naro in North Beach?"

"Who doesn't. It's an institution."

"It's been run by my family since the doors opened more than eighty years ago."

"Then, you must get a good discount."

"You're too sharp to be mixing drinks," Vinnie said. "No offense."

"No offense taken. It sounded like a compliment. I wasn't really there to mix drinks."

"Oh?"

"I get paid to find people who go missing. And sometimes to bring them back."

"Did you find who you were looking for?"

"I did, but I really can't say more about it. Client confidentiality."

"Can you talk more generally about what you do?"

"Maybe. Let's eat first," Marty said.

"I understand why this place has been around so long, the food was unbelievable."

"Would you like more wine?"

"I've had enough. Maybe coffee."

"Cannoli? I think it's the best in the city."

"I imagine you do. I'll share one with you."

Vinnie ordered the espresso and pastry.

"So, tell me about what you do. Are you a private investigator?"

"Like I said, I find people. A missing wife for her bewildered husband. A bail jumper for a bondsman. I also do some security work. I might not look it, but I'm a very good bodyguard."

"If you don't have something already lined up, I may have work for you."

"I'd rather not talk business tonight. I don't often have a chance to enjoy simple pleasures, like perfect cannoli. And I need to be going."

"Really?"

"Yes. Sorry."

"Do you need a ride somewhere?"

"No," she said, getting up from the table. "Thanks for tonight. I enjoyed the food and the company."

Vinnie took out a business card.

"If you want to talk about some work, give me a call."

Marty saw her father first thing the next morning.

"I gave him the *I get paid to find people* story, and he liked it. I think he wants to offer me a job."

"Lopez is not going to sign off on this," Jack said. "As I told you, Leone Importing is no longer on the *to-do* list—and the fate of John Agnello is not a concern of the San Francisco PD."

"Does it concern you?"

"Yes. His father was a good friend."

"Then it concerns me. I have vacation coming to me, I can look into it on my own time."

"Be careful, Martina. And try to stay clear of Sammy Orso."

"Sammy Orso?"

"He's been security and muscle for the family for many years. Orso was fiercely loyal to Roberto Leone, and to Bruno. I'm guessing Bruno's last words to Orso were *protect Vincent.*"

"Vinnie Leone is no fool, he's going to make some effort to

check me out. I used Mom's maiden name. Can we set up a dummy telephone listing and line by early tomorrow, and have calls forwarded to you?"

"Yes, I can have it up and running first thing in the morning."

Marty called Vincent.

"I'd like to talk business," she said.

"Can you be at my office in the Transamerica Building at ten tomorrow morning?"

"How about two?"

"I'll see you then."

The following morning at ten, Vincent Leone found a listing for Koslov and Banks Investigation through directory assistance. He phoned.

"This is Ted Banks."

"I'm looking for Martina Koslov."

"Miss Koslov is not available at the moment. Maybe I can help you."

"I'm considering using your services and I was wondering if you could provide any references."

"I'm afraid we can't. Our work is very confidential, our clients demand it."

"I understand."

"I can have Miss Koslov call you."

"That won't be necessary, thanks. Sorry to have bothered you."

"No bother at all," said Jack Harding.

At two, Martina was at Vincent's office.

"How much do you need to know before accepting an assignment?"

"As much as you can tell me, and I try not to break any laws."

"I'm looking for a man. Louis Agnello. He would be around ninety years old. Maybe in Colorado, under an assumed name. Maybe living with a granddaughter, Patricia, a school teacher. She may be using the same last name."

"That's a lot of maybes."

"He also has a grandson, John Agnello, who is doing time near Denver. We've been watching the prison, hoping his grandfather or cousin might turn up, but neither has visited in five years. He'll be released in a few weeks."

"I have contacts in Denver. It would take a lot of luck, but as my father always said, *you never know*. I'll see what I can do. But, if I strike out, maybe John Agnello will do the job of finding his grandfather for you."

"Do you need to know why I'm looking for the man?"

"If all you need me to do is to try finding him, I'm good."

"One more thing. I'll admit that when I invited you to dinner, employing you was not exactly what I had in mind," Vincent said, "but, if we are going to work together, it will need to be strictly business."

"You took the words right out of my mouth."

The phone on Vinnie's desk rang.

"Yes?" he said, and then, "send him in."

The man who entered the office appeared to be in his late forties, and looked as if he could easily take on three twenty-year-old men in a fistfight.

"Martina, this is Sammy Orso. Sammy is my head of security. I would like you to keep him informed about anything you may learn."

"No problem."

Marty rose from her seat, moved to Orso, and shook his hand.

Orso's hand was as cold as ice.

John. Colorado. 2005.

John Agnello had two visitors during the week before his release.

They were the only two visitors in the five years he had been locked up.

The first was a woman he didn't know but who had somehow landed on his visitor list.

They sat facing each other across a table in the large visiting room.

"Patricia sent me," she said.

"How is Patricia? And my grandfather?"

"How is your memory?" she asked, ignoring his question.

"Very good. Though that's not always a blessing."

"Twenty-two forty-five Stuart Street. At Sloan's Lake in Denver," she said. "Got it?"

"Yes."

"Good luck," she said, and left the room.

The following day, Agnello was visited by Frank Bonner's brother.

Frank sat with his son Lincoln, across the room.

The visits were arranged to give John and Lincoln a look at each other.

John Agnello was released four days later, on a Thursday in 2005.

He was given a free ride to the bus terminal in Denver.

John was picked up there by Lincoln Bonner, and they headed north for Wyoming.

That evening, he was in the safe haven at Iron Mountain.

TWENTY NINE

John. Iron Mountain. Wyoming. Thursday.

"Are you going to stick around for a while?" asked Hank Sims, as they sat around the large oak table covered with food.

"Not too long," said John Agnello.

"I thought you were bringing company."

"Things changed. We got into a little fracas outside of Fort Collins."

Hank let it pass. If John wanted to talk about it, he would in his own time. Sims reached over for the closest platter, and heaped another serving onto his dish.

"What's the matter, not hungry? You've hardly touched a thing."

"I grabbed a meal down in Cheyenne."

"Afraid we wouldn't feed you?" Hank said, turning to his wife with a smile.

"I was craving Italian food," said John. "I truly didn't expect this."

Across the tabletop were plates of food including baked manicotti, sausage, stuffed artichoke, and a fresh garden salad.

"You thought you'd be getting the boiled possum again?" said Hank's wife, Katy.

"I really appreciate this," John said to Katy Sims. "I promise I'll have a big breakfast of leftovers."

"Well, it'll save me having to make the woodchuck omelet," Katy laughed.

As Katy began clearing the dishes, Hank invited John to join him on the front porch. Agnello turned to her as he rose from his chair.

"Need a hand, Kate?"

"Since when," she said playfully. "I'll bring coffee out."

The two men settled into the handmade redwood chairs on the open porch. Hank took out his tobacco and papers and began to roll a cigarette.

Hank handed the smoke to John and started putting another together for himself as his guest looked out over the landscape. John had spent his late teens and early twenties here, learning how to rebuild car engines and break horses. Hank and Katy lived on eighty acres between Iron Mountain and Diamond, Wyoming, running along Chugwater Creek. Hank bred and sold horses, and sometimes raced them. Katy put motor vehicles back together again, mostly trucks, sold them and often raced them.

If there was one thing the two loved as much as each other and their three children, it was horsepower.

The house stood on a small rise backed against the creek at its widest point and protected by trees in front. Hank had always joked that even if John's adversaries could find him in this secluded spot, they could never get near enough to do any harm. Hank had built himself a virtual fortress, and he owned the firearms to defend it.

The Sims children were all grown and out on their own, but they made regular sojourns to this peaceful hideaway where they could forget the urban rat race. For a short time at least.

Hank and Katy were expecting their daughter, Amy, to arrive any day.

Amy Sims was a successful journalist in Chicago and she visited the Sims homestead more frequently than her two brothers, who were often tied down by more traditional jobs and small children. Amy often visited to find solitude—and inspiration for her occasional attempts at fiction.

John had harbored a secret crush on Amy throughout his four-year stay with the Sims family nearly twenty years earlier.

Just one of the many things that had made it so difficult for him to leave.

"How about some rhubarb pie?" called Katy from inside the house.

"That I could handle," said John.

"So, what's the plan, Johnny?" asked Hank.

"It's not settled. I'll need a little time to work it all out. For a while, all I want to do is hang out with the horses."

"Take all the time you need. You're welcome to remain here as long as you like."

Lincoln. Denver. Thursday.

When Lincoln Bonner exited Interstate 25 at Colfax Avenue and headed east to downtown Denver he had every intention of driving directly home, but at the last minute he decided to stop in at the station first. Captain Matthews was going to hear about the incident in Wellington soon enough, if he hadn't already heard from Sheriff Melville. Lincoln figured he may as well get it written up while he still had a vague recollection of the fabrication and leave it waiting for Matthews to find on his desk first thing in the morning.

Bonner made a few more detours on his way home, to stock up on food and beer. Not certain when he would be returning, he had taken an extended weekend off from the job and had left the cupboards bare. As he pulled out of the Argonaut Liquors parking lot and drove in the direction of the supermarket, he thought he might take advantage of the time and do some hiking for a few days. Then again, maybe he would just kick back with a good book and catch a Rockies game.

Lincoln loaded the groceries into the bed of his truck and

drove back toward downtown. It amazed him how much the city had changed in the years since he had first moved here. Relocating to Denver from the small town of Cheyenne Wells to study at the University of Colorado had been a tremendous adjustment for the eighteen-year-old country boy. The traffic, the people, the skyscrapers, the food, and the college-level academics all contributed to making it a very foreign place. Lincoln was impressionable and eager to fit in and, as is often the case with the young and fairly innocent, he made poor judgments in his attempts to cease feeling and looking like an outsider.

When he finally realized the seriousness and the danger of the mistakes he had made, it was far too late to avoid turning to his father for help.

Walking the downtown streets on a scouting mission before his studies began, Lincoln had come upon a half-empty former warehouse north of the Sixteenth Street Mall. He tracked down the leasing agent and rented a two-thousand-square-foot open space with fourteen-foot ceilings for only four hundred dollars a month.

Lincoln spent the late summer, before classes began, converting the space into a residence with the help of his father and friends from home.

Lincoln's new space occupied the entire second story and sat above a furniture upholstery shop. Large windows looked down on Eighteenth Street not far from Union Station. As close as it was to the heart of downtown Denver, it was fairly quiet during the day and abandoned at night. That was then.

Seventeen years later, Lincoln continued living in the building, defying the zoning restrictions that designated it a property for commercial use only.

Now the LoDo section of Denver was the rage. Shops and galleries lined the streets around him, the furniture shop had been replaced by a fashionable coffeehouse slash bookstore, and from the same windows he could hit Coors Field with a rock. Loft apartments with much less room were renting for thousands a month. In truth, he liked it better when it was an unknown and somewhat feared corner of the city. More than once he had thought about finding another home, but the convenience of the location was difficult for him to give up. He could hoof it to the university, which he usually did both as student and now as a part-time criminology instructor. He could walk to just about any kind of restaurant, and he was less than a block from the popular Wynkoop Brewery.

He could stroll over to the ballpark whenever the team was at home and always pick up a free pass to the game.

He could hop down the stairs anytime he cared for an espresso or if he needed something to read.

Lincoln had also changed over the years, and to his surprise he now found it oddly comforting to look out and see lots of other humans below.

Bonner pulled into the small parking area on the west side of the building. He would have to remember to roll the chain link gate shut tomorrow and lock it against the baseball fans coming to the stadium. Lincoln grabbed his provisions and walked the stairs up to his loft. Hungry, but in no mood to cook, he had picked up a rotisserie chicken from the supermarket deli. He chopped the bird in half, threw a tomato and some fresh spinach on the side, uncapped a Sam Adams, and called it dinner. After a quick shower, he settled into his recliner with a fresh cup of coffee, his pack of Camels, and another book about the Alamo.

Lincoln soon closed the book and glanced around the room. As large and open as it was, he was feeling confined. He could hear the faint sound of a guitar coming from the coffeehouse below. Lincoln threw on a pair of shoes and went down to take a walk, maybe stop in at the brewery.

It was a cool, dry evening and quiet for a Thursday night. As he wandered toward Wynkoop Street, he remembered that plans for his free day tomorrow would have to include a visit to his father.

And he wondered how John Agnello was faring.

Lincoln never noticed the man who had been standing in the shadows across the street from his building and who now began to follow.

THIRTY

John. Wyoming. Friday.

"Up and at 'em, kid. The day's a' wasting."

John Agnello opened his eyes to find Hank standing in the doorway and he checked the clock on the bedside table. It was 6:00 a.m. It had been a long time since he had slept in a real bed, and he went out like a light only minutes after settling into this one the night before. He hopped up and went to splash some water on his face, then joined Hank and Katy in the large kitchen. The table was piled with food again—eggs, bacon, fried potatoes and onions, and homemade bread.

"You can have the leftover Italian food for lunch or dinner, and I'm saving the woodchuck for when Amy arrives," said Katy.

John dug in greedily.

"We're taking a run up to Chugwater this morning for engine parts and groceries if you care to come along," Hank said. "If you'd rather hop on a horse we would understand."

"I would."

"Take the Appaloosa, he could use the exercise. Call him Teach and he usually knows who you're talking to."

Less than an hour later, John was trotting along the creek on the Appaloosa.

He stopped to allow Teach to drink from the clear water.

John was headed toward the small cabin where he and the Sims boys had spent many summer overnights during their teens, doing everything teenage boys do. It was a one-room affair with a loft for sleeping and an outhouse in back. The cabin sat close to the Creekside and was shaded by elm and oak trees. There was a small wood stove for cold nights, which could also be used for cooking.

Hank had offered to build onto the cabin, insulate and bring in running water, in the hope they could persuade John to stop his running and settle there. It was very tempting, but when all was said and done, John had decided to try his luck out in the world.

He was twenty-one years old.

His luck didn't last long.

Years of drifting through Europe, knowing that back home he was being hunted like human prey.

Then five years behind bars.

As John approached the cabin, he wondered why he had been so anxious to abandon this safe and peaceful place. And why, with all he knew about his chances, he was planning to do the same again.

Agnello dismounted and left Teach loose to graze.

He stepped onto the wide-planked porch fronting the cabin, took a deep breath of the clean air, and stepped inside.

Lincoln. Denver. Friday.

At about the same time, a little more than one hundred miles south, Lincoln Bonner pulled his truck out of the parking area and locked the gate behind him. This time, Lincoln noticed the man across the street looking completely out of place and pretending to be interested in the window display of a small boutique. He placed his revolver on the seat beside a few books he had picked out for Frank and started for Broadway.

Lincoln could see the man slip into the alley along his building and soon he spotted the car following. He opened the glove box for a pencil and pad of paper and jotted down the license plate number. He didn't imagine he was in any immediate danger—at least not until a few questions were answered.

He would have to make sure that when the time came, he would be doing the asking.

He would watch. Wait for his opportunity to turn the tables. Lincoln's mind drifted on to other thoughts, centered on the strong emotions that always accompanied a journey to visit his father.

John. Wyoming.

John Agnello used a short piece of firewood to prop up the small stove, lifting the rear left leg eight inches above the floor. He worked a piece of flat stone out from under the leg, dusted off the shallow covering of dirt, and removed the metal box from the hole dug into the ground. John opened the box to find everything as he had left it.

The gun wrapped in cloth with two clips, and the cash in a plastic bag.

In a second plastic bag were all he had left of family photographs. Several pictures of his mother, father, and brother, Joseph—all long deceased.

John looked through the photos, lingering on a candid shot of Joey combing his hair on the stoop in front of their house in Brooklyn. He put the photographs back into the bag and into the box, returned the box to its resting placed, replaced the stone, and set the stove down again.

John briefly surveyed the cabin, as if for the last time, picked up his stash, and walked outside.

Teach stood facing the door as John came out into the bright sunlight. The Appaloosa seemed to be waiting for him.

"Be patient, boy," John said as he dropped the gun, ammunition clips, and stack of hundred-dollar bills into the saddlebag and climbed on Teach's back. "One more good run and we can head back for lunch."

San Francisco.

Sammy Orso learned the name of the Denver cop who was with John Agnello when the men he had sent to tail Agnello wound up on the losing end of the gun battle in Wellington.

Augie DiNapoli was no genius, but he had at least managed to jot down the license plate number of Lincoln Bonner's truck.

Orso called the third man he had sent to Denver, and gave him the cop's address.

Then it was time to deal with DiNapoli.

"So, Augie, was it your brilliant idea to recreate OK Corral in bumfuck Colorado?"

Sammy Orso did nothing to mask his discontent.

His interrogation of Augie DiNapoli was turning heads in the otherwise quiet restaurant.

"It was Paulie's idea. I tried to talk him out of it."

Two men sat at the bar watching every move at the table unblinkingly, waiting for a sign from Orso as if he were a third base coach.

"Now why did I know you were going to lay it on your late friend Paulie Sacco?" Sammy said, lowering his volume but retaining his intensity. "Did he happen to elucidate his rationale?"

"Huh?"

"Did he say why the fuck you just didn't do what I told you to do? Follow Agnello and then tell me where he was?"

"He thought we could get the drop on Agnello and bring him in."

"So, Paulie didn't understand the meaning of *just follow*. What did *you* think it meant?"

"With all respect, Mr. Orso, you told me I'm not being paid to think."

If Orso weren't so angry and worried, he might have gotten a kick out of DiNapoli's back pedaling.

"Vincent Leone is going to be very unhappy, Augie," Sammy said. "And with Paulie gone, I'm afraid you'll have to face the brunt of his displeasure."

"Can you do something to get me off the hook?"

"I don't know. Now, get out of here."

Sammy wasn't looking forward to having to report to Vinnie that they had lost John Agnello in Colorado. The Cadillac had been discovered in Cheyenne, but from there the trail was cold. Orso hoped they could pry some information out of the Denver cop before Vinnie returned to San Francisco from his business trip to New York.

Sacco and DiNapoli had screwed up royally, and they were Sammy's responsibility. Leone might be a bit more amiable if he heard both had paid for their digression.

Orso nodded to his two men at the bar, and they followed Augie DiNapoli out of the restaurant.

John. Wyoming.

John sponged down, brushed, and fed the Appaloosa and went to the house to feed himself.

He sat down to reheated manicotti and hot Italian sausage and browsed through the local newspaper.

The news was mostly bad, particularly concerning the wildfires that still raged throughout Colorado, Wyoming, and Montana.

"How'd Teach treat you?" said Hank, coming through the kitchen door with an armful of grocery bags.

"Great. He's a beautiful animal."

"Speaking of beautiful, good grub, don't you think?" asked Hank.

"As good as my mother's."

"I wouldn't go that far, but Katy did learn everything she knows about Sicilian vittles from your mom and would be very flattered."

"Where is Katy?"

"She couldn't wait to get under that fifty-three Chevy truck. Did you get to the cabin?"

"Yes, I did."

"If you need anything you couldn't find there, just let me know."

"Thanks, but I think I'm okay."

"Are you going to visit the old man?"

"I thought I would go tomorrow," John said, "but I'm afraid he may not know me."

"You'll be surprised by the things Louis Agnello knows, especially about the enemy."

John was reminded of what Signor Caravella had said as he was leaving the restaurant in Cheyenne.

Attenti il leone. Beware the lion.

Lincoln. Colorado.

In the prison visitor hall, Frank Bonner stopped his son in the middle of the apology and instead expressed his own regrets.

"You did the best you could, Lincoln. I really appreciate your help, and I'm sorry to have put you in danger."

"Agnello probably made it to where he wanted to go. I told him he could call me if he needed more help."

"Knowing John, I don't expect you'll hear from him. He's a lot better than I am at keeping others out of the line of fire."

And a lot better than I am, Lincoln was sadly reminded—

although he knew his father didn't mean to imply it.

"I brought a few books," said Lincoln, pushing them across the table.

"Great, I've been wanting to read this," said Frank Bonner, picking up the latest biography of Lyndon Johnson. "I'm not sure about the other. What could anyone possibly say about *The Siege of the Alamo* that we haven't heard already?"

"You'll be surprised," assured his son.

Lincoln decided to tell his father that he was being followed.

"Be very careful, son. These people who are looking for John Agnello are ruthless."

"Why didn't they just hit him while he was in here? I'm sure they had the means."

"My guess is it wouldn't satisfy Vincent Leone," said Frank. "I think the bastard is determined to get his hands on John personally—at any cost. And John understands it will ultimately come down to a face-to-face confrontation."

"John never did get to tell me what this feud with the Leones was really all about."

"It's a very long story, and they're going to chase you out of here any minute now. Thank you for coming, and for the books. And thanks for taking care of John, you did good."

Lincoln headed back toward the city.

The car that had tailed him from home was following behind.

As he crossed from Arapahoe into Denver County, he called the station to have the plates run.

"What's the matter," said Detective Jim Sykes, "can't stay away for a day without having to check out what you're missing?"

"Not exactly, do me a favor and run this."

He read the license plate number to Jim.

"That's a rental car," said Sykes.

"I know that, Jim. Find out who rented it, if you can tear yourself away from *The Young and the Restless* for a minute."

A few minutes later Sykes was back.

"Phillip Gambino from Oakland, in town on business."

"Monkey business. Look, I'm at First Avenue coming toward downtown on Santa Fe. Send a squad car to stop this guy at Thirteenth and Washington, I'll lead him over that way. Have the uniforms make up an excuse for pulling him over, and keep him sitting there for a while."

"Are you going to tell me what this is about?"

"What do you think, Jim?"

"Okay, forget I asked. I'll send a cruiser."

Lincoln was stopped at the traffic light at Thirteenth and Logan when the squad car pulled up behind the rental car with its roof lights flashing.

When the traffic light went to green, he drove ahead as the rental pulled to the curb and waited for the uniformed officer to reach the driver's window.

Lincoln turned left onto Emerson and started back to his place to prepare for Gambino's return.

After the imposed delay, Gambino pulled his car around to Nineteenth Street—behind Lincoln's building. He stepped out of the vehicle and started toward his usual post across from Bonner's front window on Eighteenth. As Gambino moved through the alley connecting the two streets, Lincoln came up behind him and pressed a gun to his head.

"You like that ear, Phil?"

"Pretty much," Gambino answered.

"Then stand very still and use it to listen carefully. I don't know where John Agnello is. Last time I saw him, he was driving off in one of your pal's rented gas-guzzlers and that was that. I did all I'm going to do for Agnello and only as a favor to someone else. Personally, I don't care if all you greaseballs kill each other off completely. You can tell whoever sent you that I'm a dead end, I don't like being stalked, and that I belong to a hard-ass gang called the Denver Police Department. If I see your face again, Phil, I'm going to call out the posse."

Lincoln tickled the man's ear with the barrel of the revolver.

"Any questions?" Bonner asked.

"None."

"Good. Now beat it. I have to run and grab my cap and mitt for the baseball game."

THIRTY ONE

San Francisco. Saturday.

Vincent Leone sat behind the large desk in his office early Saturday morning, gazing out of the huge windows overlooking the San Francisco Bay.

The offices of Leone Importing Company occupied an entire floor of the Transamerica Building in the downtown Financial District, and the company also operated warehouses throughout the city and beyond. Leone was catching up on work after a successful trip to New York City, where he had solidified an arrangement with a newly contracted supplier of Italian-made men's suits.

Leone had been distracted throughout the negotiations by thoughts about John Agnello's release from prison during his absence. He anxiously awaited word from Sammy Orso. Leone flew in late the night before and was surprised Orso did not come along with the driver who picked him up at the airport.

Vincent suspected it was a foreboding of bad news.

His suspicions were confirmed when his office receptionist announced Orso's arrival and Sammy walked into Vinnie's private office a moment later.

"Save the song and dance, Sammy. What happened?"

"They lost him in Colorado."

"Who is *they?*"

"Sacco and DiNapoli. Paulie was killed. They left Augie out cold on the road and took the car. Agnello was travelling with a Denver cop."

"Where's DiNapoli now?"

"Asleep with the fishes."

"Don't get cute, Sammy, I'm absolutely in no mood and those were your guys. Did anyone find the car?"

"It was found in Cheyenne. Agnello could have hopped a train or plane to anywhere from there."

"What about the cop in Denver?"

"He helped Agnello get out of town, but I don't think he knows where to."

"I'm interested in what you *think*, Sammy. Keep an eye on him."

"It's covered," said Orso. "I sent Marty into Denver last night. She said she would find a way to get close to the cop."

"We found John Agnello in Denver five years ago. He must have a secure hideout somewhere in Colorado or Wyoming or fucking Montana, and I think he'll rest for a while to plan his next move. It must be in the middle of fucking nowhere because when he got away from New York, he disappeared completely. Agnello was a just teenager, for Christ's sake," Vinnie shouted. "Brooklyn was his entire world. He must have gone to someone his old man knew. Find out."

"His father was in Vietnam, maybe it was an old Army buddy."

"Just fucking find out, Sammy. I don't want any more surprises. If he gets anywhere near San Francisco, I want to know the very minute he does."

"Won't he have to report to a parole officer in Colorado?"

"Who the fuck knows, and why are you asking fucking questions? What is it about *find out* that you don't understand?"

"We should have killed Agnello while he was in the joint."

"Sammy, if I've said it once, I've said it a thousand times. And if I have to say it again it will be the last thing you ever hear from me. I want John Agnello alive. If he dies before I get my hands on him, I don't care if he walks in front of a bus, I'm going to hold you accountable. Now get out of here and do your job."

Sammy Orso backed out of the office.

Vinnie Leone decided it was time he paid a visit to his grandfather.

John. Wyoming.

John Agnello walked into the kitchen to find Hank and Katy already working on a large breakfast. He poured some coffee and joined them at the table.

"How can you guys eat so much and stay so healthy and trim?"

"It's called physical labor, Johnny," said Hank. "Katy can bench-press a two-eighty-three, eight-cylinder Chevy engine. That's why she's so trusting—she can throw a person pretty far."

"Would you like to wear those eggs, Henry?" said Katy, trying to sound tough but unable to hide her good humor.

"No, ma'am," said Hank, laughing.

"Will you be going down to see your grandfather today?" asked Katy.

"Thought I would," said John.

"Do you think they're looking for you down there?" asked Hank.

"I doubt it. It's probably the last place Leone would think to look. He would sooner expect me to show up at his door than go back to Denver."

"He might have someone watching the detective who drove you out."

"I don't plan to be anywhere near Bonner. I'll be in and out real fast. I just want to see Louis while I'm still around. I'll be back by dinner time, so get those badger steaks out of the freezer."

"Take the Pontiac," said Katy.

"I couldn't," said Agnello.

"Are you afraid if you put a scratch on it I'll have to break your legs?" Katy asked.

"It crossed my mind."

"Take the goat, John. The ride is worth the risk," said Hank.

"All right, you talked me into it. Thank you, Katy. I will wear my kid gloves. I'll be back tonight."

An hour later, John Agnello sat behind the wheel of Katy's 1968 Pontiac GTO convertible trying not to think too much about all the love and care she had put into restoring the vehicle to immaculate showroom condition.

John drove quickly through Cheyenne and picked up I-25 South toward Denver.

Once on the Interstate, John had to control the impulse to confirm what he was sure the car could do on the open road.

The last thing he needed today was to be pulled over by the Colorado State Police for speeding.

Lincoln. Denver.

At the same time, Lincoln Bonner walked down to the street, grabbed a copy of the *Denver Post* from a vending machine in front of his building, and entered the coffee shop below his apartment. He picked up a cup of coffee and a croissant from the counter and sank into one of the comfortable armchairs scattered in back along the two walls of used books. The previous evening had been clear and crisp, a perfect night for the baseball game, but this morning was overcast. Lincoln opened the newspaper to the leisure section, thinking about catching a movie matinee.

He looked up as a very attractive young woman settled into

a similar chair nearby. She wore her long black hair in braids, a white sleeveless shirt that accentuated her dark complexion, a denim skirt that stopped just above her knees, and a pair of tall cowboy boots. She removed her sunglasses to reveal piercing blue eyes.

Lincoln watched as she unfolded a map of the city, realized he was staring, and turned back to the movie listings. He reached for his coffee on the small table beside him, fighting the urge to look back at the woman, when she spoke to him from her seat.

"I hate to bother you," she said, "but I'm new in town and I was hoping you could help me with directions."

"No bother at all, why don't I slide my chair over there."

"Here comes the rain," said Lincoln, gazing out of the window.

Lincoln had spent nearly an hour talking with her in the coffeehouse—giving her a general overview of the city from landmarks to politics.

"My name is Lincoln, by the way. What friends I have call me Linc."

"I'm Martina. If you're in the market for a new friend, I'll call you Linc and you can call me Marty."

John. Sloan's Lake.

The small house stood across from Sloan's Lake in west Denver.

John Agnello walked up to the front door, passing the mailbox that displayed the name *Lamb.*

John rang the doorbell and moments later his cousin Patricia stood before him.

"You look good, John," she said, giving Agnello a warm embrace. "I really wanted to visit you out at the prison."

"I know, Patty. There were reasons why I didn't want you

to come."

"He's across at the lake, feeding the ducks. Why don't you go over and bring him back? I'll put up some coffee."

John spotted the old man as he crossed to the park, sitting on a wooden bench at the edge of the lake. He sat down beside Louis Agnello.

"*Buongiorno*," John said.

The old man turned to the voice and his face lit up in recognition.

"Vittorio, *come stai figlio*."

"It's John, Grandfather."

"*Naturalmente. Mi scusa.* You remind me so much of your father."

"Patricia has started the coffee."

"*Bene, vieni a casa*," the old man said as he dropped what remained of the stale bread onto the grass for the birds and rose from the bench.

THIRTY TWO

Lincoln. Denver. Saturday.

The second hour passed more quickly than the first as they talked and watched the rain pound the street outside the café.

And had fun trying to refold her map.

They had learned a lot about each other since he had slid his chair across to hers, or so it seemed. Lincoln did volunteer he came from a small rural town on Colorado's Eastern Plains, had come to Denver to attend university, and now worked for the city. However, at least for the moment, he omitted the specifics of his work. It wasn't that he was self-conscious about being a police detective, or that he had any reason to be secretive.

Bonner simply didn't wear his badge on his sleeve.

Martina revealed much more about herself. She was employed by a designer of expensive Italian men's suits and had come to Denver to obtain purchase orders from local clothiers. Marty had come to town early to become familiar with the terrain, and would spend the week making contacts. She had taken a room at the Brown Palace Hotel—a room she was told was once occupied by Wyatt Earp. Her work would consume weekday business hours, but her evenings would be free. The company she represented was exploring the possibility of opening an office in Denver, to help in handling increased sales in the Rocky Mountain region. Martina was hoping to get a thorough taste of the city while on this trip, and to get a sense of how she might like relocating from New York.

"Who knows," she said, "we may become neighbors."

The rain had let up, the midday sun was breaking through, and Lincoln did have the day off.

He decided that sitting in a movie theater alone wasn't his best option.

"If you want a real taste of Denver, I'd like to take you to Adelitas Cocina Y Cantina for lunch," said Lincoln. "Some of the best Mexican food this side of Nogales, and I'm pretty sure it's nothing like what you can find on the Upper West Side. No offense meant."

"None taken. Sounds great, can we walk?"

"We could, but strolling four miles down Broadway isn't the best walking tour in Denver."

"I live in New York City," Martina said. "I have absolutely no problem with public transportation."

"My truck is a few hundred feet from here. I live in a loft right above us."

"Great location. This is like the SoHo of Denver. How did you manage to land right in the middle of it?"

"Completely by accident. When I first moved here it was more like the back streets of Cow Town."

"Things change," she said.

"Hopefully not the menu at Adelitas."

Vinnie. Stinson Beach.

Vinnie Leone pulled up to the house on Stinson Beach, just north of Sausalito across the bay from San Francisco. Vincent stepped out of his car and greeted one of the two men who Sammy Orso had enlisted as security at his grandfather's home.

The rear of the large house faced the Pacific Ocean.

Vinnie's grandmother greeted him at the door with an embrace, told him her husband was out back, and immediately set to preparing food. Vinnie had long ago given up asking her not to bother. She was already taking platters out of the refrigerator as Leone passed through the kitchen and continued through the back door.

Salvatore Leone sat sipping wine on one of two high-backed cedar chairs his father Vincenzo had constructed by hand in 1923, eighty-two years before. Two years after Salvatore was born. The chairs had moved with him from Russian Hill when he had relocated from the city to the beach. On a wrought-iron table with a glass top sat a bottle of Chianti and an empty crystal goblet.

The old man looked out to the sea as Vinnie walked up to greet him.

"*Buongiorno, Nonno.*"

Salvatore looked up and smiled.

"Vincenzo, *bene. Prego, si accomodi,*" Salvatore said, indicating the empty seat. "Take wine. Is my wife preparing a meal?"

"Yes, Grandfather. *Grazie,*" Vinnie said, as he settled into the cedar chair. "You look very well, how do you feel?"

"*Benissimo.*"

Vinnie poured wine into the empty glass and he took a long drink and a deep breath before saying what he had come to say.

"John Agnello is out of prison."

The old man looked deeply into Vinnie's eyes, reached over and grabbed Vinnie's forearm forcefully.

"Bring him, and his grandfather, to me."

"Soon," said Vinnie.

"*Per favore,* more *vino,*" said Salvatore Leone, holding out his empty wine glass.

John. Sloan's Lake.

Patricia served coffee and homemade cookies when John and Louis returned from the park, and left them to speak in private.

"How have you been, Grandfather?" John Agnello asked.

"How have I been? Locked inside of this house in the middle of nowhere, where I cannot even find decent Italian bread—or see my own family name on the door."

"There's no other way. You're safe here. You have your backyard for *bocce,* the lake, and Patricia bakes well enough. You are alive."

"I have outlived my wife and my two sons—that is my reward for a long life."

"Please, Grandfather, I've come for your help."

"How can I help you?"

"I don't know what to do."

"You will do what you must do. As long as Vincent Leone remains alive, you will be as you were in the prison you have just come from."

"Will this killing ever end?"

"I fear it will only end when one of you is dead. It is up to you to choose who will survive."

"And what about you and Salvatore Leone. How will that end?"

"Two old men, each dying alone."

"You were raised as brothers."

"Yes. We are also cousins. Vincenzo Leone was a good father to us both. Cursed was the day Roberto Leone arrived bearing the hatred and savagery of the Old Country. I remember seeing my true father, outside the house in San Francisco. I was just seven years old. He stood talking with the devil, Roberto Leone. I did not know until many years later that he was my father. And I never saw him again."

PART FIVE

TESTIMONY

We know the past and its great events,
the present in its multitudinous complications,
chiefly through faith in the testimony of others.

—Matthew Simpson

THIRTY THREE

San Francisco. Wednesday.

Naro, *famiglia* Leone's *ristorante*, had been located at the same corner in the area of San Francisco known as North Beach for more than eighty years and, for nearly its entire history, the landmark dining establishment was run exclusively by the women of the family.

The current proprietress was Connie Leone, a strong, proud woman who asked very little of her only son but did insist Vincent come for dinner at the restaurant on Wednesday evenings. It was a timeless tradition, held sacred by his mother. And unless business took him away from the city, Vinnie honored it religiously. He always arrived alone, never scheduled meetings during these visits, and always tried to coax his mother into sitting for a while.

Six days after Sammy Orso's men had lost track of John Agnello in Colorado, Vinnie sat at a table near the kitchen listening to Connie complain about how he wasn't eating enough. Vinnie caught sight of Orso trying to get his attention from across the room. Leone ignored Orso until his mother ran back to work at her stove, then waved Sammy over to the table.

"This had better be important," Vinnie said. "Sit down."

Sammy took a seat, almost reached for a piece of bread but caught himself.

"We got him."

"You have John Agnello?"

"Well, not exactly."

"Sammy, don't upset me."

"Henry Lowell Sims was in Vito Agnello's company in Vietnam."

"Come on, Sammy, don't torture me."

"After they got back, Sims was the best man at Agnello's wedding."

"Jesus Christ, Sammy. Why the fuck is it that every time I talk with you lately I feel like a dental surgeon? Get to the fucking point before I shove this fork into your eyeball."

"This guy Sims has a ranch in Wyoming, up the road from Cheyenne."

"Find the Rizzo brothers," said Vinnie Leone calmly, "and I'll meet you all in front of the restaurant in exactly one hour."

Sammy jumped up and rushed out to his car.

Leone turned his attention back to his plate of linguini with red clam sauce.

Denver.

Lincoln and Martina sat among six thousand people listening to classical music and looking out to the Denver skyline in the distance.

Lincoln had been with Marty all but one night that week and had enjoyed every minute.

And that was very unusual.

The one evening they were apart was the night before. Lincoln had been on duty with his partner, Jim Sykes, on a stakeout.

The Denver police were investigating a group suspected of illegal hand gun sales, based on the information obtained from a fifteen-year-old boy who was picked up trying to enter a high school with a concealed 9mm.

Lincoln had confessed his occupation to Marty over lunch at the Mexican restaurant the day they met, after the hostess had playfully greeted Lincoln as *Marshal Bonner* when they walked in.

Martina didn't seem to mind.

"You should arrest the cook. The chili relleños are so delicious they should be against the law," she said, which was as close as she came to an allusion to his work.

Lincoln's only trepidation in spending all this time with Martina was his concern over being able to *entertain* this Big City professional woman.

Denver wasn't exactly cosmopolitan. Lincoln opted to show her the things she wouldn't find in New York City—as opposed to the new Denver clubs, shops, and eating places, which he felt certain she would see as fair imitations.

He decided to show her what had survived, the small out of the way places he'd discovered when he was a student that managed to maintain their unique mid-sized Western city charm all these years. It appeared to be working. Marty seemed genuinely impressed.

Lincoln stole a glance at Martina as Yo Yo Ma played Mozart on his cello and the lights of the city sparkled in the east as brightly as the stars did in the clear sky overhead.

The look on her face convinced him the concert at Red Rocks Amphitheater was another winning choice.

"I would love to sleep under these stars," Martina said.

"That can be easily arranged," Lincoln said.

San Francisco.

"You'll fly into Cheyenne tonight, rent a vehicle and find an out-of-the-way motel between Cheyenne and Iron Mountain," said Vinnie Leone, turning to face the Rizzo brothers who sat in the back seat of the car, while Sammy Orso unconsciously tapped on the steering wheel. "In the morning you drive into the town, if there is one, and ask around. Hank Sims sells horses, pretend you're in the market for a graduation present for your daughter. Whatever. All I want to find out is if John Agnello is up there."

"Whose daughter should it be?"

If Vinnie didn't know better he would have thought Jimmy Rizzo was joking.

"Let it be Richie's kid, you can be the uncle."

"Good," said Jimmy.

Great, thought Vinnie.

"You want us to nab him, Mr. Leone?"

"What did I just say, Richie? If you find him walking down a deserted road alone with his hands in the air, I don't want you anywhere close to him. Just get near enough to be able to tell me he's there. And if even one hair on his head is out of place when I see him, I don't even want to think about how upset it would make me."

"How about me, Vincent?" asked Sammy.

"You are going to get these two to the airport, each equipped with a cellular telephone, and you are going to know where they are every single minute. *Capisce?*"

"Got it."

"I truly hope so," Vinnie said, as he climbed out of the car. "Get going."

Wyoming.

John Agnello and Amy Sims sat on the front porch of her parents' house while Hank helped Katy with the dinner dishes.

Amy had arrived at the ranch earlier in the day and was surprised to find Agnello on hand.

Amy may have been pleased to see him if she weren't reminded of his insane circumstance every time she looked at him.

"I suppose you'll be off on your crusade soon," Amy said.

"You make it sound Medieval."

"It is Medieval," she said, almost angrily.

"It's self-defense, Amy."

"No, John, it isn't. I've learned a little about the law in my journalistic work. It's not self-defense when you go out looking for it."

"You don't know Vinnie Leone, Amy," said John. "He will find me. The Leones always find me. The option of letting it go was taken from me a long time ago. And for Vincent also, for that matter. We're both locked into an unavoidable showdown that was ordained long before either of us was born."

"You make it sound Biblical."

"That's stretching it a bit. In the entire scheme of things, the story of the Leones and the Agnellos isn't that earth shattering—but in my more romantic moments, I like to think Shakespeare would have appreciated it."

Denver.

Lincoln and Martina were side by side on sleeping bags under a quilted blanket, gazing up at the clear sky from their campsite on the roof of Bonner's building.

"Not bad," she said.

"We got lucky, it's not always this clear. And when there's a ballgame at Coors Field, the stars disappear. I was going to bring an alarm clock up here."

"I don't have anywhere to be before noon. Do you?"

"I have to meet Jim Sykes at seven, but the rooster will wake me up."

"You're kidding, right?"

"Yes. But the six-ten into Union Station will do the job."

"Thanks for the concert. It was beautiful out there."

"A little different from Madison Square Garden."

"A lot different, although the Garden does have its charms. Who knows, maybe I'll get to take you sometime."

"Who knows?" said Lincoln.

It was all he could think of to say.

THIRTY FOUR

Denver. Thursday.

Lincoln woke at dawn to find Marty close beside him, her head resting on his chest.

He tried to slip out without waking her, but the moment he moved her eyes popped open.

It took a few seconds for Martina to remember where she was, the stadium looming nearby doing the trick.

"Oh," she said.

"It's very early," Lincoln said sitting up. "Why don't you get some more sleep? You can move inside to the bedroom if you like."

"I think I could use a few more winks, but I'd rather stay up here. I love this roof. I'd like to take it back to New York City, if I had any place to put it."

"Stay as long as you like. If you're still here around noon, I could come back and we can have lunch."

Lincoln headed down to the apartment. When he left the building, Martina called Sammy Orso.

"I'm on Bonner. If Agnello comes near him I'll know."

"We have a possible lead," Orso said. "Agnello may be in Wyoming. The Rizzo brothers are checking it out."

"Well, Sammy, you know what they say."

"What do they say?"

"One way, or the other."

After the call, Martina decided on a little more sleep.

Wyoming.

Another morning and another huge breakfast, eggs, ham, bacon, and buttered toast all around—except for Amy who sat in front of a bowl of yogurt and fresh fruit.

"How do you expect to get through the day with a start like that," said Hank Sims. "I've seen more substantial meals in a Gerber baby food jar."

"Just because it wasn't running around the barnyard screaming for mercy last week doesn't mean it's not substantial, Dad," Amy said. "If you keep eating like this every day, Mom will have to hook up the GTO fuel pump to your aorta."

"Do you think you two can talk about something you have more control over than what the other chooses for breakfast, like maybe the weather or the price of gold," said Katy, half seriously.

Through all the playful bantering, John Agnello sat at the table delighting in their performance.

The Jeep Wrangler rolled to a stop at the gas pump in front of the Iron Mountain Country Store.

It was one of the six landmarks along the one block stretch that constituted the town center.

Adjacent to the Country Store stood Howard's Hardware, with its two small tractor mowers and one snowmobile out front.

On the opposite side of Howard's, which happened to be the owner's first *and* last name, was the Interdenominational Church of Iron Mountain.

Across Main Street was Chugwater Pharmacy, named for the creek that ran through the town and doubling as the town post office.

Neighboring the drug store stood the Park Diner, the early morning meeting place for the working men of the town—the carpenters, the ranchers, the storekeepers, the sheriff and his deputies, and the banker who managed the First Wyoming National Bank of Iron Mountain next door.

It was Howard Howard who first noticed the Jeep come to a stop across the street, and who commented to his breakfast mates at the window table in the Park Diner.

"Get a load of those two," he said. "They look like they just came off the set of *Westworld*."

Jimmy and Richie Rizzo had stepped out of the Jeep, each wearing plaid shirts and blue jeans, looking as out of place as a pair of rabbis at a pig roast.

The group at the table watched.

"Those guys give new meaning to the word wrong," added Bill Phillips.

Phillips picked up his napkin and buffed his deputy sheriff's badge, inspiring laughs all around the table.

"You think we should go and find out how they got themselves so lost?" asked Gabe Sanders, who worked horses with Hank Sims.

"Maybe if we're lucky they'll save us the trouble and come over here," said the banker, George Hanson.

"Good call, George," said Howard, "here they come."

The Rizzo brothers walked into the diner and took an empty table near the others. Sally Page took their matching orders of coffee and the breakfast special and walked back to the counter to put it in. Jimmy and Richie Rizzo both lit cigarettes, then looked at each other, each holding a burnt match when they found no ashtray on the table.

"There you go," said Gabe, walking up and placing a plastic ashtray on the table between them. "You guys lost?"

Jimmy Rizzo was about to say something when his brother jumped in, noticing the three other men at the table Gabe had come from.

"We're actually up from Denver on a shopping trip," Richie said.

"This isn't exactly the Sixteenth Street Mall," said Gabe,

donning his best amiable smile. "The only thing we have up here you couldn't find in Denver is clean air."

"And horses."

"Horses?"

"We're shopping for a graduation present for my daughter. We heard this was the place to look."

"Now, that's something I know something about," said Gabe. "Mind if I sit?"

"Not at all," said Richie. "Can we buy you a cup of coffee?"

"Thanks, I have one already," Gabe said, motioning over toward the table where Howard, George, and Bill sat waiting to get the story. "I'll be back in a minute."

Sally came up to the table with the plates of food and a pot of coffee as Gabe moved to fetch his cup.

"What's the scoop?" asked Howard.

"They say they're in the market for a horse."

"What do you think?" asked Bill.

"They look and sound more the Cadillac type, although stranger things have happened. Pass that cup," said Gabe.

"Keep in touch," George Hanson said with a snicker as he handed Gabe the mug and Sanders headed back to join the Rizzos.

Gabe sat down at the table, prepared to talk horses and give the tinhorns the benefit of the doubt, when Jimmy Rizzo opened his mouth for the first time and with a dozen words sent up the red flag.

"We heard that Hank Sims was the man to see about horses," Jimmy said.

"We thought maybe you could tell us how to find him," added Richie Rizzo, eliminating all doubt.

"Sure could, in fact I can take you to his door," said Gabe. "You boys enjoy the grub before it gets cold and, when you're ready, I'll lead you out to Hank's place."

"Great," said Richie.

Sanders returned to the other table, spoke a few words to his friends, then walked over to the pay telephone to call Hank Sims.

"That was Gabe Sanders calling from the Park Diner," said Hank, walking back from the phone on the kitchen wall. "Two apes disguised as humans walked in looking for a man with a horse."

"Jesus," said John. "How did they find this place?"

"Vinnie Leone must have learned I stood up for your dad at his wedding. I have to give him credit, his old man never got that far eighteen years ago."

"I guess I'd better get out of here."

"I said you could stay as long as you like and I meant it. Nobody is going to get anywhere near this place uninvited."

"I appreciate the offer, but it's time I get started. I'll head to Denver and catch a flight to the West Coast. Vincent Leone seems anxious to see me."

"Can you drive John down to Denver," Katy asked her daughter.

"Of course," Amy said.

"No need to rush," said Hank. "The boys will take the gorillas for a ride to chase a wild goose and give them a little talking to."

"You sure you don't mind, Amy?" asked John.

"Not at all, give me half an hour."

The Rizzo brothers, in the rented Jeep, followed Gabe Sanders' pickup truck out of town toward Morton Pass and *away* from the Sims Ranch. Seated beside Gabe were Bobby Jackson and Stu Fisher, who had walked into the Park Diner just in time to join the fun. Fifteen miles out, just past the cut off that connected back to Route 34, the road abruptly ended and Richie Rizzo stopped the Jeep behind the pickup.

Gabe, Bobby, and Stu climbed out of the truck and they

walked back to the Jeep.

Bobby had grabbed the rifle from the rack over the seat.

Sanders walked up to the driver's window while Bobby and Stu moved to the other side.

"What's this?" asked Richie Rizzo.

"This is where we tell you to get out of Dodge. We know you're here after John Agnello, but you missed him. I spoke to Hank Sims and he said Agnello is gone and he's not coming back. You want a horse for your kid, I suggest you try Montana."

"I don't know what you're talking about," said Richie.

"Let me put it simply. If you're still in Laramie County an hour from now, you'll wish you never heard the word Wyoming. Trust me boys, it's not worth it. Agnello isn't around here anymore. Don't try anything stupid," Gabe said, seeing Jimmy Rizzo reaching down to the floor of the Jeep. "Bobby there is a deputy sheriff and he's really good with that scattergun."

Richie reached over and put a hand on his brother's knee.

"Thanks for the advice," Richie Rizzo said to Gabe. "You guys have a nice day."

Gabe and the others watched as Richie turned the Jeep around and drove off.

"Think they got the message?" asked Stu.

"Oh, yeah," said Bobby Jackson, resting the barrel of the rifle on his shoulder as they returned to the pickup truck.

Jimmy Rizzo called Sammy Orso as the Jeep passed through Main Street in Iron Mountain heading to Route 211 back toward Cheyenne.

Howard Howard spotted Amy and John in the GTO, passing through town in the same direction twenty minutes later.

Richie and Jimmy Rizzo stopped at the motel near the Cheyenne Airport just long enough to check out and lose the ridiculous cowboy outfits.

They each slipped on their street clothes consisting of gabardine slacks, silk socks, Italian loafers, and cashmere polo shirts that matched exactly except for color.

From the motel, they went to trade the rented Jeep for a Cadillac.

Sammy Orso had told them to drive down to Denver, guessing John Agnello might be headed that way.

"If we drive the rental to Denver, do we have to drive it back up here?" asked Jimmy Rizzo, on the cell phone with Orso.

"You pay a little more for a one-way rental, Jimmy, then they get some high school kid to drive the car back up for five dollars an hour and a bus ticket home. Sound like a good job to you?"

"Not really."

"Then you'd better start doing yours or you could find yourself shagging cars for a living," was all Sammy said before hanging up.

After switching vehicles, the Rizzo brothers hopped onto Interstate 25.

Thirty miles ahead of them, Amy pulled the GTO into a truck stop off Interstate 25 in Colorado. John wanted to make a phone call to Bonner in Denver—thinking he could use Lincoln's help to get a flight to California. He pulled out the card Lincoln had given him when they last parted and headed for a row of pay phones while Amy ordered coffees to go.

John called the number at Lincoln Bonner's precinct house. Jim Sykes answered.

"He walked out a few minutes ago," said Jim. "He told me he was headed to his place to meet someone for lunch. Need the phone number?"

"I've got it, thanks."

. . .

Martina had slept later than she thought she would up on the roof and woke up with the late morning sun beating down on her. She moved down to the apartment and used the shower, browsed through Lincoln's bookshelf, and checked the food situation.

Martina decided she would treat Lincoln to a homemade lunch and found enough in the refrigerator and among the vegetables in a basket on the kitchen counter to throw together a pasta primavera. She was about to run down to the street for a sourdough baguette and a newspaper when the phone rang.

"Is Lincoln in?" asked John Agnello.

"Not at the moment, but I'm expecting him. Can I take a message?"

"Sure. Tell him John called and I'm on my way down. I'll call after seven."

"Will do," said Martina.

"Thanks."

Martina placed the phone down, sighed deeply, then picked up the receiver again to telephone Sammy Orso in San Francisco.

Ten minutes later, Sammy was on the phone to Vincent Leone.

"Marty called again. Agnello is on his way into Denver and is planning to call on Bonner. I have Richie and Jimmy on their way in to stake out Bonner's place. Marty's going to try to stay on the inside until Agnello shows."

"Nobody is going to go stupid on me, right, Sammy?"

"Don't worry, Boss. Marty has it covered. I warned the Rizzos not to think about inhaling unless Marty says breathe."

"Keep me posted. A lot," Vinnie said.

When Lincoln arrived home at noon, Martina was gone.

Marty had left a note saying she wanted to get her business out of the way early so they could enjoy the evening and she mentioned the call from John Agnello.

Marty promised to prepare an authentic Sicilian dinner and added she would bring the Chianti when she returned at seven.

Lincoln whipped together a cheese and tomato sandwich and headed back to work.

Martina watched him leave from the inside of a shop across from his building.

After Lincoln left, Marty stationed herself in an armchair at the window of the coffee shop below his apartment to look out for Richie and Jimmy Rizzo. When she spotted the Cadillac passing slowly up Eighteenth Street, Martina stepped out front. When the sedan came around again, she jumped into the back seat and told Richie to turn and head out Wazee Street.

She told Richie to position himself in the coffee shop and asked Jimmy to remain in the car across Eighteenth Street. Marty said she'd be returning at seven and urged them to stay at their posts until she said otherwise.

Having been warned by Sammy Orso that Marty was to be obeyed, the Rizzo brothers followed her instructions.

Amy and John spent the late morning and afternoon at Horsetooth Reservoir in Fort Collins. They had decided not to ride into Denver until evening. After an early dinner near the university campus, they picked up Interstate 25 again, arriving in downtown Denver just past six-thirty.

They settled at a table in the far rear of the Wynkoop Brewery, a short distance up Eighteenth Street from Lincoln's apartment, and ordered beers.

Lincoln returned home at six-forty-five.

Richie Rizzo sat in the coffeehouse below Lincoln's loft, playing with a cell phone and waiting to hear from Marty.

Lincoln spotted him easily. The large man in polyester sitting among the local patrons stood out like an orange in a bowl of apples.

Martina arrived at seven and immediately began working on dinner.

She was about to put a large pot of water up to boil when the telephone rang.

John Agnello calling from the Wynkoop.

"I need a favor," said Lincoln after taking the call.

"Sure."

"I need you to walk down to the brewery on Wynkoop to meet John, the man who called earlier. I'd go myself but I'm being watched."

"Sounds a little ominous."

"I don't have time to explain, but you'll be safe. I doubt anyone will follow you, they'll stick with me. Take John to your hotel and wait for me to phone. I hate to involve you, but I really don't have a choice."

"It's no problem. It's kind of exciting really."

Lincoln thanked her and she headed down to the street.

Jimmy sat in the rental car at Eighteenth and Market. Richie called his brother when he saw Martina walk by the window of the coffee shop.

"Where the hell is she going?"

"I have no idea, but she said to stay put," Richie said, "and Sammy told us her word was the law."

"Fuck," said Jimmy Rizzo, slamming the cell phone to the seat of the Cadillac.

At the Wynkoop Brewery, Amy was lifting a beer mug to her lips when she saw a woman walking slowly toward their table.

When the woman reached them she stopped and looked deeply into John Agnello's eyes.

"John?" she asked.

"Do I know you?"

"I'm Martina Harding. Your father and my father were friends."

"You're Jack's daughter?"

"Yes."

"What are you doing here?"

"I'm a detective with the San Francisco Police Department and I'm here to take you to California."

THIRTY FIVE

Denver.

John introduced Martina to Amy. Marty went into action.

"I know you have questions, John, but there's no time. There are two gorillas up the street getting really curious about where I am," Martina said. "Do you know where to find your grandfather?"

"Yes."

"Give me the address. Amy, can you take John to his grandfather?"

"Of course."

John wrote down the address for Marty.

"And I need an empty pizza box," said Marty, as the waitress walked up.

Amy went off with the waitress to pick up a box and settle the bill.

"John, call Lincoln. Tell him there's a man in the coffee shop below his place, and one in a car at Eighteenth and Market. They will both be armed. Ask Lincoln to have them picked up and held for as long as possible, and to keep them off the phone," Marty said. "Tell Lincoln I'll meet him back at his apartment and I'll explain. Go out to your grandfather's house after you speak to Lincoln, and I'll meet you there as soon as I can."

Amy came back to the table with an empty box and handed it to Marty.

"Call Lincoln now, John," Marty said, and she headed for the door.

After receiving the call from John, Lincoln rang Jim Sykes at the police station.

Lincoln walked down to the street and into the coffee shop. Richie Rizzo sat at the counter, gazing out to the side-walk. When Lincoln came in, Richie turned away.

Lincoln took a seat beside Rizzo.

Martina walked slowly on Eighteenth Street. When she passed the coffee shop, she glanced in and saw Lincoln sitting beside Richie. She walked to the alley entrance of Lincoln's building and took the stairs up to the loft.

John and Amy left the brewery and jumped into the GTO.

John directed her to Speer Boulevard and out toward Sloan's Lake.

Detective Jim Sykes parked his unmarked car on Larimer Street and moved on foot toward the Cadillac parked on Eighteenth near Market Street.

"Waiting for someone?" asked Lincoln.

"Just having a cappuccino," said Richie. "Is that against the law?"

"No, but carrying a concealed weapon is."

"What are you talking about?"

"Put both of your hands on the counter," said Lincoln, taking out his detective shield. "Very slowly."

"You've got no probable cause."

"This is Denver, that outfit you're wearing breaks about a dozen dress codes. Do it."

Richie put his hands on the counter and Lincoln proceeded to handcuff him.

Jim Sykes tapped on the window of the Cadillac.

"Can I please see your license and registration," he asked, showing his shield when Jimmy Rizzo rolled down the window.

"What for?"

"This is a no standing area, would you step out of the car please, sir."

"What for?"

"I think I see a firearm under your jacket," Jim Sykes said, as he pulled out his own weapon. "Step out slowly."

Marty called Sammy Orso from Lincoln's apartment.

"The police picked up Richie and Jimmy," she said.

"How the fuck?"

"They stood out like sore thumbs, Sammy. Bonner must have spotted one or both of them."

"Where were you?"

"Bonner sent me out for food, I couldn't say no. I'm guessing he wanted to wait for the call from Agnello. When I came back, I saw the cops grab your boys."

"Any sign of Agnello?"

"No."

"Where are you now?"

"I'm at Bonner's place, waiting for him to get back here. They won't be able to keep Richie and Jimmy long. When the Rizzos call you, tell them to sit tight until I contact them. I'll stick with Bonner."

"Fuck."

"Relax, Sammy. Now that they took the Rizzos off the street, I'm sure Bonner will give Agnello the safe sign to come in. I'm on top of it."

"Don't let Vinnie down, Marty. He hates to be disappointed."

"Don't worry, Sammy. I'll call you."

Two squad cars rolled up to the Cadillac. Sykes had Jimmy Rizzo out of the car and cuffed. He sent one of the units down to the coffee shop.

"Take Mr. Rizzo down to the station, and make him comfortable," Sykes said, "I'll be right behind you."

Sykes walked down to the coffee shop where Lincoln was turning Richie Rizzo over to the uniformed officers in the other unit. Sykes sent them back to the station also.

"Well?" asked Sykes.

"Hold them as for long as you can, without a phone call," said Lincoln. "I imagine the guns are licensed, but they're not licensed to carry them concealed here in Colorado. Write them up for the appropriate citation and fine—and hold the firearms. We can ship the weapons to California, and they can pick them up from the police back there."

"Where are you off to?" asked Sykes.

"There's a young lady up in my place that has some serious explaining to do. I'll phone you later at the station."

"Are you sure you don't need backup going up there?"

"I think I can handle it, thanks. Just keep those two apes tied up for a while."

"I remember the first time I ever saw your father," Amy said as she pulled the GTO up to the curb in front of Louis Agnello's house at Sloan's Lake. "I must have been six years old. My parents brought me and my brothers to New York to visit your family. I can still recall how much the city frightened me, how my father held me in his arms on the crowded subway. I remember you and your brother, Joey. How tough you seemed, the strange language you used. Your mother prepared a lunch that was like a banquet. Even the food scared me—it was all so alien to me. And then, late in the afternoon, your father returned home from work. My father introduced him to us as our Uncle Vito. He knelt down and looked me straight in the eyes and he told me there was nothing to be afraid of. And at that moment, all of my fears disappeared."

"My father could do that," said John Agnello. "Let's go inside and hope my grandfather can do the same."

THIRTY SIX

Jim Sykes started to his car, and Lincoln moved toward the entrance to his loft.

Before Lincoln reached the alley, Marty was down on the street.

"Can you give me a ride to Sloan's Lake?" she asked.

"I was hoping for some answers."

"How about I give it a try on the way over?"

"Sure."

They walked to the parking area on the opposite side of the building and climbed into Lincoln's truck.

As Lincoln made the turn toward Speer Boulevard, Marty began.

"I'm a detective with the San Francisco Police Department. For the past several months I've been undercover, most recently working for a man named Vincent Leone."

"And Vincent Leone sent you here to kill John Agnello?"

"Leone wants John alive, and he also wants John's grandfather, Louis. Vincent wants to present Louis and John Agnello as gifts to *his* grandfather."

"Puts both you and John in a tough spot."

"It's the spot I planned to be in."

"Tell me about you and John."

"It's a little complicated."

"Okay."

Marty ran through the generations of interactions between the Hardings and the Agnellos.

"We lost track of John when he was seventeen years old and had to go into hiding. Then, five years ago, we learned Johnny was doing prison time here in Colorado."

"That's more than a little complicated."

They sat together in the living room of the house at Sloan's Lake.

Amy Sims, Martina Harding, Lincoln Bonner, John Agnello, and John's grandfather, Louis.

Louis had been talking for more than an hour.

John's cousin, Patricia, came in from the kitchen carrying a fresh pot of coffee.

"Grandfather," Patricia said, "it's very late. You need to get to bed."

"I remained in New York City for the Falco trial," Louis said, disregarding Patricia. "Your father and your grandmother would not allow me to leave, John. I will never forget my son Vito's excitement as the day in November approached when the authorities would shut down Falco and Leone. The trials commenced in February, in both New York and San Francisco. In March, we received word that Roberto Leone had died at the San Quentin prison hospital, several days after a heart attack."

"It's terrible to say, but the death of Roberto Leone must have been a great relief to your family," said Lincoln.

"It might have been," said Louis, "except we inherited a new and equally vicious enemy in Bruno Leone, as we tragically learned a few weeks later on Easter Sunday."

"Grandfather, please," said Patricia, "it's late."

"Will you all be staying here tonight?" Louis asked.

"No," said Martina. "Amy will be returning to Wyoming. Lincoln will go home and drop me at my hotel. I need to pick up my things there. I need to talk with you and John in the morning."

Louis Agnello wished them a good night before he reluctantly allowed Patricia to take him up to his room.

"I would like to talk with John for a while before we leave," Lincoln said, after Patricia and Louis had left the group. "If that's alright with you, John."

"Sure, let's walk around the lake."

"Can you tell me about Easter Sunday?" Lincoln asked, when they reached the lake shore.

John related what he could remember about that day in 1982.

"I was eleven years old, and I didn't understand what was happening. I only came to comprehend the intensity of the feud between the Leones and our family much later. But I did know, after that day, my father and I would never be the same.

"My grandmother passed away less than two weeks later. She had been diagnosed that Easter Sunday with a very aggressive form of lung cancer but, as I came to believe when I was older, it was the loss of her son and grandson which caused her to give up any fight for her life. My father was devastated. He lost a wife, son, brother, and then his mother. My grandfather had been subject to such loss many times before and he helped my father, and me, get through tough times. For my father, the obsessive need to find Carlo Silveri also helped to take his mind away from the tragedy. There was no doubt Bruno Leone was behind the attack, but only Silveri could provide the proof. My dad now insisted—with no room for argument—that my grandfather leave New York City to a place where Bruno Leone could not locate him and stage another attempt. Though not officially in the Witness Protection Program, the government did provide a highly classified new identity for my grandfather and he was relocated to Englewood, Colorado, as Louis Ford.

"Patricia came to live with my father and me. When she graduated high school, she came out here to study at the University of Denver—also using the name Ford—and stayed with our grandfather. Patricia married a lieutenant in the Marine Corps who she met at a friend's wedding. They moved to Beaufort, North Carolina, where he was stationed and where she began teaching. When her husband was killed in Afghanistan, Patricia came back to Denver to teach here and care for Louis."

"Did your father find Silveri?" Lincoln asked.

"Actually, it was Martina's father who finally located Carlo Silveri in San Francisco—but it didn't turn out as my dad had hoped."

"If you need any more help, don't hesitate to ask," Lincoln said.

"I guess I'll know better when Marty tells Louis and me what she needs to tell us."

They had settled onto a bench and were sitting quietly looking out to the lake when Amy and Martina approached.

"I need to get back to Wyoming, and then Chicago," Amy said, as she and Marty reached them. "You know you can call my parents, and call me for that matter, if you need anything at all."

John thanked both Lincoln and Amy for their offers, but said he hoped they would no longer need to be involved.

"We should get going, also," Marty said to Lincoln. "Can you run me back here in the morning?"

"Sure," Lincoln said.

John embraced both women and shook Lincoln's hand.

"What is it you need to talk to Louis and me about?" John asked Marty.

"It will wait until morning, when we're all together. Now, we should get some rest. There may be very little rest for us in the near future."

The three left John alone at the lake.

. . .

"I need to pick up my things at the hotel and make a phone call before you take me back to Sloan's Lake tomorrow morning," Marty said, when they reached Lincoln's loft.

"No problem."

"How long can you hold the Rizzos?"

"Their weapons are licensed, so not for long. I think we can put them through red tape until mid-afternoon. But I can personally put them on a plane back to California and tell them they can pick up their guns from the San Francisco PD at their convenience—if they pay the postage."

"Great. Can we go up to the roof?"

They went up to the roof.

"Tell me about your father," Marty asked.

Lincoln told her of the trouble he had put himself in during college, and what Frank had done to rescue him.

"I had to stand by and watch him indicted, tried, convicted, and put away for life. I have been trying, somehow, to make up for it ever since."

"So, you joined the police department."

"Straight out of college."

"He did what he needed to do for his son. I'm sure he has no regrets and that he's proud of you. I would love to meet him sometime."

"Anytime you like."

"Did you ever find out what was in those small packages?"

"Never."

Marty then told Lincoln about the folder she had among her things at the hotel—several documents that held the answers to an eighty year old mystery. She spoke with a mixture of excitement and sadness. Lincoln let her speak without interruption.

"What will you do?" he asked.

"I have some ideas, but ultimately it will be up to Louis and John."

THIRTY SEVEN

Friday.

Lincoln Bonner sat in his truck in front of the Brown Palace Hotel while Martina ran in to pick up her bag. Up in her room, she called Sammy Orso.

"I just got a call from Richie Rizzo. He said the Denver PD is releasing them in a few hours and putting them on a plane."

"I know," Marty said. "I need to talk with Vincent."

"Vincent told you that you need to talk with me."

"I know that, also. But I need to talk with Vincent, and I don't have time to argue."

There was no sound from the other end of the line for several minutes. Finally, Vincent spoke.

"Richie and Jimmy are being put on a plane."

"I know that, Vinnie. It's all right, they just get in my way. I was going to ask you to call them back anyway. Hold the tips of your thumb and index finger a half-inch apart. That's how close I am to finding John Agnello, and probably his grandfather as well. Just give me some time."

"If you find them, you'll need some muscle to get them here. I can send Sammy and a few of his men."

"No. It won't work. They won't come to you without a fight, and you'll wind up with one or both of them dead. I can get them out there myself, it's what I do. Trust me."

"How much time?"

"I'm not sure. A week? I can do this."

"Okay. I'll give you a week. Then I'm sending in the troops. Keep in touch, Marty."

"Absolutely."

Twenty minutes later, in front of the house on Sloan's Lake, Lincoln asked Marty again if they needed his help.

"You've done much more than we had the right to ask. Even after finding out how easily I can lie. Please let my father know when the Rizzo brothers will be arriving in San Francisco."

"I'll call him as soon as they're on the plane. Will I see you again?"

"You will, if I have anything to say about it."

Marty gave him a quick kiss on the cheek, jumped out of the truck, and walked into the house.

Marty found Louis and John in the kitchen. John was pouring coffee into two cups.

"Good morning. Have a seat. Coffee?"

"Sure. Have any doughnuts?" Marty said, sitting at the table with Louis. "Just kidding."

John brought cups to Marty and Louis. Then poured another for himself and joined them.

"Last night, I meant to ask about your grandfather," Louis said.

Martina reached into her bag, pulled out a manila folder, and placed it on the table.

"I saw my grandfather two weeks ago," Marty said, "and he gave me this."

New Jersey and San Francisco.
Several weeks earlier.

When Phil Nolan walked into the Woodbridge Township Police Building, Officer Bob Steele rose from his seat at the front desk.

He picked something up from behind the desk.

"I have something for you, Chief."

"My birthday isn't until next month, Bob, but I appreciate the thought. What made you think I would like a briefcase that looks as if it went down with the *Titanic*?"

"Do you know the Costco they're planning to build out on Rahway Avenue?"

"Yes, Bob, I do. I hear complaints every day from our good citizens. How it's going to kill the mom and pop businesses. As if there's anything I can do about it."

"I heard they sell paper towels in packages of twenty-four."

"We should pick up a package when they open. As often as this place gets cleaned it should last us about ten years. What's your point? Are you leading to the story of that briefcase?"

"Yes."

"Then by all means, clue me in."

"A backhoe operator dug it up where they're clearing land for the store."

"Okay."

"He brought it to his foreman and the foreman brought it here while you were out. He didn't want to open it, but he thought it could be returned to the owner. Should I bring it to your office?"

"No, put it on your desk. You may want to lay it on some newspaper. But not today's paper, I haven't read it yet. I need coffee. Can I bring you a cup?"

"No, thank you."

"Okay. Put it on your desk, Bob. I'll be right back, and we'll check it out together."

Chief Nolan returned, sat at Bob's desk, placed the coffee down, and reached for the briefcase.

"It has a lock." Bob said, standing near the desk.

"I doubt it will be a problem, Bob. And please sit down, you're in my light."

288

Nolan gave the clasp a pull and it popped open easily.

In the case were some papers wrapped in plastic, and a California driver's license in a plastic sleeve. Whatever else the briefcase had held was deteriorated beyond recognition.

"See if there is anything you can find out about this guy," Nolan said, handing the driver's license to Bob.

"Should I call the San Francisco Police Department?" Steele said, after looking at the address on the license.

"Sure, Bob, that would be a fine place to start."

"This license expired in 1938."

"You'll make detective yet, Bob. Let me know how you do," Nolan said, rising from his seat. "I'll be in my office."

An hour later Bob was standing in Chief Nolan's office doorway.

"Come in. Tell me about it."

"He's deceased."

"I'm not surprised. If I did the math correctly, according his birth date he was born one hundred five years ago. Find any family?"

"A son."

"And?"

"He said he would appreciate it greatly if we could send the briefcase to him in California. He said he would pay the postage."

"That won't be necessary. We can handle the postage. We're here to serve. Did you get an address?"

"Yes."

"Go across to Abe's Grocery, try to find an empty box suitable for packing the briefcase and get it to the post office before they close."

"Yes, Chief."

"And, Bob," Nolan said, stopping Officer Steele at the door.

"Yes, sir."

"Good job. Thank you."

. . .

By the time of his retirement at seventy, Richard Harding had risen to Chief Assistant District Attorney in San Francisco.

Harding had a passion for seeing that those who broke the law were held accountable.

When his wife passed away, Harding bought a house in Sausalito and purchased a boat to dock at the marina. His second passion was sailing.

When Richard received the package from New Jersey he called his son, telling Jack he needed to see him as soon as possible.

"It has to do with your grandfather," Richard said, "and the Leones and Agnellos."

Jack called his daughter, and he and Martina went to see Richard.

When they arrived, Richard showed them the documents found wrapped in the briefcase and explained how the briefcase had been discovered and had come to him.

"It was dug up at a location close to where my father was killed in the railroad accident seventy years ago."

Richard gave his son and his granddaughter time to look over all of the documents.

There were three affidavits Theodore Harding had acquired during the week before his death. A hotel manager in North Beach, the owner of a diner on Columbus Avenue, and a resident of Russian Hill.

The three affidavits taken together indicated that Giuseppe Agnello had arrived in San Francisco around July 4, 1923, had been given directions to the home of Vincenzo Leone with hopes of locating his son, Louis, had never seen Vincenzo, and was last seen in the company of Roberto Leone.

There were also papers torn from a ledger indicating Roberto Leone, possibly without his brother Vincenzo's knowledge, had been smuggling illegal goods into the country through Leone Importing.

Finally, there was a birth certificate issued in New York City confirming, unquestionably, that Giuseppe Agnello was Louis' biological father.

"This suggests Roberto Leone may have been the last person to see Giuseppe Agnello alive," Martina said.

"It suggests something much more heinous. It suggests Roberto murdered Agnello and perhaps later, once learning Louis was Giuseppe's son, not Vincenzo's son, tried to have the young boy killed as well. Vincenzo was killed defending Louis from an assassin in New York. If Roberto did send the killer, he was directly responsible for his own brother's death."

"Why did your father carry these papers to Washington, and not use them against Roberto Leone here?" Jack asked Richard.

"My father had just begun his term as a member Congress in January and had returned to San Francisco in April to celebrate Easter with us. The affidavits were all from that time. I was only twelve, but remember my father talking about a fellow congressman he had met named Alfredo Catalano. We later learned Catalano was Louis Agnello's adoptive father. I believe my father wanted to share his findings with Catalano before deciding on any action, but he never made it back to Washington."

"If he had, it may have ended this madness between the two families seventy years ago," Martina said.

"I don't believe it would have," Richard said. "I believe my father felt, and I would agree, that the affidavits did not provide enough solid evidence to even charge Roberto Leone with murder—in spite of the fact Giuseppe Agnello's remains were found in a warehouse later connected to Leone. And as far as the ledger pages, they were basically stolen—taken without Leone's permission or a warrant."

"So, all of these papers are worthless," Jack said.

"Maybe not," Richard Harding said. "Although the feud

between the Agnellos and Leones began in Sicily, at this point, with Roberto and Bruno Leone gone, it is perpetuated by the false information Salvatore Leone had been fed since he was a young man. If he could be made to understand it was his Uncle Roberto who was actually the enemy, this hundred-year war could finally come to an end."

"So, let's get these documents to him," Martina suggested.

"It would not be enough. There is only one person who could persuade Salvatore Leone, with these documents and his own memories. Someone who was present when Vincenzo Leone was fatally wounded. Then, and only then, could there be the possibility of a truce."

"Louis Agnello," Marty said.

"Yes. We would need to find Louis Agnello, if he is still alive, and bring him with these papers to Salvatore Leone."

"That may not be completely out of the question," Marty said.

PART SIX

DESTINY

It is not in the stars to hold our destiny but in ourselves.

—William Shakespeare

*Only by joy and sorrow does a person know
anything about themselves and their destiny.
They learn what to do and what to avoid.*

—Johann Wolfgang von Goethe

THIRTY EIGHT

Sloan's Lake. Friday.

"So," said John Agnello, "the plan is to put my grandfather and Salvatore Leone in the same room, at the same time, with these documents, for the final showdown."

"It would be a lovely room," Marty said, "right on Stinson Beach looking out to the Pacific Ocean."

"Vincent Leone will not let anyone get near his grandfather without having complete control."

"I think we can get around Vinnie, but we'll need to take Sammy Orso and his boys out of the equation."

"Salvatore Leone knows nothing of this?" Louis Agnello asked, after looking through the papers found in Theodore Harding's briefcase.

"My grandfather thinks not, my father and I agree. We believe no one knew the complete truth of your father's death except Roberto Leone, and possibly his partner-in-crime, Benito Lucchese."

"Lorenzo Lucchese was the name of the man who attacked Vincenzo and me at the hotel in New York in 1924."

"How do you know that?"

"Vincenzo took papers from the assailant which identified him, and he gave them to me when he left me at Alfredo Catalano's doorstep. I still have those papers. I suppose it would not hurt to bring them along."

"Are you sure you want to do this, Grandfather. It's a very

dangerous proposition."

"If it could possibly end this madness, once and for all, it must be done. I'm tired of running and hiding, John, as I'm certain you are as well. I loved Salvatore, and I never wished him or any of his family malicious harm. And both Salvatore and I loved Vincenzo Leone deeply. These documents and the papers of Lorenzo Lucchese, though not incontrovertible proof, strongly point to the guilt of Roberto Leone. Not guilty only for the murder of my father, but also for sending the assassin who killed Vincenzo. Salvatore will either choose to accept these conclusions, or he will not. Salvatore deserves the opportunity to weigh the evidence, and I agree I am the proper person to present it to him. We will need to tell Patricia about our plans, of course. When do we leave for California?"

"Vinnie gave me a week to deliver you and John to him, but Sammy Orso doesn't trust anyone. The man is as cold as ice. He is loyal to Vinnie but, in his mind, he is still working for Roberto Leone. I believe Orso will have eyes on the airport here, and at those in San Francisco and in Oakland. If there is any hope of success, your meeting with Salvatore Leone will need to be arranged on our terms, not Vincent's or Orso's. We can't be found by Sammy Orso until we are *ready* to be found. My grandfather is on a sailing excursion heading down to Mexico. He said we could use his house in Sausalito while he's gone. We can leave tomorrow morning. I can cook dinner for us tonight, give Patricia a break."

"Believe it or not," Louis said, "I do most of the meal preparation around here."

"Great, you and I can prepare dinner together. We'll need to rent a car for the trip."

"A car?" asked John.

"As I said, the airports may not be safe. It should be fun. A road trip. We can do a little sightseeing."

"I have always wanted to visit the Grand Canyon, and Las Vegas," said Louis.

"Sure, why not."

"And we don't need to rent a vehicle. Follow me."

They walked to the garage behind the house, and Louis asked John to pull the door open.

"Wow," Marty said.

It was a 1982 Buick Riviera convertible.

Jet black, with black leather interior.

"My son, Vito, gave it to me when he moved me out here. Vito said with 330 days of sunshine each year in Denver a ragtop, which is what your father called it, John, was the way to go. I take it around the lake a few times once a week, it has been driven less than thirty thousand miles."

"Wow," Marty said, again, "this road trip *is* going to be fun."

San Francisco.

"Well? What's new?" asked Vinnie Leone, looking across his desk at Sammy Orso.

"Richie Rizzo called from the Denver Police station. He and his brother are being escorted onto a plane in a few hours. Richie gave me all the flight information."

"I would like you to pick them up at the airport personally, and I want to know how they managed to get themselves arrested."

"Vincent, when you spoke to Marty earlier today?"

"Yes?"

"Can I speak freely?"

"Yes, Sammy, what?"

"Did she say how she expects to get Louis and John Agnello out here on her own, if she can find them at all?"

"Finding people and bringing them in is what she does."

"Is it?"

"What does that mean?"

"You have a great deal of faith in someone you met in a bar less than a month ago. And you never asked me to check her out."

"*I* checked her out."

"How?"

"I spoke with her business partner, Ted Banks. Koslov and Banks Investigation."

"In person?"

"On the telephone."

"Do you have an address for them?"

"No."

"Do you still have the phone number?"

"Yes."

"Let me have it, if you don't mind."

"What are you thinking?" Vinnie asked, after giving Orso the number.

"I want to have eyes on the airports in Denver, at Oakland, and here in San Francisco. If she can get Louis and John Agnello out here, we need to know where they are at all times."

"She said she will let me know."

"When?"

"She said she would keep in touch. Are you questioning my judgment?"

"Vincent, I mean no disrespect. I just want to be sure we are in control. Please let me know if you hear from her again today. I will pick up Richie and Jimmy and find out what happened with them in Denver, and I will see what if anything I can learn about Koslov and Banks. I have nothing but the wishes and the safety of your grandfather and yourself in mind. If you trust that, please allow me to do my job and do not take offense."

"Do what you feel you need to do."

· · ·

"Carl."

"Yes, Jack?"

"Can you go out to the airport with me?"

"You know I would, partner, but I really need to get this work done for Captain Lopez today or she will have my hide. And I would like to be out of here before dark. In addition, you know how much I hate going to the airport. I don't even like going out there to put my wife on a plane to visit her mother, and those are some of my most pleasant moments."

"Because your wife is leaving?"

"Because my mother-in-law is not coming here. If you need company, take Hanover. The kid got his detective's shield over a month ago, and Lopez won't send him out. Look at the poor kid," Taylor said, pointing to Hanover at a desk across the room. "He doesn't know what to do with himself."

Jack came up behind Hanover.

"Detective Hanover."

The kid almost jumped out of his chair when Jack spoke his name.

"Detective Harding."

"It's Jack, and you're Melvin."

"I prefer Mel, sir."

"Drop the sir, Mel. It's Jack. Would you like to go for a ride?"

"With you?"

"With me."

"Yes, Jack."

"Good. Let's go."

At the airport, Harding and Hanover watched Richie and Jimmy Rizzo leave the concourse. They were easy to spot in their near matching outfits. The Rizzos headed toward the exit, the detectives following at a distance.

"I know one of those guys," Hanover said. "Jimmy Rizzo.

We busted him for drunk and disorderly, and assault charges, when I was in uniform. A brawl in a bar. Rizzo nearly destroyed the place and sent the other guy to intensive care."

"Do you think he would remember you?"

"I don't know."

"Wait in the car, I'll stay with them. When we come out, pick me up."

Richie and Jimmy walked out of the terminal.

Jack Harding came out a few moments later and watched the brothers climb into a waiting car.

Hanover pulled up, and Harding jumped into the passenger seat.

"Can you follow at a safe distance without losing them?"

"I think so," Hanover said.

"Don't think too much, Detective. Do it."

"We're being followed," Jimmy Rizzo said from the back seat, as Sammy Orso merged onto the 101.

"I can see that, Jimmy," said Orso. "Now tell me something I don't know."

"The driver is or was a cop. I had a run-in with him a while back."

"That's better. Your turn now, Richie. Tell me about the cops in Denver."

"They came down on us at the same time. It was like they knew exactly where we were. Me in the coffee shop below Bonner's place, and Jimmy in the car down the street."

"And where was Marty?"

"I'm not sure. I saw her walk by the coffee shop and then, when Bonner showed up, I saw her heading the other way carrying a pizza box. I guess she went for food."

"Did she know where you and Jimmy were?"

"Sure, she told us where to be. And you said we should do what she told us."

"Are the two cops still on our tail, Jimmy?" Orso called to the back seat.

"Yes. How do you know they're both cops?"

"Because I know who the older one is. Kind of what you might call a blast from the past. Here we are."

Orso had exited the 101 at Exit 433A and pulled over at Eighteenth Street and San Bruno Avenue.

"What are we doing here?" Richie asked.

"You and your brother are getting out."

"How do we get home from here?"

"Figure it out. And stay near your cell phones."

Hanover had pulled over a block behind the other vehicle. Harding and Hanover watched the Rizzos get out of the car. The brothers looked around as if they had been dropped off on Mars.

"What now?" Hanover asked.

"Follow Orso."

"Orso?"

"The driver of that car is Sammy Orso. The man is a legend. We have been trying to put him away for decades."

Orso pulled away.

Hanover and Harding followed.

Orso drove San Bruno Avenue to Twentieth Street and parked his vehicle between Arkansas and Connecticut streets. He left his car and walked into 1616 Twentieth Street. The sign above the front door identified the building as the Potrero Branch Library.

"This is a surprise," Harding said. "Orso doesn't impress me as much of a reader. I guess we wait."

Thirty minutes later, after several telephone calls and some internet research, Orso called Vincent Leone.

"Where are you?"

"At the hospital," Vinnie said.

"What happened?"

"My grandmother broke her hip. She climbed up on a chair and she took a fall. Eighty-three years old and she's trying to change a fucking light bulb."

"Will she be all right?"

"She'll live, but she'll be laid up in the hospital for a week or two."

"Your grandfather?"

"He stayed out at the beach."

"Vitale and Gennaro?"

"They are there with him."

"I need to speak with you right away," Orso said.

"Saint Francis Memorial on Hyde Street. Third Floor."

Orso rushed out of the library and jumped into his car.

"Here we go," Harding said.

Hanover started their car, and they followed.

Twenty minutes later, Sammy Orso was out of his vehicle again and quickly through the front entrance of Saint Francis Memorial Hospital.

"What now?" Hanover asked.

"I don't know. Do you think he's just running us around?"

"I don't know."

"We need to get back before the captain starts asking questions. If she finds out I've been trying to keep tags on Orso and Vincent Leone without her blessings she won't be happy, and if Lopez finds out I took you along the shit will hit the fan. We can't do it on company time. With Detective Taylor's help, I'm hoping we can keep both Sammy Orso and Vincent Leone in our sights most of the time."

"I can help."

"I wouldn't ask, you would be going out on a limb."

"It's better than being tied to a desk."

"Let me think about it, but not a word to anyone except

Detective Taylor or me."

"No problem. Who is Vincent Leone?"

"It is a long story, Mel. I'll tell you what I can on the way to the station."

Orso found Vincent in the third-floor visitors' lounge.

"I called the number you gave me for Koslov and Banks. It was out of service," Orso began. "I tried reaching Martina on her cell, no answer, and I called the Brown Palace Hotel in Denver. She checked out this morning. We were followed from the airport by two cops, one of them was Jack Harding."

"I know that name," Vincent said.

"You should. Harding was part of the national task force that sent your Uncle Roberto to San Quentin in 1982. Vito Agnello was also on the task force. Harding's father, Richard, worked with Louis Agnello on the Phillip Mann case, which put Roberto in Alcatraz in 1953."

"Why the fuck is Jack Harding following you? Leone Importing has been clean for years."

"It's not about Leone Importing, Vincent, it's about the Agnellos."

"What do you mean?"

"Harding has a daughter who is also a San Francisco police detective, currently on vacation. Martina Harding."

"Goddammit. What the fuck are they up to?"

"I'm not sure, Vincent. Either they are planning to send John and Louis Agnello into hiding again or planning to come out here."

"Come here why?"

"To somehow settle this once and for all."

"So, what now?"

"We have the airports covered, but I'm beginning to believe if they are headed this way it won't be by air."

"Train? Bus?"

"If it were me, I would drive."

"If they drive, how will we know where they are?"

"We won't, until they get here. So, now we need to be ready. We cover Martina's residence, and those of her father and grandfather. I want to have two more men with Salvatore out at the beach with Gennaro and Vitale. There are only so many men available who we can trust. I will need to pull Giambi out of the Denver airport today, and the others out of the airports here in San Francisco and Oakland tomorrow. I'll personally keep an eye on Jack Harding, which shouldn't be very difficult since he will probably be watching us. May I speak my mind, Vincent?"

"Yes."

"I am aware of Salvatore's wishes. I have heard it many times. Although I don't understand why, I know your grandfather wants Louis and John Agnello brought to him alive—but that is not the easiest course of action."

"What are you saying?"

"Your father, and Roberto, wanted nothing more passionately than to see Louis and John Agnello dead."

"Are you suggesting they be killed before my grandfather sees them?"

"Yes. At the first opportunity. The longer they live, the more danger they present to Salvatore. And to you."

"Jack and Martina Harding won't go outside the law."

"The Hardings may already be operating outside the police department. When it comes to supporting the Agnellos, as we've witnessed many times before, they are a law unto themselves. There's no way to predict how far they are willing to go."

"I'll have to think about that."

"It would help to know what Salvatore is thinking."

"I'll speak with him. Now I need to check on my grandmother. I want to know everything you know the minute you know it."

"You will."

. . .

"Can we talk?" Jack Harding asked at the office door.

"Sure," Captain Lopez said. "Come in and take a seat. Have you heard from Martina? How is she enjoying her time off?"

"That's what I wanted to talk with you about, and I don't think you're going to like it."

THIRTY NINE

Southern Colorado. Saturday.

The black Buick Riviera purred like a kitten.

Cruising south on Interstate 25 between Colorado Springs and Pueblo at seventy miles per hour, convertible top down.

Louis Agnello was a very healthy eighty-nine-year-old. His legs and back were strong—from his long walks around the lake once or twice a day, working in his vegetable garden in spring and summer, and shoveling snow in winter.

Louis said he was only good for three hours at a time behind the wheel and couldn't drive at night. John had only an expired Italian driver's license.

So, it had been agreed that Martina would do the bulk of the driving.

But Louis had insisted on taking the wheel for the first leg of the trip.

He promised his passengers he could get them from Denver to one of the most spectacular train rides in the country.

Just north of Pueblo, Louis exited I-25 and picked up Route 50 West to Canon City.

"That's an eyesore," Marty said, from the back seat.

"Colorado State Penitentiary," Louis said. "Jack Gilbert Graham was executed there."

"Who was he?" John asked.

"Did your father ever tell you of the day I took him and your Uncle Joe to game three of the 1955 World Series?"

"When the Dodgers finally whipped the Yankees. Dad talked about it all the time."

"Did you know I might have been killed that day if not for the ballgame?"

"Yes, my father talked about that also."

"Well, I escaped death again less than five weeks later."

"I don't recall hearing *that* story," John said.

"Your grandfather figures in that story also, Martina."

"I'm all ears."

"There was a conference of state and federal prosecutors in Denver at the beginning of November. I wasn't planning to attend, it being so soon after my colleague Jim Baldwin had been assassinated by a cousin of the Leones—but when I heard your grandfather would be there, I decided to attend. I flew out of LaGuardia on United flight six-twenty-nine. After stopping in Chicago, the plane continued to my destination in Denver. The route had two additional stops scheduled, to Portland and Seattle. Soon after leaving Denver, the plane exploded over Longmont, Colorado and crashed—killing all forty-four passengers, including Jack Gilbert Graham's mother. Graham had planted a bomb in his mother's checked suitcase, after purchasing more than thirty thousand dollars in flight insurance while at the Denver airport. Jack Graham was twenty-three years old, and apparently not very fond of Mom."

"And forty-three innocent people died," Marty said. "Insane."

"Yes, and I had spoken to some of them before I left the plane. There was no law in the books at the time against placing a bomb in a plane, so they had to prosecute Jack on a single count of premeditated murder in the death of his mother. Graham was tried, convicted, incarcerated, and finally executed at the prison here in 1957."

"All of that death because members of a family couldn't figure out how to get along," John said.

"Families can be very tricky business, John," Louis Agnello

said, pulling the Buick into a parking area. "Here we are. The Royal Gorge Railroad. You kids are going to love this."

Four hours later, they were back on Route 50 traveling west.

Marty driving.

"This car is a dream," she said.

"Not so much when you need to fill her with gasoline," Louis said.

"What next?" John asked.

"I've always wanted to see Telluride," Marty said. "I've heard it's a beautiful little city. I thought we would have dinner there and stay for the night. It's on the way."

"On the way to where?" John asked.

"On the way to the Grand Canyon."

"Will you be calling Vincent Leone?" Louis asked.

"I suppose I should. But first, I need to figure out what I'm going to say."

San Francisco. Saturday.

"Martina Harding lives in the Upper Haight. Jack Harding lives in the Richmond with his wife whose maiden name, by the way, is Koslov. Richard Harding lives in Sausalito. And both Hardings work out of the Vallejo Street Station. I can have all the locations covered, as soon as we can pull our men out of the airports."

"Do it now," Vincent Leone said. "What happens if they turn up at any of those places?"

"We try to grab Louis and John Agnello unless you want to go the other way."

"I haven't decided yet, I need to talk with my grandfather. In any event, none of the others are to be hit. We cannot be killing cops. It may have been the way things were done in

New York City, back in Roberto and my father's time, but it won't wash here and now."

"Understood. The sooner you talk to Salvatore the better."

"I'm taking him to visit my grandmother at the hospital in the morning. I'll speak with him then."

"Good. I don't suppose you've heard from Martina."

"I haven't."

"I have no idea what she would say to you, *if* she ever calls, but you may want to think about what you will say to her if she does."

"I'll do that, and Sammy."

"Yes."

"Make sure everyone understands. *No one* gets killed unless *I* say so."

Telluride.

They took neighboring rooms at the Telluride Mountainside Inn, in a setting surrounded by lush woods and mountain views, fronted by the San Miguel River.

Once checked in, they walked down into the town center to look for a restaurant.

After dinner, back at the hotel, Louis fell asleep immediately.

John watched his grandfather sleep for a while, and then went outside and tapped on Marty's door.

"Would you like to take a walk?" John asked.

"Absolutely. I'm on the telephone, give me a minute."

John walked over to a nearby picnic table, sat, and lit a cigarette.

Moments later, Marty joined him.

"That was Lincoln. I wanted him to know we were having a fine time."

"You and Lincoln got along well."

"Lincoln is a good man, and a very brave man. Battling his

demons has given him great courage."

"Frank Bonner raised his son well."

"As Vito Agnello raised his son well. Let's walk."

They strolled quietly for some time before John finally broke the silence.

"How do you think this will end?"

"How would you like it to end?"

"I'm thirty-five years old, Martina, and I haven't felt safe since I was twelve. I would just like to feel free."

"Then that should be our goal."

"Louis fell asleep instantly. It amazes me."

"That he can fall asleep so quickly?"

"That he can sleep at all, after all he's been through."

"Louis is a survivor, he has a strong will to live."

"He has lost so much. A father he never had the chance to know, and a father he grew to love. He lost two sons, a grandson, and his wife. Why would he have so strong a will to keep going?"

"Because he hasn't lost *everything.*"

"I don't understand."

"When someone we love and care for dies, John, we feel loss. *One* person is lost forever to all who were left behind. But the one who dies loses *everyone.* Your grandfather survives because he does not want to lose you and Patricia."

"I wish I had that kind of courage."

"The fact that you're here, John, convinces me you do have that kind of courage. It should convince you as well."

FORTY

Stinson Beach. Sunday.

When Vincent Leone arrived to pick up his grandfather for the trip to Saint Francis Memorial Hospital, Sammy Orso was already at Salvatore's home.

Orso had recruited two additional men for security, and he was giving them a tour of the house and property.

The regulars, Vitale and Gennaro, stood at their usual posts at the front and rear entrances.

When Vincent climbed out of his car, Sammy approached him.

"I'll send Gennaro with you into the city."

"I need to talk to my grandfather alone, and I can't see any danger. If you're correct about Marty driving from Denver, they won't be anywhere near here for at least a day or two. If old man Agnello is like my grandfather, they will need to stop every two hours for a bathroom. I'll call you when we're about to head back, so you don't worry too much."

"I'm paid to worry, Vincent. Have you heard from Marty?"

"No. And do me a favor. I'll tell you if and when she calls. Meanwhile stop asking and just keep doing what you're doing. Got it?"

"Got it."

. . .

"I think Louis and John Agnello are on their way here," Vincent said to Salvatore, as they drove south on the Shoreline Highway.

"What do you mean you *think*, Vincent?"

"The way I see it, they have two choices. Come here to confront us and see where the chips fall—or go deeper underground. Louis is close to ninety years old, and John Agnello has spent the past five years locked up. I think they've decided it's time to come up for air. We have identified the places they're likely to show up, and we have them all covered. But, there's a problem. They're being protected by San Francisco police detectives, either officially or unofficially, so it would be difficult if not impossible to take custody. It would be far easier to take them out when they're in the open."

"Take them out? You mean *gun them down?*"

"Yes."

"Absolutely not, Vincent, and it grieves me deeply that I need to repeat it again and again. I want Louis Agnello standing before me alive. Please, assure me that you have finally heard me."

"I heard you."

"Good. Please stop where we can pick up flowers for my wife."

Arizona. Sunday.

Marty had done all of the driving between Telluride and Tuba City.

They had travelled along Route 145, a section of the San Juan Skyway, winding through San Juan National Forest, following Snow Spur Creek and then the Dolores River where the Snow Spur ended.

They had stopped briefly at Trout Lake.

From Lizard Head Pass, elevation 10,222 feet, they viewed a number of thirteen and fourteen thousand footers, including El Diente Peak, Lizard Head Peak, and Mount Wilson.

The Buick Riviera, and her able captain, handled the often challenging and sometimes treacherous road gracefully.

They passed through Dolores, stopped at Cortez for lunch, and took a detour to visit Canyons of the Ancients National Monument.

A park attendant, member of the Ute Nation, informed them that ancient Pueblo peoples had constructed dwellings in the area as early as AD 750. More than six thousand distinct structures had been identified, and excavations and restorations had been ongoing since the 1920s.

John was reminded of Pompeii.

Backtracking to Cortez, they picked up Route 491 South and eventually rejoined Route 160 West at Four Corners—where Colorado, Utah, New Mexico, and Arizona met.

Much of the landscape they travelled through was within the borders of tribal reservations—Ute, Navajo, and Hopi.

The small towns they passed through after crossing into Arizona—Teec Nos Pos, Red Mesa, Kayenta, Tonalea—were inhabited primarily by Native Americans.

They were always greeted warmly and generously, particularly Louis.

"There is a great respect for elders among these peoples," Louis said. "Being an old man does have some advantages."

By early evening they had arrived at Tuba City.

They checked into the Moenkopi Inn on Legacy Lane and had dinner in a Hopi restaurant at the hotel.

Once again, Louis was asleep soon after dinner.

Once again, Marty and John talked for a while before calling it a night.

San Francisco. Monday.

"Jack, someone has been watching the house."

"I know. I spotted him out there last night," Jack told his wife.

"Is this something that should worry me?"

"We're safe. Vincent Leone is hoping Martina will show up here."

"Is our daughter in danger, Jack?"

Tuba City. Monday.

John Agnello woke up Monday morning to the knocking on his door.

"One minute," he called.

He quickly dressed and noticed Louis had already left the room.

When he stepped outside, he found Marty standing there with a wide smile on her face.

"You need to see this. Follow me."

She led him to the hotel office and stopped him in front of the window.

Louis was sitting with the proprietor of the hotel, a Hopi near to Louis' age. They were drinking coffee and eating omelets smothered in green chili.

They two old men were talking animatedly and laughing often.

"I'd hate to interrupt them," Marty said. "Let's get breakfast."

After breakfast, they found Louis sitting in front of the hotel room.

"There are few things as beautiful, or as comfortable, as a handmade redwood chair," he said.

"You made a new friend," Marty said.

"He was born less than ten miles from this spot. We were born the in same year, 1916, when his mother, a tribal princess, was fifteen. She was photographed by Edward Sheriff

Curtis when she was five years old. His name is *Mochni*, talking bird, because his first cries at birth were said to sound like those of a crow."

"We spied on you, you shared a few laughs."

"We were reminiscing about our departed wives, how funny both women could be at times."

"Grandmother made Joey and me laugh all the time, with stories about our father and Uncle Joe when they were our age."

"We should get started," Marty said. "It's a ninety-mile drive."

"I can drive ninety miles," Louis said.

"You're on."

"Will we return here this evening?"

"We can, if you like," Marty said.

"Mochni invited us all to attend the wedding of his great-granddaughter. The invitation is quite an honor. What do you think, John?"

"Sounds good to me. I'm in."

"Marty?"

"I wouldn't miss it, though I don't have proper clothing for a wedding."

"No need to worry. I'm sure the only dress anyone will notice is the bride's."

San Francisco. Monday.

When Jack Harding reached the Vallejo Street Station, Carl Taylor was waiting.

"I just came back from Martina's place. Leone has a man watching."

"There's one at my place also," Jack said. "These guys are not very proficient at making themselves invisible, even my wife spotted him."

"They're all high school dropouts. Have you heard from Marty?"

"She said she would call when they reach Las Vegas. I'm going out to my dad's place, to make sure Sammy Orso is at least trying to do his job. We meet with Captain Lopez this afternoon."

"I can hardly wait."

Sammy Orso watched Richard Harding's house in Sausalito from the marina below. Sammy saw Jack Harding's car arrive and watched Jack go into the house.

Jack found an envelope sitting on the kitchen table, with the name Louis Agnello written on the outside in his father's hand. He picked it up and took it back to his car.

Orso watched Jack drive off.

Ten minutes later, Orso heard the sound of his name from behind the bench where he sat. He turned to the voice.

"We need to talk," Jack Harding said.

"Have a seat."

"I won't be long," Jack said, coming around to the front of the bench. "We both know where we stand. You are watching us, and we are watching you. Martina is bringing Louis and John Agnello here of their own free will. Louis wants to talk with Salvatore Leone, alone. I understand the house at Stinson Beach is a lovely setting."

"That's not going to happen."

"I think the decision is Salvatore's to make. Speak to Vincent, I'll be in touch," Jack said, as he walked away.

A few minutes later, Richie Rizzo joined Orso at the bench.

"Well?" Sammy asked.

"You called it. I followed him down from the house and put the thing under his car when he came over to speak with you."

Moran Point. Grand Canyon.

Standing on the South Rim, they could see the North Rim eight miles away.

Below them, the Colorado River cut through the canyon.

"Wow," was all Marty could think to say.

"It reminds me of being out on the ocean," Louis said.

"How so?" John asked.

"It reminds me how small we are."

San Francisco.

"So, now what, Sammy?"

"The stakeouts aren't going to do us any good now. We wait to hear from Jack Harding and keep tabs on him, Taylor, and whoever else is helping them."

"Do you think you have anyone at all who can keep track of them *without* being made?"

"I admit I underestimated Harding. I assure you it won't happen again."

"Sammy, what I need are guarantees."

Orso took a small black plastic object from his pocket. It was the size of a disposable cigarette lighter.

"What is it?"

"A monitor for a tracking device planted on Jack Harding's car. It will let us know where he is at all times. I have always succeeded in my responsibility to serve and protect the Leone family. Please trust I will not fail now."

"Alright, Sammy, but my patience is wearing very thin."

"Thank you," Orso said.

"I spoke with Salvatore. If you want to thank me, get your hands on Louis Agnello and get him to me without messing a single hair on his head."

Arizona and Nevada. Tuesday.

The three travelers agreed the Hopi wedding was nothing less than magical.

Marty and John waited in the Buick while Louis and Mochni said their farewells.

"Mochni told me the Hopi tribal name came from *Hopituh Shi-nu-mu*, the peaceful people, and he presented me with my own Hopi name, *Pahana*—Lost White Brother."

They picked up Route 40 at Flagstaff, Route 93 at Kingman, and crossed into Nevada at Lake Mead. Six hours after leaving Tuba City, they were driving down the Las Vegas Strip.

"Can we stay at the Flamingo," Louis asked.

"We can stay anywhere you like," Marty said. "Why the Flamingo?"

"Have you heard of the time I met Benjamin Siegel in New York, before he came West and invented this town?"

"Bugsy Siegel?" John said.

"Yes, Bugsy Siegel. But I must be boring you both terribly with all of this ancient history."

"Are you going to torture us or tell us the story?"

"Well, John, if you insist. Ben came out to see Lansky at the restaurant where Meyer and I were having dinner..."

"I need to take a shower and make a few phone calls," Martina said, in the elevator up to their rooms.

"I will buy a roll of quarters and play the slot machines," Louis said.

"And I'm going to look for a card table. The only thing other than Frank Bonner that made the past five years almost bearable were the poker games."

"Let's meet at the Wildlife Habitat in two hours and decide about dinner."

"Wildlife Habitat?" John said.

"Flamingos and ducks and turtles," Marty said, holding the brochure she had picked up in the lobby. "Oh, boy."

"Maybe after dinner we can catch a show," John said.

"Is Wayne Newton in town?" Louis asked.

"That would be terrific, Grandfather, but he's not."

"Wayne Newton? Are you two serious?"

"I was joking, Marty," Louis said. "I prefer Barry Manilow."

"I *wasn't* joking," John said, "I checked. Wayne Newton is performing in Joliet, Illinois."

"You two would make a great comedy team. Maybe you can schedule an audition while we're here."

"We're in Las Vegas, Dad. We'll spend the night and hit the road again sometime early tomorrow. We decided we would like to stop at Big Sur, for a day or two. I'm expecting we'll arrive in the Bay Area by Thursday, Friday the latest."

"Vincent Leone knows who you are, and that you're on the way. He's been preparing. I'm looking for a safe place for you to land, both of our places *and* Sausalito are being watched. Carl and I met with the Captain. Lopez can't officially give us a green light, but she can look the other way. And she cannot give us any more bodies. It's just you, me, Taylor, and Hanover."

"Melvin?"

"He prefers Mel."

"He should. He's a little green, isn't he? Is he up for this?"

"We all start green, Martina. I've been running him around for several days. I think he'll be fine, and we can use the help."

"Okay."

"Call me again as soon as you have a more definite idea about when you'll arrive."

"I will."

. . .

Louis and John found Marty at the Wildlife Habitat pond, surrounded by pink flamingos.

"They come from Chile," Marty said.

"They look like they would rather be back in South America," John said. "Did you speak with your father?"

"I did. Vincent knows we're on the way, and now he also knows who I am. My father is working on a plan for when we get in. So, how did the *big time* gamblers do?"

"I won my last poker hand and managed to break even, and *Pahana* here hit a two-thousand-dollar jackpot at a slot machine."

"Wow," Marty said. "I hope you have fun spending it."

"I did. I bought tickets for a show at Caesar's Palace," Louis said, taking three tickets from his shirt pocket, "and what is left over should be enough to cover the cost of our rooms and the best steak and lobster we can find."

"Donny and Marie Osmond?" Marty said, playfully.

"The Red Piano."

"Elton John. Wow, again."

"Does he put on a good show?"

"From what I've heard, it could be the concert equivalent of the Royal Gorge Railroad ride," Marty said. "We should all be feeling very lucky."

"We are very lucky every morning we wake up alive," Louis said.

"Let's hope our luck holds out," John said. "Meanwhile steak, lobster, and Elton John sound damn good."

FORTY ONE

Monterey. Thursday.

After spending the night at the Cannery Row Inn, and putting a dent into the hotel's breakfast buffet, they walked down to San Carlos Beach Park.

Marty pulled up at a bench on the beach.

"I need to call my father," she said. "I'll catch up to you."

John and Louis continued walking.

"We're in Monterey. We'll be up there early this afternoon."

"Good," Jack said. "Get to 1550 Cabrillo Highway South. It's an isolated house in Half Moon Bay. Take Route One and it will become Cabrillo Highway. You will need to exit north of the house, at Main Street, and come back down on the southbound side. There is no rush, but I would like you to be there when I arrive at four. It should take two hours from where you are."

"We'll be there. Is Mom around?"

"She is. Hold on."

San Francisco International Airport.

The taxi driver had been sitting for quite a while watching the terminal exit door when a man came out and walked to the cab. The man opened the back door and climbed in.

"Going into the city?"

"Vallejo Street Police Station."

"Turning yourself in?" the cab driver said, with a laugh.

"How could you possibly have known that?" his passenger said, then he laughed also.

Vallejo Street Station.

Arriving at the station, Jack collected Taylor and Hanover.

They convened in one of the interrogation rooms.

"I need to leave soon to meet Marty. It could take ninety minutes to get down there if I run into traffic, and I told her I would be there by four. At four, you pick Vincent Leone up at the Transamerica Building and get him over to my father's place in Sausalito. Here is the address," Jack said, "and the key."

"What about Orso?" Taylor asked.

"Sammy will be busy with me."

"How do we get Leone out of his office?" Hanover asked.

"Watch me," Taylor said.

Sammy Orso phoned Vincent.

"How is your tracking device working?" Leone asked.

"Good. Harding is at the Vallejo Street Station. We're parked a few blocks away. I have Giambi and the Rizzo brothers with me."

He paid the cab driver in front, entered the police station, and walked over to the desk sergeant.

"I'd like to speak to Detective Harding."

"Which one?"

"Either."

"In that case, here's Jack Harding coming our way."

"Detective Harding," the visitor said, when Jack reached them.

"Yes?"

"I'm looking for John Agnello."

"And who are you?"

He removed a wallet from his pocket and opened it to show Harding his identification.

Jack looked at the ID, then at the man's face.

"Come with me," Harding said.

Half Moon Bay.

The house on Cabrillo Highway was fronted by a wood picket fence that opened to a gravel driveway. Jack pulled in, followed the drive around to the back of the house, and parked beside the Buick Riviera.

Before leaving the vehicle, Jack reached into the glovebox and removed a Smith and Wesson .38.

"Keep this close," he said, handing the weapon to his passenger.

Marty heard the car pull up, picked up her .357, and went to the window. Then she placed the gun down again and opened the back door.

"Nice ride," Jack said, turning from the convertible.

"You have no idea. Where did you find this place?"

"Mel Hanover. Belongs to his grandmother. The family had to put her into a nursing home."

"Sad. But it's perfect. And it's really good to see you," Marty said, embracing her father.

"Good seeing you, also."

"And you," Marty said, to the man with her father, "aren't you way out of your jurisdiction?"

"Not any further than you were in Denver."

"Come in, the boys are in the living room."

John rose from his chair when they walked in.

"This is a surprise. What brought you out here?"

"Frank told me to do what I felt I needed do," Lincoln Bonner said, shaking John's hand.

"John, Louis, this is my father, Jack," Marty said.

"I remember you as a young boy," Jack said, shaking John's hand.

"And I remember *you* as a young boy, Jack," Louis said.

"We need to be ready. Sammy Orso is on his way, surely with others."

"Do you think he was able to follow you?" Marty asked.

"They planted a tracking device on my car."

"If you knew, why didn't you remove it?" John asked.

"Because Dad didn't want to have to guess whether or not Orso was on him," Marty answered for her father. "This way we're sure they're coming. Should we be expecting them soon?"

"They'll want to look over the terrain before they make a move."

John reached into a gym bag at his feet and pulled out police special.

"Have you had that all along?" Marty asked.

"Since Wyoming, cleaned and oiled and ready to go—though I haven't pointed it at a person in many years."

"Are you really anticipating a shootout?" Lincoln asked.

"I may be able to talk Orso down if I tell him we have Vincent, but you can never tell with Sammy Orso."

"Do we have Vincent?" Marty asked.

"That depends on Carl Taylor and Mel Hanover."

San Francisco.

When Taylor and Hanover came into the offices of Leone Importing, the reception desk was unoccupied.

Mel followed Carl to the door of Vincent's private office and knocked.

"Who is it?"

Without answering, Carl opened the door and they walked in.

"I'm Detective Taylor and this is Detective Hanover. You need to come with us."

"What are you talking about? I'm not going anywhere with you."

"We picked up a Sammy Orso near the Vallejo Street Station, carrying a concealed weapon, and we're holding him. Orso claims he works for you, we need you to come down to clear it up. We insist," Taylor said.

"In that case, I'll meet you down there."

"We'll be happy to give you a ride, sir," Hanover said, "and get you back here as soon as possible."

When they were approaching the on-ramp to the Golden Gate Bridge, Vincent Leone was sure they weren't going to the Vallejo Street Station.

Half Moon Bay.

The house sat on a large lot, with no other buildings nearby. It was well concealed from the highway by a row of shore pines.

They drove around the property and spotted the two vehicles parked in back.

Sammy Orso parked a hundred yards from the house. He told the others to remain in the car.

Orso walked up the drive, stopped twenty feet from the front entrance, and called out for Jack Harding.

FORTY TWO

Jack stepped out onto the front porch.

"Did you think I wouldn't find you?"

"I knew you would find us, Sammy. What concerns me is what you have on your mind."

"I believe you have Louis and John Agnello inside. If you hand them over, we can avoid a mess."

"I would love to avoid a mess, but I don't much care for that solution."

"Salvatore Leone doesn't want them harmed, he only wants a meeting. And Vincent respects the wishes of his grandfather."

"And you?"

"I have always respected the wishes of the Leones."

"Roberto and Bruno maybe, but they were terrible role models. If all Salvatore wants to do is talk, why don't we follow you to him? But no, I'm guessing you're prepared to take the Agnellos by force if necessary, and possibly kill them both while you're at it—regardless of Salvatore and Vincent's wishes. We seem to be short on trust here, Orso. Oh, and by the way, did I mention we have Vincent?"

"You won't harm Vincent."

"Maybe not. But once we're done with you, I believe we can scare him into taking us out to Stinson Beach."

"You're making a big mistake."

"My big mistake was not finding a way to be done with you a long time ago."

With that, Orso turned and walked off to collect his men. Jack walked back into the house.

"They'll be coming soon," Jack said to the others. "I'd like two up here at the front. John and I. Marty and Lincoln in the kitchen in back."

"I'm much better working outdoors," Lincoln said.

"So am I," John said, "and having hunted with Hank Sims for years, I'm pretty good at concealment. Though I'll have to admit I'm much more effective with a rifle."

"There's a Remington 7615 pump action in the trunk of my car and a ten-round clip," Jack said, tossing his keys to John. "Louis, I would prefer you find yourself somewhere relatively safe."

"Out of your way?"

"That's not what I meant. I didn't mean to offend you."

"These men are here for me, I'm not going to hide in a bathroom. Give me your gun, John, if you won't be needing it."

Lincoln slipped out the front door.

Marty and Louis followed John to the kitchen and watched him go out and take the rifle from Jack's trunk.

"I enjoyed travelling with you, Louis," Marty said.

"Let's do it again soon," he said.

They stood, concealed by trees, on all four sides of the house.

Richie Rizzo, on the south side, felt the barrel of the gun pressed against his head.

"Drop your weapon and turn around slowly."

Richie let go of his gun and turned.

"Remember me," Lincoln said. Then he knocked Rizzo out cold with a punch in the face, the .38 in his hand doing most of the work.

Lincoln removed Richie's shirt, tore off the sleeves, gagged

Rizzo and bound his arms and legs.

Phil Giambi spotted Marty at the kitchen window and took a shot, missing her by inches. Giambi ducked behind Jack's car.

Louis opened the back door and called out to Giambi.

"If you put a scratch on my Buick, I'll kill you."

Giambi rose to take aim at the old man.

A bullet struck him square between the shoulder blades and brought him to his knees. Giambi turned and saw John pump another round into the chamber of the Remington.

Giambi dropped his gun and laid face down on the ground, with both arms spread out in front of him.

"Don't make a sound or I will shoot you again," John said. "Don't try to move and you may not bleed to death."

Jimmy Rizzo came at John quickly from the north side of the house—but before Rizzo could get off a shot, Martina took him down with two direct hits to the chest.

Lincoln responded to the shooting and joined them.

They all heard the gunfire coming from the front and rushed around the building.

They found Jack sitting on the front porch, blood running down his left arm.

"Are you all right, Dad?" Marty asked.

"Bullet went right through. Wrap it up for me, I'll live. You should see the other guy," Jack said, pointing across the front yard.

Sammy Orso lay on the ground, a hole in his forehead.

Lincoln used a torn bed sheet for a tourniquet and managed to stop the bleeding.

"We should get you to a hospital," Marty said.

"I can drive myself to a hospital, though I'd love to do it in the Riviera," Jack said, looking up at Louis.

"Be my guest."

"Thanks. Oh, I almost forgot," Jack said, pulling an envelope from his pocket and handing it to Louis. "My father left this for you. Martina, take my car and get out to Sausalito. Carl and Mel are there with Vincent Leone. You know what to do. Let's move, we don't want to be around when the local police arrive."

They were crossing to Marin County on the Golden Gate Bridge.

Marty behind the wheel. Louis seated beside her. John and Lincoln in the back seat.

Louis opened the envelope Jack Harding had given him and removed the contents.

A note and a photograph.

Louis read the note aloud.

> *Louis,*
> *This is a photograph which my father, Theodore, took on the day you and Vincenzo Leone boarded the train from San Francisco to New York City in 1924.*
> *I wish you peace, and hope we will see each other before long.*
> *Richard.*

So do I, Louis thought.

Then he silently stared at the photograph for a long time.

FORTY THREE

Detective Hanover was standing out front when they arrived.

"Thanks for letting us use the house in Half Moon Bay," Marty said. "I'm afraid it was shot up a bit. I'm sorry."

"No worries," Hanover said. "The others are inside."

Marty started in, Louis and John following.

"I'll stay out here," Lincoln said, "and enjoy the view."

Lincoln stood beside Hanover, looking out to the marina and Richardson Bay. He pulled out a package of Camel cigarettes and offered one to Hanover.

"No, thanks. Those things will kill you."

"Thank you for the warning," Lincoln said, lighting up.

They found Carl Taylor and Vincent at the kitchen table.

Vincent's hands were cuffed behind his back.

"Do me a favor, Carl," Marty said, "remove the cuffs and give us a few minutes."

Taylor removed the handcuffs and left the room.

Vincent brought his arms forward and rubbed his wrists.

"Vincent, this is Louis Agnello and his grandson, John."

"You never did pick Sammy up, did you?"

"Sammy Orso is dead. He made his last bad decision. He chose Roberto and your father over you, and gave us no choice."

"I'm not surprised. What do you want from me? Are you going to kill me too?"

"All we want from you is to get Louis in to see your grandfather."

"I won't do that."

"John, where are the papers?" Louis asked.

John reached into his bag, pulled out the folder of documents, and he handed it to Louis.

Louis sat at the table, across from Vincent, and placed the folder down in front of him.

Louis looked directly into Vincent's eyes.

"Roberto Leone murdered my father in cold blood. Later, he sent an assassin to kill me—but it went wrong, and Vincenzo Leone died fighting to save me. It is all here," Louis said, lightly tapping the folder. "Whether he accepts it or not, your grandfather needs to hear this."

Louis took out the photograph Richard Harding had left for him and placed it in front of Vincent.

"Vincenzo Leone was a great man. You are his namesake. Please look at the photograph."

Vincent picked it up from the table.

"That is your great-grandfather, Vincenzo. Standing beside him is your grandmother, Lena—with your father, Salvatore, in her arms. The older boy, standing between your great-aunts, Rosa and Maria, is me. My mother was Vincenzo's sister. We are family, Vincent."

Vincent studied the photograph for a while before handing it to Louis.

"There are still four men out at the beach," Vincent said, "and they all answer to Sammy Orso. They may not listen to me."

"All we can ask is that you try your best," Louis Agnello said, placing the photograph into the folder.

FORTY FOUR

They drove the Panoramic Highway through Muir Woods and Mount Tamalpais State Park.

Marty driving the lead car—with Vincent, Louis, and John.

Carl Taylor following with Hanover and Lincoln Bonner aboard.

An hour later, they rejoined the Shoreline Highway.

When they arrived, both cars pulled over across the road from the house.

Martina and Vincent left their vehicle and crossed to Ed Gennaro, who was standing just inside the gate.

"Ed, this is Detective Harding of the San Francisco Police Department. We need to see my grandfather."

"Where is Sammy?" Gennaro asked.

"Sammy is dead," Marty said. "I have two carloads of police with me. Be smart, get the others, and leave the premises."

"Do as she says," Vincent added.

Without another word, Gennaro walked back to the house.

Taylor, Hanover, and Bonner joined them at the gate.

"What do you think?" Carl asked.

"I'm not sure," Marty said. "We'll wait."

Ten minutes later, four men in a car approached the gate from inside.

The gate opened. The car rolled up to Vincent and stopped.

"Your grandfather is waiting in the sun room," Gennaro said.

Gennaro turned the car onto the road.

"We'll stay with them, make certain they don't try to come back," Taylor said.

"I'll join you," Lincoln said. "I'll be at the police station, Marty. Call me as soon as you can."

"I will."

The two cars drove off.

Louis and John joined Marty and Vincent at the gate.

"We can walk from here," Vincent said.

FAMILY

They followed Vincent through the house to the back.

The door to the sun room was closed.

In the room, the far wall was entirely windowed.

Salvatore Leone stood looking out to the ocean.

Vincent tapped lightly on the door.

"Yes?"

"Grandfather. Louis Agnello is here to see you."

"Send him in," Salvatore said, turning from the window. "Alone."

"I don't like the idea of my grandfather going in alone," John said, looking to Vincent. "Does *your* grandfather have a weapon?"

"I really don't know," Vincent said.

"It's all right, John," Louis said, indicating the folder in his hand. "I am armed also."

Louis opened the door and stepped into the room.

He closed the door behind him.

Salvatore stood facing Louis.

Leone raised his arm. He was holding a gun.

Louis Agnello raised the folder to his chest.

"Do you think that will stop a bullet?" Salvatore asked.

"I pray it will stop all of the bullets."

ACKNOWLEDGMENTS

I entered adolescence in 1960. Throughout that decade I was educated and nurtured among a postwar generation of dreamers professing peace, equality, compassion, acceptance, and a strong belief that we, as fellow human beings and co-habitants of this small planet, were one family.

Family has always played an important part in my life, and in my writing.

There are few things that sadden me more deeply than witnessing families torn apart by greed, jealousy, or the unwillingness to try to understand—or to at least respectfully tolerate—innocent differences in philosophies or lifestyles.

Some of the final words my mother shared with me were, "Don't ever let anything come between you and your sisters."

I am therefore indebted to my mother for her wisdom.

I thank my sisters for their boundless support and encouragement.

I thank all of the loyal friends who have forgiven me my trespasses.

I thank Eric Campbell and Down & Out Books for the opportunity to make the work accessible.

I thank the readers, who help make it all make sense.

And I thank Jake Diamond, Darlene Roman, Jimmy Pigeon, Nick Ventura, James Samson, Thomas Murphy, Louis Agnello, Salvatore Leone, and all of the other fictional characters who have slipped into my head and invited me to join them on their journeys.

J.L. Abramo
Denver, Colorado

J.L. Abramo was born and raised in the seaside paradise of Brooklyn, NY on Raymond Chandler's fifty-ninth birthday.

A long-time journalist, educator and theatre artist, Abramo earned a Bachelor of Arts degree in Sociology and Education at The City College of The City University New York and a Master's Degree in Social Psychology from The University of Cincinnati.

Abramo is the author of *Catching Water in a Net*, winner of the St. Martin's Press/Private Eye Writers of America prize for Best First Private Eye Novel; the subsequent Jake Diamond Novels: *Clutching at Straws*, *Counting to Infinity* and *Circling the Runway* (Shamus Award Winner); *Chasing Charlie Chan*, a prequel to the Jake Diamond series; and the crime novels *Gravesend*, *Brooklyn Justice* and *Coney Island Avenue*.

www.jlabramo.com
www.facebook.com/jlabramo

On the following pages are a few
more great titles from the
Down & Out Books publishing family.

For a complete list of books and to
sign up for our newsletter,
go to DownAndOutBooks.com.

Shakedown
Martin Bodenham

Down & Out Books
978-1-946502-13-1

Damon Traynor leaves a glittering career on Wall Street to set up his own private equity business. When it is the winning bidder in the multi-billion dollar auction for a government-owned defense company, his firm's future success looks certain. But soon after the deal closes, Damon makes an alarming discovery—something that makes the recent acquisition worthless. Facing financial ruin, he investigates the US treasury officials behind the transaction and finds himself locked in a deadly battle with the leader of the free world.

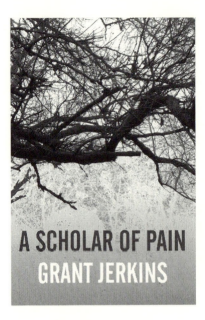

A Scholar of Pain
Grant Jerkins

ABC Group Documentation
an imprint of Down & Out Books
978-1-946502-15-5

In his debut short fiction collection, Grant Jerkins remains—as the *Washington Post* put it—"Determined to peer into the darkness and tell us exactly what he sees." Here, the depth of that darkness is on evident, oftentimes poetic, display. Read all sixteen of these deviant diversions. Peer into the darkness.

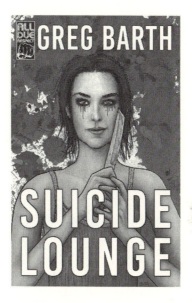

Suicide Lounge
Book 3 of the Selena Series
Greg Barth

All Due Respect, an imprint of
Down & Out Books
978-1-946502-81-0

Selena has settled in to being a crime boss with her cronies at the Red Light Lounge. But when a sadistic drug dealer attempts a bloody takeover of their territory, loyalties are strained and alliances broken. All forces are aligned against Selena, including her most lethal enemy—her own self-destructive lifestyle. Never one to back away from a fight, Selena puts all chips on the table and lets the dice fly.

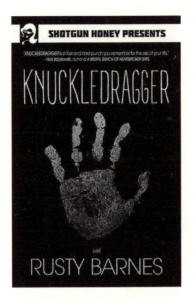

Knuckledragger
Rusty Barnes

Shotgun Honey, an imprint of
Down & Out Books
978-1-946502-07-0

Hooligan and low-level criminal enforcer Jason "Candy" Stahl has made a good life collecting money for his boss Otis. One collection trip, though, at the Diovisalvo Liquor Store, unravels events that turn Candy's life into a horror-show.

In quick succession he moves up a notch in the organization, overseeing a chop shop, while he falls in lust with Otis's girlfriend Nina, gets beaten for insubordination, and is forced to run when Otis finds out about Candy and Nina's affair.